$\mathcal{J}$ACK AND $\mathcal{J}$ILL

Also available in uniform editions:

LITTLE WOMEN

LITTLE MEN

JO'S BOYS

EIGHT COUSINS

ROSE IN BLOOM

UNDER THE LILACS

JACK AND JILL

by

Louisa May Alcott

FROM THE ORIGINAL PUBLISHER

LITTLE, BROWN AND COMPANY

BOSTON   NEW YORK   LONDON

Uniform Edition

Library of Congress Cataloging-in-Publication Data
Alcott, Louisa May, 1832–1888.
    Jack and Jill / by Louisa May Alcott.—
Uniform ed.
        p.   cm.
    "From the original publisher."
    Summary: When friends Jack and Jill are injured in a sledding accident,
their family and friends rally around them to help in their recovery.
    ISBN 0-316-03084-8
    [1. Family life—Fiction.   2. Friendship—Fiction.   3. Winter—
Fiction.]   I. Title.
PZ7.A335J25   1999
[Fic]—dc21   98-42840

10 9 8 7 6 5 4 3 2 1

MV-NY

Printed in the United States of America

To the schoolmates of

ELLSWORTH DEVENS

whose lovely character will not soon

be forgotten

This Village Story

is affectionately inscribed by their

friend

THE AUTHOR

Contents

Jack and Jill went up the hill
To coast with fun and laughter;
Jack fell down and broke his crown,
And Jill came tumbling after.

The Catastrophe

CHAPTER 1

"Clear the lulla!" was the general cry on a bright December afternoon, when all the boys and girls of Harmony Village were out enjoying the first good snow of the season. Up and down three long coasts they went as fast as legs and sleds could carry them. One smooth path led into the meadow, and here the little folk congregated; one swept across the pond, where skaters were darting about like water-bugs; and the third, from the very top of the steep hill, ended abruptly at a rail fence on the high bank above the road. There was a group of lads and lasses sitting or leaning on this fence to rest after an exciting race, and, as they reposed, they amused themselves with criticising their mates, still absorbed in this most delightful of outdoor sports.

"Here comes Frank Minot, looking as solemn as a judge," cried one, as a tall fellow of sixteen spun by, with a set look about the mouth and a keen sparkle of the eyes, fixed on the distant goal with a do-or-die expression.

"Here's Molly Loo
And little Boo!"

sang out another; and down came a girl with flying hair, carrying a small boy behind her, so fat that his short legs stuck out from the sides, and his round face looked over her shoulder like a full moon.

"There's Gus Burton; doesn't he go it?" and such a very long boy whizzed by, that it looked almost as if his heels were at the top of the hill when his head was at the bottom.

"Hurrah for Ed Devlin!" and a general shout greeted a sweet-faced lad, with a laugh on his lips, a fine color on his brown cheek, and a gay word for every girl he passed.

"Laura and Lotty keep to the safe coast into the meadow, and Molly Loo is the only girl that dares to try this long one to the pond. I wouldn't for the world; the ice can't be strong yet, though it is cold enough to freeze one's nose off," said a timid damsel, who sat hugging a post and screaming whenever a mischievous lad shook the fence.

"No, she isn't; here's Jack and Jill going like fury."

> "Clear the track
> For jolly Jack!"

sang the boys, who had rhymes and nicknames for nearly every one.

Down came a gay red sled, bearing a boy who seemed all smile and sunshine, so white were his teeth, so golden was his hair, so bright and happy his whole air. Behind him clung a little gypsy of a girl, with black eyes and hair, cheeks as red as her hood, and a face full of fun and sparkle, as she waved Jack's blue tippet like a banner with one hand, and held on with the other.

"Jill goes wherever Jack does, and he lets her. He's such a good-natured chap, he can't say 'No.' "

"To a girl," slyly added one of the boys, who had

```
    #260   10-14-2016 4:58PM
Item(s) checked out to PLUMMER, SHANYAH

TITLE: Jack and Jill
BARCODE: 39223031335550
DUE DATE: 11-11-16


          RENEW BY PHONE
           765.454.4711
```

wished to borrow the red sled, and had been politely refused because Jill wanted it.

"He's the nicest boy in the world, for he never gets mad," said the timid young lady, recalling the many times Jack had shielded her from the terrors which beset her path to school, in the shape of cows, dogs, and boys who made faces and called her " 'Fraid-cat."

"He doesn't dare to get mad with Jill, for she'd take his head off in two minutes if he did," growled Joe Flint, still smarting from the rebuke Jill had given him for robbing the little ones of their safe coast because he fancied it.

"She wouldn't! she's a dear! *You* needn't sniff at her because she is poor. She's ever so much brighter than you are, or she wouldn't always be at the head of your class, old Joe," cried the girls, standing by their friend with a unanimity which proved what a favorite she was.

Joe subsided with as scornful a curl to his nose as its chilly state permitted, and Merry Grant introduced a subject of general interest by asking abruptly,—

"Who is going to the candy-scrape to-night?"

"All of us. Frank invited the whole set, and we shall have a tip-top time. We always do at the Minots'," cried Sue, the timid trembler.

"Jack said there was a barrel of molasses in the house, so there would be enough for all to eat and some to carry away. They know how to do things handsomely;" and the speaker licked his lips, as if already tasting the feast in store for him.

"Mrs. Minot is a mother worth having," said Molly Loo, coming up with Boo on the sled; and she knew what it was to need a mother, for she had none, and tried to care for the little brother with maternal love and patience.

"She is just as sweet as she can be!" declared Merry, enthusiastically.

"Especially when she has a candy-scrape," said Joe, trying to be amiable, lest he should be left out of the party.

Whereat they all laughed, and went gayly away for a farewell frolic, as the sun was setting and the keen wind nipped fingers and toes as well as noses.

Down they went, one after another, on the various coasts, — solemn Frank, long Gus, gallant Ed, fly-away Molly Loo, pretty Laura and Lotty, grumpy Joe, sweet-faced Merry with Sue shrieking wildly behind her, gay Jack and gypsy Jill, always together, — one and all bubbling over with the innocent jollity born of healthful exercise. People passing in the road below looked up and smiled involuntarily at the red-cheeked lads and lasses, filling the frosty air with peals of laughter and cries of triumph as they flew by in every conceivable attitude; for the fun was at its height now, and the oldest and gravest observers felt a glow of pleasure as they looked, remembering their own young days.

"Jack, take me down that coast. Joe said I wouldn't dare to do it, so I must," commanded Jill, as they paused for breath after the long trudge up hill. Jill, of course, was not her real name, but had been given because of her friendship with Jack, who so admired Janey Pecq's spirit and fun.

"I guess I wouldn't. It is very bumpy and ends in a big drift; not half so nice as this one. Hop on and we'll have a good spin across the pond;" and Jack brought "Thunderbolt" round with a skilful swing and an engaging air that would have won obedience from anybody but wilful Jill.

"It is very nice, but I won't be told I don't 'dare' by any boy in the world. If you are afraid, I'll go alone." And, before he could speak, she had snatched the rope from his hand, thrown herself upon the sled, and was off, helter-skelter, down the most dangerous coast on the hill-side.

She did not get far, however; for, starting in a hurry, she did not guide her steed with care, and the red charger landed her in the snow half-way down, where she lay laughing till Jack came to pick her up.

"If you *will* go, I'll take you down all right. I'm not afraid, for I've done it a dozen times with the other fellows; but we gave it up because it is short and bad," he said, still good-natured, though a little hurt at the charge of cowardice; for Jack was as brave as a little lion, and with the best sort of bravery,—the courage to do right.

"So it is; but I *must* do it a few times, or Joe will plague me and spoil my fun to-night," answered Jill, shaking her skirts and rubbing her blue hands, wet and cold with the snow.

"Here, put these on; I never use them. Keep them if they fit; I only carry them to please mother." And Jack pulled out a pair of red mittens with the air of a boy used to giving away.

"They are lovely warm, and they do fit. Must be too small for your paws, so I'll knit you a new pair for Christmas, and make you wear them, too," said Jill, putting on the mittens with a nod of thanks, and ending her speech with a stamp of her rubber boots to enforce her threat.

Jack laughed, and up they trudged to the spot whence the three coasts diverged.

"Now, which will you have?" he asked, with a warning look in the honest blue eyes which often unconsciously controlled naughty Jill against her will.

"That one!" and the red mitten pointed firmly to the perilous path just tried.

"You will do it?"

"I will!"

"Come on, then, and hold tight."

Jack's smile was gone now, and he waited without a word while Jill tucked herself up, then took his place in front, and off they went on the brief, breathless trip straight into the drift by the fence below.

"I don't see anything very awful in that. Come up and have another. Joe is watching us, and I'd like to show him that *we* aren't afraid of anything," said Jill, with a defiant glance at a distant boy, who had paused to watch the descent.

"It is a regular 'go-bang,' if that is what you like," answered Jack, as they plowed their way up again.

"It is. You boys think girls like little mean coasts without any fun or danger in them, as if we couldn't be brave and strong as well as you. Give me three go-bangs and then we'll stop. My tumble doesn't count, so give me two more and then I'll be good."

Jill took her seat as she spoke, and looked up with such a rosy, pleading face that Jack gave in at once, and down they went again, raising a cloud of glittering snow-dust as they reined up in fine style with their feet on the fence.

"It's just splendid! Now, one more!" cried Jill, excited by the cheers of a sleighing party passing below.

Proud of his skill, Jack marched back, resolved to make the third "go" the crowning achievement of the afternoon, while Jill pranced after him as lightly as if the big boots were the famous seven-leagued ones, and chattering about the candy-scrape and whether there would be nuts or not.

So full were they of this important question, that they piled on hap-hazard, and started off still talking so busily that Jill forgot to hold tight and Jack to steer carefully. Alas, for the candy-scrape that never was to be! alas, for poor "Thunderbolt" blindly setting forth on the last trip he ever made! and oh, alas, for Jack and Jill, who wilfully chose the wrong road and ended their fun for the winter! No one knew how it happened, but instead of landing in the drift, or at the fence, there was a great crash against the bars, a dreadful plunge off the steep bank, a sudden scattering of girl, boy, sled, fence, earth, and snow, all about the road, two cries, and then silence.

"I knew they'd do it!" and, standing on the post where he had perched, Joe waved his arms and shouted: "Smash-up! Smash-up! Run! Run!" like a raven croaking over a battle-field when the fight was done.

Down rushed boys and girls ready to laugh or cry, as the case might be, for accidents will happen on the best-regulated coasting-grounds. They found Jack sitting up looking about him with a queer, dazed expression, while an ugly cut on the forehead was bleeding in a way which sobered the boys and frightened the girls half out of their wits.

"He's killed! He's killed!" wailed Sue, hiding her face and beginning to cry.

"No, I'm not. I'll be all right when I get my breath. Where's Jill?" asked Jack, stoutly, though still too giddy to see straight.

The group about him opened, and his comrade in misfortune was discovered lying quietly in the snow with all the pretty color shocked out of her face by the fall, and winking rapidly, as if half stunned. But no wounds appeared, and when asked if she was dead, she answered in a vague sort of way,—

"I guess not. Is Jack hurt?"

"Broken his head," croaked Joe, stepping aside, that she might behold the fallen hero vainly trying to look calm and cheerful with red drops running down his cheek and a lump on his forehead.

Jill shut her eyes and waved the girls away, saying, faintly, —

"Never mind me. Go and see to him."

"Don't! I'm all right," and Jack tried to get up in order to prove that headers off a bank were mere trifles to him; but at the first movement of the left leg he uttered a sharp cry of pain, and would have fallen if Gus had not caught and gently laid him down.

"What is it, old chap?" asked Frank, kneeling beside him, really alarmed now, the hurts seeming worse than mere bumps, which were common affairs among base-ball players, and not worth much notice.

"I lit on my head, but I guess I've broken my leg. Don't frighten mother," and Jack held fast to Frank's arm as he looked into the anxious face bent over him; for, though the elder tyrannized over the younger, the brothers loved one another dearly.

"Lift his head, Frank, while I tie my handkerchief round to stop the bleeding," said a quiet voice, as Ed Devlin laid a handful of soft snow on the wound; and Jack's face brightened as he turned to thank the one big boy who never was rough with the small ones.

"Better get him right home," advised Gus, who stood by looking on, with his little sisters Laura and Lotty clinging to him.

"Take Jill, too, for it's my opinion she has broken her back. She can't stir one bit," announced Molly Loo, with a droll air of triumph, as if rather pleased than otherwise to have her patient hurt the worse; for Jack's wound was very effective, and Molly had a taste for the tragic.

This cheerful statement was greeted with a wail from

Susan and howls from Boo, who had earned that name from the ease with which, on all occasions, he could burst into a dismal roar without shedding a tear, and stop as suddenly as he began.

"Oh, I am so sorry! It was my fault; I shouldn't have let her do it," said Jack, distressfully.

"It was all *my* fault; I made him. If I'd broken every bone I've got, it would serve me right. Don't help me, anybody; I'm a wicked thing, and I deserve to lie here and freeze and starve and die!" cried Jill, piling up punishments in her remorseful anguish of mind and body.

"But we want to help you, and we can settle about blame by and by," whispered Merry with a kiss; for she adored dashing Jill, and never would own that she did wrong.

"Here come the wood-sleds just in time. I'll cut away and tell one of them to hurry up." And, freeing himself from his sisters, Gus went off at a great pace, proving that the long legs carried a sensible head as well as a kind heart.

As the first sled approached, an air of relief pervaded the agitated party, for it was driven by Mr. Grant, a big, benevolent-looking farmer, who surveyed the scene with the sympathetic interest of a man and a father.

"Had a little accident, have you? Well, that's a pretty likely place for a spill. Tried it once myself and broke the bridge of my nose," he said, tapping that massive feature with a laugh which showed that fifty years of farming had not taken all the boy out of him. "Now then, let's see about this little chore, and lively, too, for it's late, and these parties ought to be housed," he added, throwing down his whip, pushing back his cap, and nodding at the wounded with a reassuring smile.

"Jill first, please, sir," said Ed, the gentle squire of

dames, spreading his overcoat on the sled as eagerly as ever
Raleigh laid down his velvet cloak for a queen to walk upon.

"All right. Just lay easy, my dear, and I won't hurt you
a mite if I can help it."

Careful as Mr. Grant was, Jill could have screamed
with pain as he lifted her; but she set her lips and bore it
with the courage of a little Indian; for all the lads were looking on, and Jill was proud to show that a girl could bear as
much as a boy. She hid her face in the coat as soon as she was
settled, to hide the tears that would come, and by the time
Jack was placed beside her, she had quite a little cistern of
salt water stored up in Ed's coat-pocket.

Then the mournful procession set forth, Mr. Grant
driving the oxen, the girls clustering about the interesting
invalids on the sled, while the boys came behind like a guard
of honor, leaving the hill deserted by all but Joe, who had
returned to hover about the fatal fence, and poor "Thunderbolt," split asunder, lying on the bank to mark the spot
where the great catastrophe occurred.

Two Penitents
CHAPTER 2

Jack and Jill never cared to say much about the night
which followed the first coasting party of the season, for it
was the saddest and the hardest their short lives had ever
known. Jack suffered most in body; for the setting of the
broken leg was such a painful job, that it wrung several
sharp cries from him, and made Frank, who helped, quite
weak and white with sympathy, when it was over. The
wounded head ached dreadfully, and the poor boy felt as if

bruised all over, for he had the worst of the fall. Dr. Whiting spoke cheerfully of the case, and made so light of broken
legs, that Jack innocently asked if he should not be up in a
week or so.

"Well, no; it usually takes twenty-one days for bones
to knit, and young ones make quick work of it," answered
the doctor, with a last scientific tuck to the various bandages, which made Jack feel like a hapless chicken trussed
for the spit.

"Twenty-one days! Three whole weeks in bed! I
shouldn't call that quick work," groaned the dismayed patient, whose experience of illness had been limited.

"It is a forty days' job, young man, and you must make
up your mind to bear it like a hero. We will do our best; but
next time, look before you leap, and save your bones.
Good-night; you'll feel better in the morning. No jigs, remember;" and off went the busy doctor for another look at
Jill, who had been ordered to bed and left to rest till the
other case was attended to.

Any one would have thought Jack's plight much the
worse, but the doctor looked more sober over Jill's hurt
back than the boy's compound fractures; and the poor little
girl had a very bad quarter of an hour while he was trying to
discover the extent of the injury.

"Keep her quiet, and time will show how much damage is done," was all he said in her hearing; but if she had
known that he told Mrs. Pecq he feared serious consequences, she would not have wondered why her mother
cried as she rubbed the numb limbs and placed the pillows
so tenderly.

Jill suffered most in her mind; for only a sharp stab
of pain now and then reminded her of her body; but her

remorseful little soul gave her no peace for thinking of Jack, whose bruises and breakages her lively fancy painted in the darkest colors.

"Oh, don't be good to me, Mammy; I made him go, and now he's hurt dreadfully, and may die; and it is all my fault, and everybody ought to hate me," sobbed poor Jill, as a neighbor left the room after reporting in a minute manner how Jack screamed when his leg was set, and how Frank was found white as a sheet, with his head under the pump, while Gus restored the tone of his friend's nerves, by pumping as if the house was on fire.

"Whist, my lass, and go to sleep. Take a sup of the good wine Mrs. Minot sent, for you are as cold as a clod, and it breaks my heart to see my Janey so."

"I can't go to sleep; I don't see how Jack's mother could send me anything when I've half killed him. I want to be cold and ache and have horrid things done to me. Oh, if I ever get out of this bed I'll be the best girl in the world, to pay for this. See if I ain't!" and Jill gave such a decided nod that her tears flew all about the pillow like a shower.

"You'd better begin at once, for you won't get out of that bed for a long while, I'm afraid, my lamb," sighed her mother, unable to conceal the anxiety that lay so heavy on her heart.

"Am I hurt badly, Mammy?"

"I fear it, lass."

"I'm *glad* of it; I ought to be worse than Jack, and I hope I am. I'll bear it well, and be good right away. Sing, Mammy, and I'll try to go to sleep to please you."

Jill shut her eyes with sudden and unusual meekness, and before her mother had crooned half a dozen verses of an old ballad, the little black head lay still upon the pillow, and repentant Jill was fast asleep with a red mitten in her hand.

Mrs. Pecq was an Englishwoman who had left Montreal at the death of her husband, a French Canadian, and had come to live in the tiny cottage which stood near Mrs. Minot's big house, separated only by an arbor-vitae hedge. A sad, silent person, who had seen better days, but said nothing about them, and earned her bread by sewing, nursing, work in the factory, or anything that came in her way, being anxious to educate her little girl. Now, as she sat beside the bed in the small, poor room, that hope almost died within her, for here was the child laid up for months, probably, and the one ambition and pleasure of the solitary woman's life was to see Janey Pecq's name over all the high marks in the school-reports she proudly brought home.

"She'll win through, please Heaven, and I'll see my lass a gentlewoman yet, thanks to the good friend in yonder, who will never let her want for care," thought the poor soul, looking out into the gloom where a long ray of light streamed from the great house warm and comfortable upon the cottage, like the spirit of kindness which made the inmates friends and neighbors.

Meantime, that other mother sat by her boy's bed as anxious but with better hope, for Mrs. Minot made trouble sweet and helpful by the way in which she bore it; and her boys were learning of her how to find silver linings to the clouds that must come into the bluest skies.

Jack lay wide awake, with hot cheeks, and throbbing head, and all sorts of queer sensations in the broken leg. The soothing potion he had taken did not affect him yet, and he tried to beguile the weary time by wondering who came and went below. Gentle rings at the front door, and mysterious tappings at the back, had been going on all the evening; for the report of the accident had grown astonishingly in its travels, and at eight o'clock the general belief was that Jack had broken both legs, fractured his skull, and lay at the point of death, while Jill had dislocated one shoulder, and was bruised black and blue from top to toe. Such being the case, it is no wonder that anxious playmates and neighbors haunted the door-steps of the two houses, and that offers of help poured in.

Frank, having tied up the bell and put a notice in the lighted side-window, saying, "Go to the back door," sat in the parlor, supported by his chum, Gus, while Ed played softly on the piano, hoping to lull Jack to sleep. It did soothe him, for a very sweet friendship existed between the tall youth and the lad of thirteen. Ed went with the big fellows, but always had a kind word for the smaller boys; and affectionate Jack, never ashamed to show his love, was often seen with his arm round Ed's shoulder, as they sat together in the pleasant red parlors, where all the young people were welcome and Frank was king.

"Is the pain any easier, my darling?" asked Mrs. Minot, leaning over the pillow, where the golden head lay quiet for a moment.

"Not much. I forget it listening to the music. Dear old Ed is playing all my favorite tunes, and it is very nice. I guess he feels pretty sorry about me."

"They all do. Frank could not talk of it. Gus wouldn't go home to tea, he was so anxious to do something for us. Joe brought back the bits of your poor sled, because he didn't like to leave them lying round for any one to carry off, he said, and you might like them to remember your fall by."

Jack tried to laugh, but it was rather a failure, though he managed to say, cheerfully, —

"That was good of old Joe. I wouldn't lend him 'Thunderbolt' for fear he'd hurt it. Couldn't have smashed it up better than I did, could he? Don't think I want any pieces to remind me of *that* fall. I just wish you'd seen us, mother! It must have been a splendid spill,—to look at, any way."

"No, thank you; I'd rather not even try to imagine my precious boy going heels over head down that dreadful hill. No more pranks of that sort for some time, Jacky;" and Mrs. Minot looked rather pleased on the whole to have her venturesome bird safe under her maternal wing.

"No coasting till some time in January. What a fool I was to do it! Go-bangs always are dangerous, and that's the fun of the thing. Oh dear!"

Jack threw his arms about and frowned darkly, but never said a word of the wilful little baggage who had led him into mischief; he was too much of a gentleman to tell on a girl, though it cost him an effort to hold his tongue, because Mamma's good opinion was very precious to him, and he longed to explain. She knew all about it, however, for Jill had been carried into the house reviling herself for the mishap, and, even in the midst of her own anxiety for her boy, Mrs. Minot understood the state of the case without more words. So she now set his mind at rest by saying, quietly,—

"Foolish fun, as you see, dear. Another time, stand firm and help Jill to control her headstrong will. When you learn to yield less and she more, there will be no scrapes like this to try us all."

"I'll remember, mother. I hate not to be obliging, but I guess it would have saved us lots of trouble if I'd said No in the beginning. I tried to, but she *would* go. Poor Jill! I'll take better care of her next time. Is she very ill, Mamma?"

"I can tell you better to-morrow. She does not suffer much, and we hope there is no great harm done."

"I wish she had a nice place like this to be sick in. It must be very poky in those little rooms," said Jack, as his eye roved round the large chamber where he lay so cosey, warm, and pleasant, with the gay chintz curtains draping doors and windows, the rosy carpet, comfortable chairs, and a fire glowing in the grate.

"I shall see that she suffers for nothing, so don't trouble your kind heart about her to-night, but try to sleep; that's what you need," answered his mother, wetting the bandage on his forehead, and putting a cool hand on the flushed cheeks.

Jack obediently closed his eyes and listened while the boys sang "The Sweet By and By," softening their rough young voices for his sake till the music was as soft as a lullaby. He lay so still his mother thought he was off, but presently a tear slipped out and rolled down the red cheek, wetting her hand as it passed.

"My blessed boy, what is it?" she whispered, with a touch and a tone that only mothers have.

The blue eyes opened wide, and Jack's own sunshiny smile broke through the tears that filled them as he said with a sniff,—

"Everybody is so good to me I can't help making a noodle of myself."

"You are not a noodle!" cried Mamma, resenting the epithet. "One of the sweet things about pain and sorrow is that they show us how well we are loved, how much kindness there is in the world, and how easily we can make others happy in the same way when they need help and sympathy. Don't forget that, little son."

"Don't see how I can, with you to show me how nice it is. Kiss me good-night, and then 'I'll be good,' as Jill says."

Nestling his head upon his mother's arm, Jack lay quiet till, lulled by the music of his mates, he drowsed away into the dreamless sleep which is Nurse Nature's healthiest soothing sirup for weary souls and bodies.

Ward No. 1
CHAPTER 3 ᧿

*F*or some days, nothing was seen and little was heard of the "dear sufferers," as the old ladies called them. But they were not forgotten; the first words uttered when any of the young people met were: "How is Jack?" "Seen Jill yet?" and all waited with impatience for the moment when they could be admitted to their favorite mates, more than ever objects of interest now.

Meantime, the captives spent the first few days in sleep, pain, and trying to accept the hard fact that school and play were done with for months perhaps. But young spirits are wonderfully elastic and soon cheer up, and healthy young bodies heal fast, or easily adapt themselves to new conditions. So our invalids began to mend on the fourth day, and to drive their nurses distracted with efforts to amuse them, before the first week was over.

The most successful attempt originated in Ward No. 1, as Mrs. Minot called Jack's apartment, and we will give our sympathizing readers some idea of this place, which became the stage whereon were enacted many varied and remarkable scenes.

Each of the Minot boys had his own room, and there collected his own treasures and trophies, arranged to suit his convenience and taste. Frank's was full of books, maps, machinery, chemical messes, and geometrical drawings, which adorned the walls like intricate cobwebs. A big chair, where

he read and studied with his heels higher than his head, a basket of apples for refreshment at all hours of the day or night,
and an immense inkstand, in which several pens were always
apparently bathing their feet, were the principal ornaments
of his scholastic retreat.

Jack's hobby was athletic sports, for he was bent on
having a strong and active body for his happy little soul to
live and enjoy itself in. So a severe simplicity reigned in his
apartment; in summer, especially, for then his floor was
bare, his windows were uncurtained, and the chairs uncush-
ioned, the bed being as narrow and hard as Napoleon's. The
only ornaments were dumb-bells, whips, bats, rods, skates,
boxing-gloves, a big bath-pan and a small library, consisting
chiefly of books on games, horses, health, hunting, and travels. In winter his mother made things more comfortable by
introducing rugs, curtains, and a fire. Jack, also, relented
slightly in the severity of his training, occasionally indulging
in the national buck-wheat cake, instead of the prescribed
oatmeal porridge, for breakfast, omitting his cold bath when
the thermometer was below zero, and dancing at night, instead of running a given distance by day.

Now, however, he was a helpless captive, given over
to all sorts of coddling, laziness, and luxury, and there was
a droll mixture of mirth and melancholy in his face, as he
lay trussed up in bed, watching the comforts which had
suddenly robbed his room of its Spartan simplicity. A delicious couch was there, with Frank reposing in its depths,
half hidden under several folios which he was consulting
for a history of the steam-engine, the subject of his next
composition.

A white-covered table stood near, with all manner of
dainties set forth in a way to tempt the sternest principles.

Vases of flowers bloomed on the chimney-piece, — gifts from anxious young ladies, left with their love. Frivolous story-books and picture-papers strewed the bed, now shrouded in effeminate chintz curtains, beneath which Jack lay like a wounded warrior in his tent. But the saddest sight for our crippled athlete was a glimpse, through a half-opened door, at the beloved dumb-bells, bats, balls, boxing-gloves, and snow-shoes, all piled ignominiously away in the bath-pan, mournfully recalling the fact that their day was over, now, at least for some time.

He was about to groan dismally, when his eye fell on a sight which made him swallow the groan, and cough instead, as if it choked him a little. The sight was his mother's face, as she sat in a low chair rolling bandages, with a basket beside her in which were piles of old linen, lint, plaster, and other matters, needed for the dressing of wounds. As he looked, Jack remembered how steadily and tenderly she had stood by him all through the hard times just past, and how carefully she had bathed and dressed his wound each day in spite of the effort it cost her to give him pain or even see him suffer.

"That's a better sort of strength than swinging twenty-pound dumb-bells or running races; I guess I'll try for that kind, too, and not howl or let her see me squirm when the doctor hurts," thought the boy, as he saw that gentle face so pale and tired with much watching and anxiety, yet so patient, serene, and cheerful, that it was like sunshine.

"Lie down and take a good nap, mother dear, I feel first-rate, and Frank can see to me if I want anything. Do, now," he added, with a persuasive nod toward the couch, and a boyish relish in stirring up his lazy brother.

After some urging, Mamma consented to go to her

room for forty winks, leaving Jack in the care of Frank, begging him to be as quiet as possible if the dear boy wished to sleep, and to amuse him if he did not.

Being worn out, Mrs. Minot lengthened her forty winks into a three hours' nap, and as the "dear boy" scorned repose, Mr. Frank had his hands full while on guard.

"I'll read to you. Here's Watt, Arkwright, Fulton, and a lot of capital fellows, with pictures that will do your heart good. Have a bit, will you?" asked the new nurse, flapping the leaves invitingly, — for Frank had a passion for such things, and drew steam-engines all over his slate, as Tommy Traddles drew hosts of skeletons when low in his spirits.

"I don't want any of your old boilers and stokers and whirligigs. I'm tired of reading, and want something regularly jolly," answered Jack, who had been chasing white buffaloes with "The Hunters of the West," till he was a trifle tired and fractious.

"Play cribbage, euchre, anything you like;" and Frank obligingly disinterred himself from under the folios, feeling that it *was* hard for a fellow to lie flat a whole week.

"No fun; just two of us. Wish school was over, so the boys would come in; doctor said I might see them now."

"They'll be along by and by, and I'll hail them. Till then, what shall we do? I'm your man for anything, only put a name to it."

"Just wish I had a telegraph or a telephone, so I could talk to Jill. Wouldn't it be fun to pipe across and get an answer!"

"I'll make either you say;" and Frank looked as if trifles of that sort were to be had for the asking.

"Could you, really?"

"We'll start the telegraph first, then you can send

things over if you like," said Frank, prudently proposing the surest experiment.

"Go ahead, then. I'd like that, and so would Jill, for I know she wants to hear from me."

"There's one trouble, though; I shall have to leave you alone for a few minutes while I rig up the ropes;" and Frank looked sober, for he was a faithful boy, and did not want to desert his post.

"Oh, never mind; I won't want anything. If I do I can pound for Ann."

"And wake mother. I'll fix you a better way than that;" and, full of inventive genius, our young Edison spliced the poker to part of a fishing-rod in a jiffy, making a long-handled hook which reached across the room.

"There's an arm for you; now hook away, and let's see how it works," he said, handing over the instrument to Jack, who proceeded to show its unexpected capabilities by hooking the cloth off the table in attempting to get his handkerchief, catching Frank by the hair when fishing for a book, and breaking a pane of glass in trying to draw down the curtain.

"It's so everlasting long, I can't manage it," laughed Jack, as it finally caught in his bed-hangings, and nearly pulled them, ring and all, down upon his head.

"Let it alone, unless you need something very much, and don't bother about the glass. It's just what we want for the telegraph wire or rope to go through. Keep still, and I'll have the thing running in ten minutes;" and, delighted with the job, Frank hurried away, leaving Jack to compose a message to send as soon as it was possible.

"What in the world is that flying across the Minots' yard,—a brown hen or a boy's kite?" exclaimed old Miss

Hopkins, peering out of her window at the singular perfor-
mances going on in her opposite neighbor's garden.

First, Frank appeared with a hatchet and chopped a
clear space in the hedge between his own house and the cottage; next, a clothes line was passed through this aperture
and fastened somewhere on the other side; lastly, a small
covered basket, slung on this rope, was seen hitching along,
drawn either way by a set of strings; then, as if satisfied with
his job, Frank retired, whistling "Hail Columbia."

"It's those children at their pranks again. I thought
broken bones wouldn't keep them out of mischief long,"
said the old lady, watching with great interest the mysterious basket travelling up and down the rope from the big
house to the cottage.

If she had seen what came and went over the wires of
the "Great International Telegraph," she would have
laughed till her spectacles flew off her Roman nose. A letter
from Jack, with a large orange, went first, explaining the
new enterprise:—

> DEAR JILL,—It's too bad you can't come over to see me.
> I am pretty well, but awful tired of keeping still. I want to
> see you ever so much. Frank has fixed us a telegraph, so we
> can write and send things. Won't it be jolly! I can't look
> out to see him do it; but, when you pull your string, my
> little bell rings, and I know a message is coming. I send you
> an orange. Do you like *gorver* jelly? People send in lots of
> goodies, and we will go halves. Good-by.
>
> JACK.

Away went the basket, and in fifteen minutes it came
back from the cottage with nothing in it but the orange.

"Hullo! is she mad?" asked Jack, as Frank brought the
despatch for him to examine.

But, at the first touch, the hollow peel opened, and

out fell a letter, two gum-drops, and an owl made of a pea-
nut, with round eyes drawn at the end where the stem
formed a funny beak. Two bits of straw were the legs, and
the face looked so like Dr. Whiting that both boys laughed
at the sight.

"That's so like Jill; she'd make fun if she was half dead.
Let's see what she says;" and Jack read the little note, which
showed a sad neglect of the spelling-book:—

DEAR JACKY,—I can't stir and it's horrid. The telly graf is
very nice and we will have fun with it. I never ate any
gorver jelly. The orange was first rate. Send me a book to
read. All about bears and ships and crockydiles. The doctor
was coming to see you, so I sent him the quickest way.
Molly Loo says it is dreadful lonesome at school without
us. Yours truly,

JILL.

Jack immediately despatched the book and a sample of
guava jelly, which unfortunately upset on the way, to the
great detriment of "The Wild Beasts of Asia and Africa." Jill
promptly responded with the loan of a tiny black kitten,
who emerged spitting and scratching, to Jack's great delight; and he was cudgelling his brains as to how a fat white
rabbit could be transported, when a shrill whistle from
without saved Jill from that inconvenient offering.

"It's the fellows; do you want to see them?" asked
Frank, gazing down with calm superiority upon the three
eager faces which looked up at him.

"Guess I do!" and Jack promptly threw the kitten
overboard, scorning to be seen by any manly eye amusing
himself with such girlish toys.

Bang! went the front door; tramp, tramp, tramp, came
six booted feet up the stairs; and, as Frank threw wide the

door, three large beings paused on the threshold to deliver the courteous "Hullo!" which is the established greeting among boys on all social occasions.

"Come along, old fellows; I'm ever so glad to see you!" cried the invalid, with such energetic demonstrations of the arms that he looked as if about to fly or crow, like an excited young cockerel.

"How are you, Major?"

"Does the leg ache much, Jack?"

"Mr. Phipps says you'll have to pay for the new rails."

With these characteristic greetings, the gentlemen cast away their hats and sat down, all grinning cheerfully, and all with eyes irresistibly fixed upon the dainties, which proved too much for the politeness of ever-hungry boys.

"Help yourselves," said Jack, with a hospitable wave. "All the dear old ladies in town have been sending in nice things, and I can't begin to eat them up. Lend a hand and clear away this lot, or we shall have to throw them out of the window. Bring on the doughnuts and the tarts and the shaky stuff in the entry closet, Frank, and let's have a lark."

No sooner said than done. Gus took the tarts, Joe the doughnuts, Ed the jelly, and Frank suggested "spoons all round" for the Italian cream. A few trifles in the way of custard, fruit, and wafer biscuits were not worth mentioning; but every dish was soon emptied, and Jack said, as he surveyed the scene of devastation with great satisfaction, —

"Call again to-morrow, gentlemen, and we will have another bout. Free lunches at 5 P.M. till further notice. Now tell me all the news."

For half an hour, five tongues went like mill clappers, and there is no knowing when they would have stopped if the little bell had not suddenly rung with a violence that made them jump.

"That's Jill; see what she wants, Frank;" and while his brother sent off the basket, Jack told about the new invention, and invited his mates to examine and admire.

They did so, and shouted with merriment when the next despatch from Jill arrived. A pasteboard jumping-jack, with one leg done up in cotton-wool to preserve the likeness, and a great lump of molasses candy in a brown paper, with accompanying note:—

> DEAR SIR,—I saw the boys go in, and know you are having a nice time, so I send over the candy Molly Loo and Merry brought me. Mammy says I can't eat it, and it will all melt away if I keep it. Also a picture of Jack Minot, who will dance on one leg and waggle the other, and make you laugh. I wish I could come, too. Don't you hate grewel? I do.—In haste,
>
> J. P.

"Let's all send her a letter," proposed Jack, and out came pens, ink, paper, and the lamp, and every one fell to scribbling. A droll collection was the result, for Frank drew a picture of the fatal fall with broken rails flying in every direction, Jack with his head swollen to the size of a balloon, and Jill in two pieces, while the various boys and girls were hit off with a sly skill that gave Gus legs like a stork, Molly Loo hair several yards long, and Boo a series of visible howls coming out of an immense mouth in the shape of o's. The oxen were particularly good, for their horns branched like those of the moose, and Mr. Grant had a patriarchal beard which waved in the breeze as he bore the wounded girl to a sled very like a funeral pyre, the stakes being crowned with big mittens like torches.

"You ought to be an artist. I never saw such a dabster as you are. That's the very moral of Joe, all in a bunch on the fence, with a blot to show how purple his nose was," said Gus, holding up the sketch for general criticism and admiration.

"I'd rather have a red nose than legs like a grass-hopper; so you needn't twit, Daddy," growled Joe, quite unconscious that a blot actually did adorn his nose, as he labored over a brief despatch.

The boys enjoyed the joke, and one after the other read out his message to the captive lady:—

"DEAR JILL,—Sorry you ain't here. Great fun. Jack pretty lively. Laura and Lot would send love if they knew of the chance. Fly round and get well.

Gus."

"DEAR GILLIFLOWER,—Hope you are pretty comfortable in your 'dungeon cell.' Would you like a serenade when the moon comes? Hope you will soon be up again, for we miss you very much. Shall be very happy to help in any way I can. Love to your mother. Your true friend,

E. D."

"MISS PECQ.

Dear Madam,—I am happy to tell you that we are all well, and hope you are the same. I gave Jem Cox a licking because he went to your desk. You had better send for your books. You won't have to pay for the sled or the fence. Jack says he will see to it. We have been having a spread over here. First-rate things. I wouldn't mind breaking a leg, if I had such good grub and no chores to do. No more now, from yours, with esteem,

JOSEPH P. FLINT."

Joe thought that an elegant epistle, having copied portions of it from the "Letter Writer," and proudly read it off to the boys, who assured him that Jill would be much impressed.

"Now, Jack, hurry up and let us send the lot off, for

we must go," said Gus, as Frank put the letters in the basket, and the clatter of tea-things was heard below.

"I'm not going to show mine. It's private and you
mustn't look," answered Jack, patting down an envelope
with such care that no one had a chance to peep.

But Joe had seen the little note copied, and while the
others were at the window working the telegraph he caught
up the original, carelessly thrust by Jack under the pillow,
and read it aloud before any one knew what he was about.

> "MY DEAR,—I wish I could send you some of my good
> times. As I can't, I send you much love, and I hope you
> will try and be patient as I am going to, for it was our fault,
> and we must not make a fuss now. Ain't mothers sweet?
> Mine is coming over to-morrow to see you and tell me
> how you are. This round thing is a kiss for good-night.
>   YOUR JACK."

"Isn't that spoony? You'd better hide your face, I
think. He's getting to be a regular mollycoddle, isn't he?"
jeered Joe, as the boys laughed, and then grew sober, seeing
Jack's head buried in the bedclothes, after sending a pillow
at his tormentor.

It nearly hit Mrs. Minot, coming in with her patient's
tea on a tray, and at sight of her the guests hurriedly took
leave, Joe nearly tumbling downstairs to escape from
Frank, who would have followed, if his mother had not said
quickly,—

"Stay, and tell me what is the matter."

"Only teasing Jack a bit. Don't be mad, old boy; Joe
didn't mean any harm, and it *was* rather soft, now wasn't
it?" asked Frank, trying to appease the wounded feelings of
his brother.

"I charged you not to worry him. Those boys were too

much for the poor dear, and I ought not to have left him,"
said Mamma, as she vainly endeavored to find and caress the
yellow head burrowed so far out of sight that nothing but
one red ear was visible.

"He liked it, and we got on capitally till Joe roughed
him about Jill. Ah, Joe's getting it now! I thought Gus and
Ed would do that little job for me," added Frank, running to
the window as the sound of stifled cries and laughter
reached him.

The red ear heard also, and Jack popped up his head to
ask, with interest, —

"What are they doing to him?"

"Rolling him in the snow, and he's howling like fun."

"Serves him right," muttered Jack, with a frown.
Then, as a wail arose suggestive of an unpleasant mixture of
snow in the mouth and thumps on the back, he burst out
laughing, and said, good-naturedly, "Go and stop them,
Frank; I won't mind, only tell him it was a mean trick.
Hurry! Gus is so strong he doesn't know how his pounding
hurts."

Off ran Frank, and Jack told his wrongs to his mother.
She sympathized heartily, and saw no harm in the affectionate little note, which would please Jill, and help her to bear
her trials patiently.

"It isn't silly to be fond of her, is it? She is so nice and
funny, and tries to be good, and likes me, and I won't be
ashamed of my friends, if folks do laugh," protested Jack,
with a rap of his teaspoon.

"No, dear, it is quite kind and proper, and I'd rather
have you play with a merry little girl than with rough boys
till you are big enough to hold your own," answered
Mamma, putting the cup to his lips that the reclining lad
might take his broma without spilling.

"Pooh! I don't mean that; I'm strong enough now to
take care of myself," cried Jack, stoutly. "I can thrash Joe any
day, if I like. Just look at my arm; there's muscle for you!"
and up went a sleeve, to the great danger of overturning the
tray, as the boy proudly displayed his biceps and expanded
his chest, both of which were very fine for a lad of his years.
"If I'd been on my legs, he wouldn't have dared to insult me,
and it was cowardly to hit a fellow when he was down."

Mrs. Minot wanted to laugh at Jack's indignation, but
the bell rang, and she had to go and pull in the basket, much
amused at the new game.

Burning to distinguish herself in the eyes of the big
boys, Jill had sent over a tall, red flannel night-cap, which
she had been making for some proposed Christmas plays,
and added the following verse, for she was considered a
gifted rhymester at the game parties: —

> "When it comes night,
>   We put out the light.
>   Some blow with a puff,
>   Some turn down and snuff;
>   But neat folks prefer
>   A nice extinguis*her*,
>   So here I send you back
>   One to put on Mr. Jack."

"Now, I call that regularly smart; not one of us could
do it, and I just wish Joe was here to see it. I want to send
once more, something good for tea; she hates gruel so;" and
the last despatch which the Great International Telegraph
carried that day was a baked apple and a warm muffin, with
"J. M.'s best regards."

Ward No. 2

Chapter 4 ᧡

*T*hings were not so gay in Ward No. 2, for Mrs. Pecq was very busy, and Jill had nothing to amuse her but flying visits from the girls, and such little plays as she could invent for herself in bed. Fortunately, she had a lively fancy, and so got on pretty well, till keeping still grew unbearable, and the active child ached in every limb to be up and out. That, however, was impossible, for the least attempt to sit or stand brought on the pain that took her breath away and made her glad to lie flat again. The doctor spoke cheerfully, but looked sober, and Mrs. Pecq began to fear that Janey was to be a cripple for life. She said nothing, but Jill's quick eyes saw an added trouble in the always anxious face, and it depressed her spirits, though she never guessed half the mischief the fall had done.

The telegraph was a great comfort, and the two invalids kept up a lively correspondence, not to say traffic in light articles, for the Great International was the only aerial express in existence. But even this amusement flagged after a time; neither had much to tell, and when the daily health bulletins had been exchanged, messages gave out, and the basket's travels grew more and more infrequent. Neither could read all the time, games were soon used up, their mates were at school most of the day, and after a week or two the poor children began to get pale and fractious with the confinement, always so irksome to young people.

"I do believe the child will fret herself into a fever, mem, and I'm clean distraught to know what to do for her. She never used to mind trifles, but now she frets about the

oddest things, and I can't change them. This wall-paper is
well enough, but she has taken a fancy that the spots on it
look like spiders, and it makes her nervous. I've no other
warm place to put her, and no money for a new paper. Poor
lass! there are hard times before her, I'm fearing."

Mrs. Pecq said this in a low voice to Mrs. Minot, who
came in as often as she could, to see what her neighbor
needed; for both mothers were anxious, and sympathy
drew them to one another. While one woman talked, the
other looked about the little room, not wondering in the
least that Jill found it hard to be contented there. It was very
neat, but so plain that there was not even a picture on the
walls, or an ornament upon the mantel, except the necessary clock, lamp, and match-box. The paper *was* ugly, being
a deep buff with a brown figure that did look very like spiders sprawling over it, and might well make one nervous to
look at day after day.

Jill was asleep in the folding-chair Dr. Whiting had
sent, with a mattress to make it soft. The back could be
raised or lowered at will; but only a few inches had been
gained as yet, and the thin hair pillow was all she could bear.
She looked very pretty as she lay, with dark lashes against
the feverish cheeks, lips apart, and a cloud of curly black
locks all about the face pillowed on one arm. She seemed
like a brilliant little flower in that dull place, — for the
French blood in her veins gave her a color, warmth, and
grace which were very charming. Her natural love of beauty
showed itself in many ways: a red ribbon had tied up her
hair, a gay but faded shawl was thrown over the bed, and
the gifts sent her were arranged with care upon the table by
her side among her own few toys and treasures. There was
something pathetic in this childish attempt to beautify the

poor place, and Mrs. Minot's eyes were full as she looked at the tired woman, whose one joy and comfort lay there in such sad plight.

"My dear soul, cheer up, and we will help one another through the hard times," she said, with a soft hand on the rough one, and a look that promised much.

"Please God, we will, mem! With such good friends, I never should complain. I try not to do it, but it breaks my heart to see my little lass spoiled for life, most like;" and Mrs. Pecq pressed the kind hand with a despondent sigh.

"We won't say, or even think, that, yet. Everything is possible to youth and health like Janey's. We must keep her happy, and time will do the rest, I'm sure. Let us begin at once, and have a surprise for her when she wakes."

As she spoke, Mrs. Minot moved quietly about the room, pinning the pages of several illustrated papers against the wall at the foot of the bed, and placing to the best advantage the other comforts she had brought.

"Keep up your heart, neighbor. I have an idea in my head which I think will help us all, if I can carry it out," she said, cheerily, as she went, leaving Mrs. Pecq to sew on Jack's new night-gowns, with swift fingers, and the grateful wish that she might work for these good friends for ever.

As if the whispering and rustling had disturbed her, Jill soon began to stir, and slowly opened the eyes which had closed so wearily on the dull December afternoon. The bare wall with its brown spiders no longer confronted her, but the colored print of a little girl dancing to the tune her father was playing on a guitar, while a stately lady, with satin dress, ruff, and powder, stood looking on, well pleased. The quaint figure, in its belaced frock, quilted petticoat, and red-heeled shoes, seemed to come tripping toward her in such a life-like way, that she almost saw the curls blow back, heard the rustle of the rich brocade, and caught the sparkle of the little maid's bright eyes.

"Oh, how pretty! Who sent them?" asked Jill, eagerly, as her eye glanced along the wall, seeing other new and interesting things beyond: an elephant-hunt, a ship in full sail, a horse-race, and a ball-room.

"The good fairy who never comes empty-handed. Look round a bit and you will see more pretties, — all for you, my dearie;" and her mother pointed to a bunch of purple grapes in a green leaf plate, a knot of bright flowers pinned on the white curtain, and a gay little double gown across the foot of the bed.

Jill clapped her hands, and was enjoying her new pleasures, when in came Merry and Molly Loo, with Boo, of course, trotting after her like a fat and amiable puppy. Then the good times began; the gown was put on, the fruit tasted, and the pictures were studied like famous works of art.

"It's a splendid plan to cover up that hateful wall. I'd stick pictures all round and have a gallery. That reminds me! Up in the garret at our house is a box full of old fashion-books my aunt left. I often look at them on rainy days, and they are very funny. I'll go this minute and get every one. We can pin them up, or make paper dolls;" and away rushed Molly Loo, with the small brother waddling behind, for, when he lost sight of her, he was desolate indeed.

The girls had fits of laughter over the queer costumes of years gone by, and put up a splendid procession of ladies in full skirts, towering hats, pointed slippers, powdered hair, simpering faces, and impossible waists.

"I do think this bride is perfectly splendid, the long train and veil are so sweet," said Jill, revelling in fine clothes as she turned from one plate to another.

"I like the elephants best, and I'd give anything to go

on a hunt like that!" cried Molly Loo, who rode cows, drove any horse she could get, had nine cats, and was not afraid of the biggest dog that ever barked.

"I fancy 'The Dancing Lesson;' it is so sort of splendid, with the great windows, gold chairs, and fine folks. Oh, I would like to live in a castle with a father and mother like that," said Merry, who was romantic, and found the old farmhouse on the hill a sad trial to her high-flown ideas of elegance.

"Now, that ship, setting out for some far-away place, is more to my mind. I weary for home now and then, and mean to see it again some day;" and Mrs. Pecq looked longingly at the English ship, though it was evidently outward bound. Then, as if reproaching herself for discontent, she added: "It looks like those I used to see going off to India with a load of missionaries. I came near going myself once, with a lady bound for Siam; but I went to Canada with her sister, and here I am."

"I'd like to be a missionary and go where folks throw their babies to the crocodiles. I'd watch and fish them out, and have a school, and bring them up, and convert all the people till they knew better," said warm-hearted Molly Loo, who befriended every abused animal and forlorn child she met.

"We needn't go to Africa to be missionaries; they have 'em nearer home and need 'em, too. In all the big cities there are a many, and they have their hands full with the poor, the wicked, and the helpless. One can find that sort of work anywhere, if one has a mind," said Mrs. Pecq.

"I wish we had some to do here. I'd like to go round with baskets of tea and rice, and give out tracts and talk to people. Wouldn't you, girls?" asked Molly, much taken with the new idea.

"It would be rather nice to have a society all to ourselves, and have meetings and resolutions and things," answered Merry, who was fond of little ceremonies, and
always went to the sewing circle with her mother.

"We wouldn't let the boys come in. We'd have it a secret society, as they do their temperance lodge, and we'd
have badges and pass-words and grips. It would be fun if we
can only get some heathen to work at!" cried Jill, ready for
fresh enterprises of every sort.

"I can tell you some one to begin on right away," said
her mother, nodding at her. "As wild a little savage as I'd
wish to see. Take her in hand, and make a pretty-mannered
lady of her. Begin at home, my lass, and you'll find missionary work enough for a while."

"Now, Mammy, you mean me! Well, I will begin; and
I'll be so good, folks won't know me. Being sick makes
naughty children behave in story-books. I'll see if live ones
can't;" and Jill put on such a sanctified face that the girls
laughed and asked for their missions also, thinking they
would be the same.

"You, Merry, might do a deal at home helping mother,
and setting the big brothers a good example. One little girl
in a house can do pretty much as she will, especially if she
has a mind to make plain things nice and comfortable, and
not long for castles before she knows how to do her own
tasks well," was the first unexpected reply.

Merry colored, but took the reproof sweetly, resolving to do what she could, and surprised to find how many
ways seemed open to her after a few minutes' thought.

"Where shall I begin? I'm not afraid of a dozen crocodiles after Miss Bat;" and Molly Loo looked about her with a
fierce air, having had practice in battles with the old lady
who kept her father's house.

"Well, dear, you haven't far to look for as nice a little heathen as you'd wish;" and Mrs. Pecq glanced at Boo, who sat on the floor staring hard at them, attracted by the dread word "crocodile." He had a cold and no handkerchief, his little hands were red with chilblains, his clothes shabby, he had untidy darns in the knees of his stockings, and a head of tight curls that evidently had not been combed for some time.

"Yes, I know he is, and I try to keep him decent, but I forget, and he hates to be fixed, and Miss Bat doesn't care, and father laughs when I talk about it."

Poor Molly Loo looked much ashamed as she made excuses, trying at the same time to mend matters by seizing Boo and dusting him all over with her handkerchief, giving a pull at his hair as if ringing bells, and then dumping him down again with the despairing exclamation: "Yes, we're a pair of heathens, and there's no one to save us if I don't."

That was true enough; for Molly's father was a busy man, careless of everything but his mills. Miss Bat was old and lazy, and felt as if she might take life easy after serving the motherless children for many years as well as she knew how. Molly was beginning to see how much amiss things were at home, and old enough to feel mortified, though, as yet, she had done nothing to mend the matter except be kind to the little boy.

"You will, my dear," answered Mrs. Pecq, encouragingly, for she knew all about it. "Now you've each got a mission, let us see how well you will get on. Keep it secret, if you like, and report once a week. I'll be a member, and we'll do great things yet."

"We won't begin till after Christmas; there is so much to do, we never shall have time for any more. Don't tell, and we'll start fair at New Year's, if not before," said Jill, taking the lead as usual. Then they went on with the gay ladies, who certainly were heathen enough in dress to be in sad need of conversion,—to common-sense at least.

"I feel as if I was at a party," said Jill, after a pause occupied in surveying her gallery with great satisfaction, for dress was her delight, and here she had every conceivable style and color.

"Talking of parties, isn't it too bad that we must give up our Christmas fun? Can't get on without you and Jack, so we are not going to do a thing, but just have our presents," said Merry, sadly, as they began to fit different heads and bodies together, to try droll effects.

"I shall be all well in a fortnight, I know; but Jack won't, for it will take more than a month to mend his poor leg. May be they will have a dance in the boys' big room, and he can look on," suggested Jill, with a glance at the dancing damsel on the wall, for she dearly loved it, and never guessed how long it would be before her light feet would keep time to music again.

"You'd better give Jack a hint about the party. Send over some smart ladies, and say they have come to his Christmas ball," proposed audacious Molly Loo, always ready for fun.

So they put a preposterous green bonnet, top-heavy with plumes, on a little lady in yellow, who sat in a carriage; the lady beside her, in winter costume of velvet pelisse and ermine boa, was fitted to a bride's head with its orange flowers and veil, and these works of art were sent over to Jack, labelled "Miss Laura and Lotty Burton going to the Minots' Christmas ball,"—a piece of naughtiness on Jill's part, for she knew Jack liked the pretty sisters, whose gentle manners made her own wild ways seem all the more blamable.

No answer came for a long time, and the girls had

almost forgotten their joke in a game of Letters, when "Tingle, tangle!" went the bell, and the basket came in heavily laden. A roll of colored papers was tied outside, and within was a box that rattled, a green and silver horn, a roll of narrow ribbons, a spool of strong thread, some large needles, and a note from Mrs. Minot:——

DEAR JILL,——I think of having a Christmas tree so that our invalids can enjoy it, and all your elegant friends are cordially invited. Knowing that you would like to help, I send some paper for sugar-plum horns and some beads for necklaces. They will brighten the tree and please the girls for themselves or their dolls. Jack sends you a horn for a pattern, and will you make a ladder-necklace to show him how? Let me know if you need anything.

YOURS IN HASTE,
ANNA MINOT.

"She knew what the child would like, bless her kind heart," said Mrs. Pecq to herself, and something brighter than the most silvery bead shone on Jack's shirt-sleeve, as she saw the rapture of Jill over the new work and the promised pleasure.

Joyful cries greeted the opening of the box, for bunches of splendid large bugles appeared in all colors, and a lively discussion went on as to the best contrasts. Jill could not refuse to let her friends share the pretty work, and soon three necklaces glittered on three necks, as each admired her own choice.

"I'd be willing to hurt my back dreadfully, if I could lie and do such lovely things all day," said Merry, as she reluctantly put down her needle at last, for home duties waited to be done, and looked more than ever distasteful after this new pleasure.

"So would I! Oh, do you think Mrs. Minot will let you

fill the horns when they are done? I'd love to help you then. Be sure you send for me!" cried Molly Loo, arching her neck like a proud pigeon to watch the glitter of her purple and gold necklace on her brown gown.

"I'm afraid you couldn't be trusted, you love sweeties so, and I'm sure Boo couldn't. But I'll see about it," replied Jill, with a responsible air.

The mention of the boy recalled him to their minds, and looking round they found him peacefully absorbed in polishing up the floor with Molly's pocket-handkerchief and oil from the little machine-can. Being torn from this congenial labor, he was carried off shining with grease and roaring lustily.

But Jill did not mind her loneliness now, and sang like a happy canary while she threaded her sparkling beads, or hung the gay horns to dry, ready for their cargoes of sweets. So Mrs. Minot's recipe for sunshine proved successful, and mother-wit made the wintry day a bright and happy one for both the little prisoners.

Secrets

CHAPTER 5

There were a great many clubs in Harmony Village, but as we intend to interest ourselves with the affairs of the young folks only, we need not dwell upon the intellectual amusements of the elders. In summer, the boys devoted themselves to base-ball, the girls to boating, and all got rosy, stout, and strong, in these healthful exercises. In winter, the lads had their debating club, the lasses a dramatic ditto. At the former, astonishing bursts of oratory were heard; at the latter, everything was boldly attempted, from

Romeo and Juliet to Mother Goose's immortal melodies. The two clubs frequently met and mingled their attractions in a really entertaining manner, for the speakers made good actors, and the young actresses were most appreciative listeners to the eloquence of each budding Demosthenes.

Great plans had been afoot for Christmas or New Year, but when the grand catastrophe put an end to the career of one of the best "spouters," and caused the retirement of the favorite "singing chambermaid," the affair was postponed till February, when Washington's birthday was always celebrated by the patriotic town, where the father of his country once put on his night-cap, or took off his boots, as that ubiquitous hero appears to have done in every part of the United States.

Meantime the boys were studying Revolutionary characters, and the girls rehearsing such dramatic scenes as they thought most appropriate and effective for the 22d. In both of these attempts they were much helped by the sense and spirit of Ralph Evans, a youth of nineteen, who was a great favorite with the young folks, not only because he was a good, industrious fellow, who supported his grandmother, but also full of talent, fun, and ingenuity. It was no wonder every one who really knew him liked him, for he could turn his hand to anything, and loved to do it. If the girls were in despair about a fire-place when acting "The Cricket on the Hearth," he painted one, and put a gas-log in it that made the kettle really boil, to their great delight. If the boys found the interest of their club flagging, Ralph would convulse them by imitations of the "Member from Cranberry Centre," or fire them with speeches of famous statesmen. Charity fairs could not get on without him, and in the store where he worked he did many an ingenious job, which made him valued for his mechanical skill, as well as for his energy and integrity.

Mrs. Minot liked to have him with her sons, because they also were to paddle their own canoes by and by, and she believed that, rich or poor, boys make better men for learning to use the talents they possess, not merely as ornaments, but tools with which to carve their own fortunes; and the best help toward this end is an example of faithful work, high aims, and honest living. So Ralph came often, and in times of trouble was a real rainy-day friend. Jack grew very fond of him during his imprisonment, for the good youth ran in every evening to get commissions, amuse the boy with droll accounts of the day's adventures, or invent lifts, bed-tables, and foot-rests for the impatient invalid. Frank found him a sure guide through the mechanical mysteries which he loved, and spent many a useful half-hour discussing cylinders, pistons, valves, and balance-wheels. Jill also came in for her share of care and comfort; the poor little back lay all the easier for the air-cushion Ralph got her, and the weary headaches found relief from the spray atomizer, which softly distilled its scented dew on the hot forehead till she fell asleep.

Round the beds of Jack and Jill met and mingled the school-mates of whom our story treats. Never, probably, did invalids have gayer times than our two, after a week of solitary confinement; for school gossip crept in, games could not be prevented, and Christmas secrets were concocted in those rooms till they were regular conspirators' dens, when they were not little Bedlams.

After the horn and bead labors were over, the stringing of pop-corn on red, and cranberries on white, threads, came next, and Jack and Jill often looked like a new kind of spider in the pretty webs hung about them, till reeled off to bide their time in the Christmas closet. Paper flowers followed, and gay garlands and bouquets blossomed, regardless of the snow and frost without. Then there was a great scribbling of names, verses, and notes to accompany the steadily increasing store of odd parcels which were collected at the Minots', for gifts from every one were to ornament the tree, and contributions poured in as the day drew near.

But the secret which most excited the young people was the deep mystery of certain proceedings at the Minot house. No one but Frank, Ralph, and Mamma knew what it was, and the two boys nearly drove the others distracted by the tantalizing way in which they hinted at joys to come, talked strangely about birds, went measuring round with foot-rules, and shut themselves up in the Boys' Den, as a certain large room was called. This seemed to be the centre of operations, but beyond the fact of the promised tree no ray of light was permitted to pass the jealously guarded doors. Strange men with paste-pots and ladders went in, furniture was dragged about, and all sorts of boyish lumber was sent up garret and down cellar. Mrs. Minot was seen pondering over heaps of green stuff, hammering was heard, singular bundles were smuggled upstairs, flowering plants betrayed their presence by whiffs of fragrance when the door was opened, and Mrs. Pecq was caught smiling all by herself in a back bedroom, which usually was shut up in winter.

"They are going to have a play, after all, and that green stuff was the curtain," said Molly Loo, as the girls talked it over one day, when they sat with their backs turned to one another, putting last stitches in certain bits of work which had to be concealed from all eyes, though it was found convenient to ask one another's taste as to the color, materials, and sizes of these mysterious articles.

"I think it is going to be a dance. I heard the boys doing their steps when I went in last evening to find out whether Jack liked blue or yellow best, so I could put the bow on his pen-wiper," declared Merry, knitting briskly away at the last of the pair of pretty white bed-socks she was making for Jill right under her inquisitive little nose.

"They wouldn't have a party of that kind without Jack and me. It is only an extra nice tree, you see if it isn't," answered Jill from behind the pillows which made a temporary screen to hide the toilet mats she was preparing for all her friends.

"Every one of you is wrong, and you'd better rest easy, for you won't find out the best part of it, try as you may." And Mrs. Pecq actually chuckled as she, too, worked away at some bits of muslin, with her back turned to the very unsocial-looking group.

"Well, I don't care, we've got a secret all our own, and won't ever tell, will we?" cried Jill, falling back on the Home Missionary Society, though it was not yet begun.

"Never!" answered the girls, and all took great comfort in the idea that one mystery would not be cleared up, even at Christmas.

Jack gave up guessing, in despair, after he had suggested a new dining-room where he could eat with the family, a private school in which his lessons might go on with a tutor, or a theatre for the production of the farces in which he delighted.

"It is going to be used to keep something in that you are very fond of," said Mamma, taking pity on him at last.

"Ducks?" asked Jack, with a half pleased, half puzzled air, not quite seeing where the water was to come from.

Frank exploded at the idea, and added to the mystification by saying,—

"There will be one little duck and one great donkey in it."

Then, fearing he had told the secret, he ran off, quacking and braying derisively.

"It is to be used for creatures that I, too, am fond of, and you know neither donkeys nor ducks are favorites of mine," said Mamma, with a demure expression, as she sat turning over old clothes for the bundles that always went to poor neighbors, with a little store of goodies, at this time of the year.

"I know! I know! It is to be a new ward for more sick folks, isn't it, now?" cried Jack, with what he thought a great proof of shrewdness.

"I don't see how I could attend to many more patients till this one is off my hands," answered Mamma, with a queer smile, adding quickly, as if she too was afraid of letting the cat out of the bag: "That reminds me of a Christmas I once spent among the hospitals and poor-houses of a great city with a good lady who, for thirty years, had made it her mission to see that these poor little souls had one merry day. We gave away two hundred dolls, several great boxes of candy and toys, besides gay pictures, and new clothes to orphan children, sick babies, and half-grown innocents. Ah, my boy, that was a day to remember all my life, to make me doubly grateful for my blessings, and very glad to serve the helpless and afflicted, as that dear woman did."

The look and tone with which the last words were uttered effectually turned Jack's thoughts from the great secret, and started another small one, for he fell to planning what he would buy with his pocket-money to surprise the little Pats and Biddies who were to have no Christmas tree.

Surprises

CHAPTER 6

"Is it pleasant?" was the question Jill asked before she was fairly awake on Christmas morning.

"Yes, dear; as bright as heart could wish. Now eat a bit, and then I'll make you nice for the day's pleasure. I only hope it won't be too much for you," answered Mrs. Pecq, bustling about, happy, yet anxious, for Jill was to be carried over to Mrs. Minot's, and it was her first attempt at going out since the accident.

It seemed as if nine o'clock would never come, and Jill, with wraps all ready, lay waiting in a fever of impatience for the doctor's visit, as he wished to superintend the moving. At last he came, found all promising, and having bundled up his small patient, carried her, with Frank's help, in her chair-bed to the ox-sled, which was drawn to the next door, and Miss Jill landed in the Boys' Den before she had time to get either cold or tired. Mrs. Minot took her things off with a cordial welcome, but Jill never said a word, for, after one exclamation, she lay staring about her, dumb with surprise and delight at what she saw.

The great room was entirely changed; for now it looked like a garden, or one of the fairy scenes children love, where in-doors and out-of-doors are pleasantly combined. The ceiling was pale blue, like the sky; the walls were covered with a paper like a rustic trellis, up which climbed morning-glories so naturally that the many-colored bells seemed dancing in the wind. Birds and butterflies flew among them, and here and there, through arches in the trellis, one seemed to look into a sunny summer world, contrasting curiously with the wintry landscape lying beyond the real windows, festooned with evergreen garlands, and curtained only by stands of living flowers. A green drugget covered the floor like grass, rustic chairs from the garden stood about, and in the middle of the room a handsome hemlock waited for its pretty burden. A Yule-log blazed on the wide hearth, and over the chimney-piece, framed in holly, shone the words that set all hearts to dancing, "Merry Christmas!"

"Do you like it, dear? This is our surprise for you and Jack, and here we mean to have good times together," said Mrs. Minot, who had stood quietly enjoying the effect of her work.

"Oh, it is so lovely I don't know what to say!" and Jill put up both arms, as words failed her, and grateful kisses were all she had to offer.

"Can you suggest anything more to add to the pleasantness?" asked the gentle lady, holding the small hands in her own, and feeling well repaid by the child's delight.

"Only Jack;" and Jill's laugh was good to hear, as she glanced up with merry, yet wistful eyes.

"You are right. We'll have him in at once, or he will come hopping on one leg;" and away hurried his mother, laughing, too, for whistles, shouts, thumps, and violent demonstrations of all kinds had been heard from the room where Jack was raging with impatience, while he waited for his share of the surprise.

Jill could hardly lie still when she heard the roll of another chair-bed coming down the hall, its passage enlivened with cries of "Starboard! Port! Easy now! Pull away!" from

Ralph and Frank, as they steered the recumbent Columbus on his first voyage of discovery.

"Well, I call that handsome!" was Jack's exclamation, when the full beauty of the scene burst upon his view. Then he forgot all about it and gave a whoop of pleasure, for there beside the fire was an eager face, two hands beckoning, and Jill's voice crying, joyfully,—

"I'm here! I'm here! Oh, do come, quick!" Down the long room rattled the chair, Jack cheering all the way, and brought up beside the other one, as the long-parted friends exclaimed, with one accord,—

"Isn't this jolly!"

It certainly did look so, for Ralph and Frank danced a wild sort of fandango round the tree, Dr. Whiting stood and laughed, while the two mothers beamed from the doorway, and the children, not knowing whether to laugh or to cry, compromised the matter by clapping their hands and shouting, "Merry Christmas to everybody!" like a pair of little maniacs.

Then they all sobered down, and the busy ones went off to the various duties of the day, leaving the young invalids to repose and enjoy themselves together.

"How nice you look," said Jill, when they had duly admired the pretty room.

"So do you," gallantly returned Jack, as he surveyed her with unusual interest.

They did look very nice, though happiness was the principal beautifier. Jill wore a red wrapper, with the most brilliant of all the necklaces sparkling at her throat, over a nicely crimped frill her mother had made in honor of the day. All the curly black hair was gathered into a red net, and a pair of smart little moccasins covered the feet that had not stepped for many a weary day. Jack was not so gay, but had made himself as fine as circumstances would permit. A gray dressing-gown, with blue cuffs and collar, was very becoming to the blonde youth; an immaculate shirt, best studs, sleeve-buttons, blue tie, and handkerchief wet with cologne sticking out of the breast-pocket, gave an air of elegance in spite of the afghan spread over the lower portions of his manly form. The yellow hair was brushed till it shone, and being parted in the middle, to hide the black patch, made two engaging little "quirls" on his forehead. The summer tan had faded from his cheeks, but his eyes were as blue as the wintry sky, and nearly every white tooth was visible as he smiled on his partner in misfortune, saying cheerily, —

"I'm ever so glad to see you again; guess we are over the worst of it now, and can have good times. Won't it be fun to stay here all the while, and amuse one another?"

"Yes, indeed; but one day is so short! It will be stupider than ever when I go home to-night," answered Jill, looking about her with longing eyes.

"But you are not going home to-night; you are to stay ever so long. Didn't Mamma tell you?"

"No. Oh, how splendid! Am I really? Where will I sleep? What will Mammy do without me?" and Jill almost sat up, she was so delighted with the new surprise.

"That room in there is all fixed for you. I made Frank tell me so much. Mamma said I might tell you, but I didn't think she would be able to hold in if she saw you first. Your mother is coming, too, and we are all going to have larks together till we are well."

The splendor of this arrangement took Jill's breath away, and before she got it again, in came Frank and Ralph with two clothes-baskets of treasures to be hung upon the tree. While they wired on the candles the children asked questions, and found out all they wanted to know about the new plans and pleasures.

"Who fixed all this?"

"Mamma thought of it, and Ralph and I did it. He's the man for this sort of thing, you know. He proposed cutting out the arches and sticking on birds and butterflies just where they looked best. I put those canaries over there, they looked so well against the blue;" and Frank proudly pointed out some queer orange-colored fowls, looking as if they were having fits in the air, but very effective, nevertheless.

"Your mother said you might call this the Bird Room. We caught a scarlet-tanager for you to begin with, didn't we, Jack?" and Ralph threw a *bonbon* at Jill, who looked very like a bright little bird in a warm nest.

"Good for you! Yes, and we are going to keep her in this pretty cage till we can both fly off together. I say, Jill, where shall we be in our classes when we do get back?" and Jack's merry face fell at the thought.

"At the foot, if we don't study and keep up. Doctor said I might study sometimes, if I'd lie still as long as he thought best, and Molly brought home my books, and Merry says she will come in every day and tell me where the lessons are. I don't mean to fall behind, if my backbone is cracked," said Jill, with a decided nod that made several black rings fly out of the net to dance on her forehead.

"Frank said he'd pull me along in my Latin, but I've been lazy and haven't done a thing. Let's go at it and start fair for New Year," proposed Jack, who did not love study as the bright girl did, but was ashamed to fall behind her in anything.

"All right. They've been reviewing, so we can keep up when they begin, if we work next week, while the rest have a holiday. Oh, dear, I do miss school dreadfully;" and Jill sighed for the old desk, every blot and notch of which was dear to her.

"There come our things, and pretty nice they look, too," said Jack; and his mother began to dress the tree, hanging up the gay horns, the gilded nuts, red and yellow apples and oranges, and festooning long strings of pop-corn and scarlet cranberries from bough to bough, with the glittering necklaces hung where the light would show their colors best.

"I never saw such a splendid tree before. I'm glad we could help, though we were ill. Is it all done now?" asked Jill, when the last parcel was tied on and everybody stood back to admire the pretty sight.

"One thing more. Hand me that box, Frank, and be very careful that you fasten this up firmly, Ralph," answered Mrs. Minot, as she took from its wrappings the waxen figure of a little child. The rosy limbs were very life-like, so was the smiling face under the locks of shining hair. Both plump arms were outspread as if to scatter blessings over all, and downy wings seemed to flutter from the dimpled shoulders, making an angel of the baby.

"Is it St. Nicholas?" asked Jill, who had never seen that famous personage, and knew but little of Christmas festivities.

"It is the Christ-child, whose birthday we are celebrating. I got the best I could find, for I like the idea better than old Santa Claus; though we *may* have him, too," said Mamma, holding the little image so that both could see it well.

"It looks like a real baby;" and Jack touched the rosy foot with the tip of his finger, as if expecting a crow from the half-open lips.

"It reminds me of the saints in the chapel of the Sacred

Heart in Montreal. One little St. John looked like this, only
he had a lamb instead of wings," said Jill, stroking the flaxen
hair, and wishing she dared ask for it to play with.

"He is the children's saint to pray to, love, and imitate, for he never forgot them, but blessed and healed and
taught them all his life. This is only a poor image of the holi-
est baby ever born, but I hope it will keep his memory in
your minds all day, because this is the day for good resolutions, happy thoughts, and humble prayers, as well as play
and gifts and feasting."

While she spoke, Mrs. Minot, touching the little figure as tenderly as if it were alive, had tied a broad white ribbon round it, and, handing it to Ralph, bade him fasten it to
the hook above the tree-top, where it seemed to float as if
the downy wings supported it.

Jack and Jill lay silently watching, with a sweet sort of
soberness in their young faces, and for a moment the room
was very still as all eyes looked up at the Blessed Child. The
sunshine seemed to grow more golden as it flickered on the
little head, the flames glanced about the glittering tree as if
trying to climb and kiss the baby feet, and, without, a chime
of bells rang sweetly, calling people to hear again the lovely
story of the life begun on Christmas Day.

Only a minute, but it did them good, and presently,
when the pleasant work was over, and the workers gone,
the boys to church, and Mamma to see about lunch for the
invalids, Jack said, gravely, to Jill,—

"I think we ought to be extra good, every one is so
kind to us, and we are getting well, and going to have such
capital times. Don't see how we can do anything else to
show we are grateful."

"It isn't easy to be good when one is sick," said Jill,
thoughtfully. "I fret dreadfully, I get so tired of being still. I

want to scream sometimes, but I don't, because it would scare Mammy, so I cry. Do you cry, Jack?"

"Men never do. I want to tramp round when things bother me; but I can't, so I kick and say, 'Hang it!' and when I get very bad I pitch into Frank, and he lets me. I tell you, Jill, he's a good brother!" and Jack privately resolved then and there to invite Frank to take it out of him in any form he pleased as soon as health would permit.

"I rather think we *shall* grow good in this pretty place, for I don't see how we can be bad if we want to, it is all so nice and sort of pious here," said Jill, with her eyes on the angel over the tree.

"A fellow can be awfully hungry, I know that. I didn't half eat breakfast, I was in such a hurry to see you, and know all about the secrets. Frank kept saying I couldn't guess, that you had come, and I never would be ready, till finally I got mad and fired an egg at him, and made no end of a mess."

Jack and Jill went off into a gale of laughter at the idea of dignified Frank dodging the egg that smashed on the wall, leaving an indelible mark of Jack's besetting sin, impatience.

Just then Mrs. Minot came in, well pleased to hear such pleasant sounds, and to see two merry faces, where usually one listless one met her anxious eyes.

"The new medicine works well, neighbor," she said to Mrs. Pecq, who followed with the lunch tray.

"Indeed it does, mem. I feel as if I'd taken a sup myself, I'm that easy in my mind."

And she looked so, too, for she seemed to have left all her cares in the little house when she locked the door behind her, and now stood smiling with a clean apron on, so fresh and cheerful, that Jill hardly knew her own mother.

"Things taste better when you have some one to eat

with you," observed Jack, as they devoured sandwiches, and drank milk out of little mugs with rose buds on them.

"Don't eat too much, or you won't be ready for the next surprise," said his mother, when the plates were empty, and the last drop gone down throats dry with much chatter.

"More surprises! Oh, what fun!" cried Jill. And all the rest of the morning, in the intervals of talk and play, they tried to guess what it could be.

At two o'clock they found out, for dinner was served in the Bird Room, and the children revelled in the simple feast prepared for them. The two mothers kept the little bed-tables well supplied, and fed their nurslings like maternal birds, while Frank presided over the feast with great dignity, and ate a dinner which would have astonished Mamma, if she had not been too busy to observe how fast the mince pie vanished.

"The girls said Christmas was spoiled because of us; but I don't think so, and they won't either, when they see this splendid place and know all about our nice plans," said Jill, luxuriously eating the nut-meats Jack picked out for her, as they lay in Eastern style at the festive board.

"I call this broken bones made easy. I never had a better Christmas. Have a raisin? Here's a good fat one." And Jack made a long arm to Jill's mouth, which began to sing "Little Jack Horner," as an appropriate return.

"It would have been a lonesome one to all of us, I'm thinking, but for your mother, boys. My duty and hearty thanks to you, mem," put in grateful Mrs. Pecq, bowing over her coffee-cup as she had seen ladies bow over their wine-glasses at dinner parties in Old England.

"I rise to propose a health, Our Mothers." And Frank

stood up with a goblet of water, for not even at Christmas time was wine seen on that table.

"Hip, hip, hurra!" called Jack, baptizing himself with a good sprinkle, as he waved his glass and drank the toast with a look that made his mother's eyes fill with happy tears.

Jill threw her mother a kiss, feeling very grown up and elegant to be dining out in such style. Then they drank every one's health with much merriment, till Frank declared that Jack would float off on the deluge of water he splashed about in his enthusiasm, and Mamma proposed a rest after the merry-making.

"Now the best fun is coming, and we have not long to wait," said the boy, when naps and rides about the room had whiled away the brief interval between dinner and dusk, for the evening entertainment was to be an early one, to suit the invalids' bed-time.

"I hope the girls will like their things. I helped to choose them, and each has a nice present. I don't know mine, though, and I'm in a twitter to see it," said Jill, as they lay waiting for the fun to begin.

"I do; I chose it, so I know you will like one of them, anyway."

"Have I got more than one?"

"I guess you'll think so when they are handed down. The bell was going all day yesterday, and the girls kept bringing in bundles for you; I see seven now," and Jack rolled his eyes from one mysterious parcel to another hanging on the laden boughs.

"I know something, too. That square bundle is what you want ever so much. I told Frank, and he got it for his present. It is all red and gold outside, and every sort of color inside; you'll hurrah when you see it. That roundish one is yours too; I made them," cried Jill, pointing to a flat package tied to the stem of the tree, and a neat little roll in which were the blue mittens that she had knit for him.

"I can wait;" but the boy's eyes shone with eagerness, and he could not resist firing two or three pop-corns at it to see whether it was hard or soft.

"That barking dog is for Boo, and the little yellow sled, so Molly can drag him to school, he always tumbles down so when it is slippery," continued Jill, proud of her superior knowledge, as she showed a small spotted animal hanging by its tail, with a red tongue displayed as if about to taste the sweeties in the horn below.

"Don't talk about sleds, for mercy's sake! I never want to see another, and you wouldn't, either, if you had to lie with a flat-iron tied to your ankle, as I do," said Jack, with a kick of the well leg and an ireful glance at the weight attached to the other that it might not contract while healing.

"Well I think plasters, and liniment, and rubbing, as bad as flat-irons any day. I don't believe you have ached half so much as I have, though it sounds worse to break legs than to sprain your back," protested Jill, eager to prove herself the greater sufferer, as invalids are apt to be.

"I guess you wouldn't think so if you'd been pulled round as I was when they set my leg. Caesar, how it did hurt!" and Jack squirmed at the recollection of it.

"You didn't faint away as I did when the doctor was finding out if my *vertebrums* were hurt, so now!" cried Jill, bound to carry her point, though not at all clear what vertebrae were.

"Pooh! Girls always faint. Men are braver, and I didn't faint a bit in spite of all that horrid agony."

"You howled; Frank told me so. Doctor said *I* was a brave girl, so you needn't brag, for you'll have to go on a crutch for a while. I know that."

"You may have to use two of them for years, may be. I heard the doctor tell my mother so. I shall be up and about long before you will. Now then!"

Both children were getting excited, for the various pleasures of the day had been rather too much for them, and there is no knowing but they would have added the sad surprise of a quarrel to the pleasant ones of the day, if a cheerful whistle had not been heard, as Ralph came in to light the candles and give the last artistic touches to the room.

"Well, young folks, how goes it? Had a merry time so far?" he asked, as he fixed the steps and ran up with a lighted match in his hand.

"Very nice, thank you," answered a prim little voice from the dusk below, for only the glow of the fire filled the room just then.

Jack said nothing, and two red sulky faces were hidden in the dark, watching candle after candle sputter, brighten, and twinkle, till the trembling shadows began to flit away like imps afraid of the light.

"Now he will see my face, and I know it is cross," thought Jill, as Ralph went round the last circle, leaving another line of sparks among the hemlock boughs.

Jack thought the same, and had just got the frown smoothed out of his forehead, when Frank brought a fresh log, and a glorious blaze sprung up, filling every corner of the room, and dancing over the figures in the long chairs till they had to brighten whether they liked it or not. Presently the bell began to ring and gay voices to sound below: then Jill smiled in spite of herself as Molly Loo's usual cry of "Oh, dear, where *is* that child?" reached her, and Jack could not help keeping time to the march Ed played, while Frank and Gus marshalled the procession.

"Ready!" cried Mrs. Minot, at last, and up came the

troop of eager lads and lasses, brave in holiday suits, with faces to match. A unanimous "O, o, o!" burst from twenty tongues, as the full splendor of the tree, the room, and its inmates, dawned upon them; for not only did the pretty Christ-child hover above, but Santa Claus himself stood below, fur-clad, white-bearded, and powdered with snow from the dredging-box.

Ralph was a good actor, and, when the first raptures were over he distributed the presents with such droll speeches, jokes, and gambols, that the room rang with merriment, and passers-by paused to listen, sure that here, at least, Christmas was merry. It would be impossible to tell about all the gifts or the joy of the receivers, but every one was satisfied, and the king and queen of the revels so overwhelmed with little tokens of good-will, that their beds looked like booths at a fair. Jack beamed over the handsome postage-stamp book which had long been the desire of his heart, and Jill felt like a millionaire, with a silver fruit-knife, a pretty work-basket, and—oh! coals of fire on her head!— a ring from Jack.

A simple little thing enough, with one tiny turquoise forget-me-not, but something like a dew-drop fell on it when no one was looking, and she longed to say, "I'm sorry I was cross; forgive me, Jack." But it could not be done then, so she turned to admire Merry's bed-shoes, the pots of pansies, hyacinths, and geranium which Gus and his sisters sent for her window garden, Molly's queer Christmas pie, and the zither Ed promised to teach her how to play upon.

The tree was soon stripped, and pop-corns strewed the floor as the children stood about picking them off the red threads when candy gave out, with an occasional cranberry by way of relish. Boo insisted on trying the new sled at once, and enlivened the trip by the squeaking of the spotted dog, the toot of a tin trumpet, and shouts of joy at the splendor of the turn-out.

The girls all put on their necklaces, and danced about like fine ladies at a ball. The boys fell to comparing skates, balls, and cuff-buttons on the spot, while the little ones devoted all their energies to eating everything eatable they could lay their hands on.

Games were played till nine o'clock, and then the party broke up, after they had taken hands round the tree and sung a song written by one whom you all know, — so faithfully and beautifully does she love and labor for children the world over.

THE BLESSED DAY.

"What shall little children bring
    On Christmas Day, on Christmas Day?
What shall little children bring
    On Christmas Day in the morning?
This shall little children bring
    On Christmas Day, on Christmas Day;
Love and joy to Christ their king,
    On Christmas Day in the morning!

"What shall little children sing
    On Christmas Day, on Christmas Day?
What shall little children sing
    On Christmas Day in the morning?
The grand old carols shall they sing
    On Christmas Day, on Christmas Day;
With all their hearts, their offerings bring
    On Christmas Day in the morning."

Jack was carried off to bed in such haste that he had only time to call out, "Good-night!" before he was rolled away, gaping as he went. Jill soon found herself tucked up in the great white bed she was to share with her mother, and lay looking about the pleasant chamber, while Mrs. Pecq ran home for a minute to see that all was safe there for the night.

After the merry din the house seemed very still, with only a light step now and then, the murmur of voices not far away, or the jingle of sleigh-bells from without, and the little girl rested easily among the pillows, thinking over the pleasures of the day, too wide-awake for sleep. There was no lamp in the chamber, but she could look into the pretty Bird Room, where the fire-light still shone on flowery walls, deserted tree, and Christ-child floating above the green. Jill's eyes wandered there and lingered till they were full of regretful tears, because the sight of the little angel recalled the words spoken when it was hung up, the good resolution she had taken then, and how soon it was broken.

"I said I couldn't be bad in that lovely place, and I was a cross, ungrateful girl after all they've done for Mammy and me. Poor Jack *was* hurt the worst, and he *was* brave, though he did scream. I wish I could go and tell him so, and hear him say, 'All right.' Oh, me, I've spoiled the day!"

A great sob choked more words, and Jill was about to have a comfortable cry, when some one entered the other room, and she saw Frank doing something with a long cord and a thing that looked like a tiny drum. Quiet as a bright-eyed mouse, Jill peeped out wondering what it was, and suspecting mischief, for the boy was laughing to himself as he stretched the cord, and now and then bent over the little object in his hand, touching it with great care.

"May be it's a torpedo to blow up and scare me; Jack likes to play tricks. Well, I'll scream loud when it goes off, so he will be satisfied that I'm dreadfully frightened," thought Jill, little dreaming what the last surprise of the day was to be.

Presently a voice whispered,—

"I say! Are you awake?"

"Yes."

"Any one there but you?"

"No."

"Catch this, then. Hold it to your ear and see what you'll get."

The little drum came flying in, and, catching it, Jill, with some hesitation, obeyed Frank's order. Judge of her amazement when she caught in broken whispers these touching words:—

"Sorry I was cross. Forgive and forget. Start fair to-morrow. All right. Jack."

Jill was so delighted with this handsome apology, that she could not reply for a moment, then steadied her voice, and answered back in her sweetest tone,—

"I'm sorry, too. Never, never, will again. Feel much better now. Good-night, you dear old thing."

Satisfied with the success of his telephone, Frank twitched back the drum and vanished, leaving Jill to lay her cheek upon the hand that wore the little ring and fall asleep, saying to herself, with a farewell glance at the children's saint, dimly seen in the soft gloom, "I will not forget. I will be good!"

Jill's Mission
CHAPTER 7

*T*he good times began immediately, and very little studying was done that week in spite of the virtuous resolutions made by certain young persons on Christmas-day. But, dear me, how was it possible to settle down to lessons in the delightful Bird Room, with not only its own charms to distract one, but all the new gifts to enjoy, and a dozen calls a day to occupy one's time?

"I guess we'd better wait till the others are at school, and just go in for fun this week," said Jack, who was in great spirits at the prospect of getting up, for the splints were off, and he hoped to be promoted to crutches very soon.

"*I* shall keep my Speller by me and take a look at it every day, for that is what I'm most backward in. But I intend to devote myself to you, Jack, and be real kind and useful. I've made a plan to do it, and I mean to carry it out, any way," answered Jill, who had begun to be a missionary, and felt that this was a field of labor where she could distinguish herself.

"Here's a home mission all ready for you, and you can be paying your debts beside doing yourself good," Mrs. Pecq said to her in private, having found plenty to do herself.

Now Jill made one great mistake at the outset, — she forgot that she was the one to be converted to good manners and gentleness, and devoted her efforts to looking after Jack, finding it much easier to cure other people's faults than her own. Jack was a most engaging heathen, and needed very little instruction; therefore Jill thought her task would be an easy one. But three or four weeks of petting and play had rather demoralized both children, so Jill's Speller, though tucked under the sofa pillow every day, was seldom looked at, and Jack shirked his Latin shamefully. Both read all the story-books they could get, held daily levees in the Bird Room, and all their spare minutes were spent in teaching Snowdrop, the great Angora cat, to bring the ball when they dropped it in their game. So Saturday came, and both were rather the worse for so much idleness, since daily duties and studies are the wholesome bread which feeds the mind better than the dyspeptic plum-cake of sensational reading, or the unsubstantial *bon-bons* of frivolous amusement.

It was a stormy day, so they had few callers, and devoted themselves to arranging the album; for these books were all the rage just then, and boys met to compare, discuss, buy, sell, and "swap" stamps with as much interest as men on 'Change gamble in stocks. Jack had a nice little collection, and had been saving up pocket-money to buy a book in which to preserve his treasures. Now, thanks to Jill's timely suggestion, Frank had given him a fine one, and several friends had contributed a number of rare stamps to grace the large, inviting pages. Jill wielded the gum-brush and fitted on the little flaps, as her fingers were skilful at this nice work, and Jack put each stamp in its proper place with great rustling of leaves and comparing of marks. Returning, after a brief absence, Mrs. Minot beheld the countenances of the workers adorned with gay stamps, giving them a very curious appearance.

"My dears! what new play have you got now? Are you wild Indians? or letters that have gone round the world before finding the right address?" she asked, laughing at the ridiculous sight, for both were as sober as judges and deeply absorbed in some doubtful specimen.

"Oh, we just stuck them there to keep them safe; they get lost if we leave them lying round. It's very handy, for I can see in a minute what I want on Jill's face and she on mine, and put our fingers on the right chap at once," answered Jack, adding, with an anxious gaze at his friend's variegated countenance, "Where the dickens *is* my New Granada? It's rare, and I wouldn't lose it for a dollar."

"Why, there it is on your own nose. Don't you remember you put it there because you said mine was not big enough to hold it?" laughed Jill, tweaking a large orange square off the round nose of her neighbor, causing it to wrinkle up in a droll way, as the gum made the operation slightly painful.

"So I did, and gave you Little Bolivar on yours. Now I'll have Alsace and Lorraine, 1870. There are seven of them, so hold still and see how you like it," returned Jack, picking the large, pale stamps one by one from Jill's forehead, which they crossed like a band.

She bore it without flinching, saying to herself with a secret smile, as she glanced at the hot fire, which scorched her if she kept near enough to Jack to help him, "This really is being like a missionary, with a tattooed savage to look after. I have to suffer a little, as the good folks did who got speared and roasted sometimes; but I won't complain a bit, though my forehead smarts, my arms are tired, and one cheek is as red as fire."

"The Roman States make a handsome page, don't they?" asked Jack, little dreaming of the part he was playing in Jill's mind. "Oh, I say, isn't Corea a beauty. I'm ever so proud of that;" and he gazed fondly on a big blue stamp, the sole ornament of one page.

"I don't see why the Cape of Good Hope has pyramids. They ought to go in Egypt. The Sandwich Islands are all right, with heads of the black kings and queens on them," said Jill, feeling that they were very appropriate to her private play.

"Turkey has crescents, Australia swans, and Spain women's heads, with black bars across them. Frank says it is because they keep women shut up so; but that was only his fun. I'd rather have a good, honest green United States, with Washington on it, or a blue one-center with old Franklin, than all their eagles and lions and kings and queens put together," added the democratic boy, with a disrespectful slap on a crowned head as he settled Heligoland in its place.

"Why does Austria have Mercury on the stamp, I wonder? Do they wear helmets like that?" asked Jill, with the brush-handle in her mouth as she cut a fresh batch of flaps.

"May be he was postman to the gods, so he is put on stamps now. The Prussians wear helmets, but they have spikes like the old Roman fellows. I like Prussians ever so much; they fight splendidly, and always beat. Austrians have a handsome uniform, though."

"Talking of Romans reminds me that I have not heard your Latin for two days. Come, lazybones, brace up, and let us have it now. I've done my compo, and shall have just time before I go out for a tramp with Gus," said Frank, putting by a neat page to dry, for he studied every day like a conscientious lad as he was.

"Don't know it. Not going to try till next week. Grind away over your old Greek as much as you like, but don't bother me," answered Jack, frowning at the mere thought of the detested lesson.

But Frank adored his Xenophon, and would not see his old friend, Caesar, neglected without an effort to defend him; so he confiscated the gum-pot, and effectually stopped the stamp business by whisking away at one fell swoop all that lay on Jill's table.

"Now then, young man, you will quit this sort of nonsense and do your lesson, or you won't see these fellows again in a hurry. You asked me to hear you, and I'm going to do it; here's the book."

Frank's tone was the dictatorial one, which Jack hated and always found hard to obey, especially when he knew he ought to do it. Usually, when his patience was tried, he strode about the room, or ran off for a race round the garden, coming back breathless, but good-tempered. Now both these vents for irritation were denied him, and he had fallen into the way of throwing things about in a pet. He longed to send Caesar to perpetual banishment in the fire blazing close by, but resisted the temptation, and answered honestly, though gruffly: "I know I did, but I don't see any use in pouncing on a fellow when he isn't ready. I haven't got my lesson, and don't mean to worry about it; so you may just give me back my things and go about your business."

"I'll give you back a stamp for every perfect lesson you get, and you won't see them on any other terms;" and, thrusting the treasures into his pocket, Frank caught up his rubber-boots, and went off swinging them like a pair of clubs, feeling that he would give a trifle to be able to use them on his lazy brother.

At this high-handed proceeding, and the threat which accompanied it, Jack's patience gave out, and catching up Caesar, as he thought, sent him flying after the retreating tyrant with the defiant declaration,—

"Keep them, then, and your old book, too! I won't look at it till you give all my stamps back and say you are sorry. So now!"

It was all over before Mamma could interfere, or Jill do more than clutch and cling to the gum-brush. Frank vanished unharmed, but the poor book dashed against the wall to fall half open on the floor, its gay cover loosened, and its smooth leaves crushed by the blow.

"It's the album! O Jack, how could you?" cried Jill,

dismayed at sight of the precious book so maltreated by the owner.

"Thought it was the other. Guess it isn't hurt much. Didn't mean to hit him, any way. He does provoke me so," muttered Jack, very red and shamefaced as his mother picked up the book and laid it silently on the table before him. He did not know what to do with himself, and was thankful for the stamps still left him, finding great relief in making faces as he plucked them one by one from his mortified countenance. Jill looked on, half glad, half sorry that her savage showed such signs of unconverted ferocity, and Mrs. Minot went on writing letters, wearing the grave look her sons found harder to bear than another person's scolding. No one spoke for a moment, and the silence was becoming awkward when Gus appeared in a rubber suit, bringing a book to Jack from Laura and a note to Jill from Lotty.

"Look here, you just trundle me into my den, please, I'm going to have a nap, it's so dull to-day I don't feel like doing much," said Jack, when Gus had done his errands, trying to look as if he knew nothing about the fracas.

Jack folded his arms and departed like a warrior borne from the battle-field, to be chaffed unmercifully for a "pepper-pot," while Gus made him comfortable in his own room.

"I heard once of a boy who threw a fork at his brother and put his eye out. But he didn't mean to, and the brother forgave him, and he never did so any more," observed Jill, in a pensive tone, wishing to show that she felt all the dangers of impatience, but was sorry for the culprit.

"Did the boy ever forgive himself?" asked Mrs. Minot.

"No, 'm; I suppose not. But Jack didn't hit Frank, and feels real sorry, I know."

"He might have, and hurt him very much. Our actions are in our own hands, but the consequences of them are not. Remember that, my dear, and think twice before you do anything."

"Yes, 'm, I will;" and Jill composed herself to consider what missionaries usually did when the natives hurled tomahawks and boomerangs at one another, and defied the rulers of the land.

Mrs. Minot wrote one page of a new letter, then stopped, pushed her papers about, thought a little, and finally got up, saying, as if she found it impossible to resist the yearning of her heart for the naughty boy,—

"I am going to see if Jack is covered up, he is so helpless, and liable to take cold. Don't stir till I come back."

"No, 'm, I won't."

Away went the tender parent to find her son studying Caesar for dear life, and all the more amiable for the little gust which had blown away the temporary irritability. The brothers were often called "Thunder and Lightning," because Frank lowered and growled and was a good while clearing up, while Jack's temper came and went like a flash, and the air was all the clearer for the escape of dangerous electricity. Of course Mamma had to stop and deliver a little lecture, illustrated by sad tales of petulant boys, and punctuated with kisses which took off the edge of these afflicting narratives.

Jill meantime meditated morally on the superiority of her own good temper over the hasty one of her dear playmate, and just when she was feeling unusually uplifted and secure, alas! like so many of us, she fell, in the most deplorable manner.

Glancing about the room for something to do, she saw a sheet of paper lying exactly out of reach, where it had fluttered from the table unperceived. At first her eye rested on it as carelessly as it did on the stray stamp Frank had dropped; then, as if one thing suggested the other, she took it into her head that the paper was Frank's composition, or, better still, a note to Annette, for the two corresponded when absence or weather prevented the daily meeting at school.

"Wouldn't it be fun to keep it till he gives back Jack's stamps? It would plague him so if it was a note, and I do believe it is, for compos don't begin with two words on one side. I'll get it, and Jack and I will plan some way to pay him off, cross thing!"

Forgetting her promise not to stir, also how dishonorable it was to read other people's letters, Jill caught up the long-handled hook, often in use now, and tried to pull the paper nearer. It would not come at once, for a seam in the carpet held it, and Jill feared to tear or crumple it if she was not very careful. The hook was rather heavy and long for her to manage, and Jack usually did the fishing, so she was not very skilful; and just as she was giving a particularly quick jerk, she lost her balance, fell off the sofa, and dropped the pole with a bang.

"Oh, my back!" was all she could think or say as she felt the jar all through her little body, and a corresponding fear in her guilty little mind that some one would come and find out the double mischief she had been at. For a moment she lay quite still to recover from the shock, then as the pain passed she began to wonder how she should get back, and looked about her to see if she could do it alone. She thought she could, as the sofa was near and she had improved so much that she could sit up a little if the doctor would have let her. She was gathering herself together for the effort, when, within arm's reach now, she saw the tempting paper, and seized it with glee, for in spite of her predicament she did want to tease Frank. A glance showed that it was not the composition nor a note, but the beginning of a letter from Mrs. Minot to her sister, and Jill was about to lay it down when her own name caught her eye, and she could not resist reading it. Hard words to write of one so young, doubly hard to read, and impossible to forget.

> DEAR LIZZIE, —Jack continues to do very well, and will soon be up again. But we begin to fear that the little girl is permanently injured in the back. She is here, and we do our best for her; but I never look at her without thinking of Lucinda Snow, who, you remember, was bedridden for twenty years, owing to a fall at fifteen. Poor little Janey does not know yet, and I hope—

There it ended, and "poor little Janey's" punishment for disobedience began that instant. She thought she was getting well because she did not suffer all the time, and every one spoke cheerfully about "by and by." Now she knew the truth, and shut her eyes with a shiver as she said, low, to herself,—

"Twenty years! I couldn't bear it; oh, I couldn't bear it!"

A very miserable Jill lay on the floor, and for a while did not care who came and found her; then the last words of the letter—"I hope"—seemed to shine across the blackness of the dreadful "twenty years" and cheer her up a bit, for despair never lives long in young hearts, and Jill was a brave child.

"That is why Mammy sighs so when she dresses me, and every one is so good to me. Perhaps Mrs. Minot doesn't really know, after all. She was dreadfully scared about Jack, and he is getting well. I'd like to ask Doctor, but he might find out about the letter. Oh, dear, why didn't I keep still and let the horrid thing alone!"

As she thought that, Jill pushed the paper away, pulled herself up, and with much painful effort managed to get back to her sofa, where she laid herself down with a groan, feeling as if the twenty years had already passed over her since she tumbled off.

"I've told a lie, for I said I wouldn't stir. I've hurt my back, I've done a mean thing, and I've got paid for it. A nice missionary I am; I'd better begin at home, as Mammy told me to;" and Jill groaned again, remembering her mother's words. "Now I've got another secret to keep all alone, for I'd be ashamed to tell the girls. I guess I'll turn round and study my spelling; then no one will see my face."

Jill looked the picture of a good, industrious child as she lay with her back to the large table, her book held so that nothing was to be seen but one cheek and a pair of lips moving busily. Fortunately, it is difficult for little sinners to act a part, and, even if the face is hidden, something in the body seems to betray the internal remorse and shame. Usually, Jill lay flat and still; now her back was bent in a peculiar way as she leaned over her book, and one foot wagged nervously, while on the visible cheek was a Spanish stamp with a woman's face looking through the black bars, very suggestively, if she had known it. How long the minutes seemed till some one came, and what a queer little jump her heart gave when Mrs. Minot's voice said, cheerfully, "Jack is all right, and, I declare, so is Jill. I really believe there is a telegraph still working somewhere between you two, and each knows what the other is about without words."

"I didn't have any other book handy, so I thought I'd study awhile," answered Jill, feeling that she deserved no praise for her seeming industry.

She cast a sidelong glance as she spoke, and seeing that Mrs. Minot was looking for the letter, hid her face and lay so still she could hear the rustle of the paper as it was taken from the floor. It was well she did not also see the quick look the lady gave her as she turned the letter and found a red stamp sticking to the under side, for this unlucky little witness told the story.

Mrs. Minot remembered having seen the stamp lying close to the sofa when she left the room, for she had had half a mind to take it to Jack, but did not, thinking Frank's plan had some advantages. She also recollected that a paper flew off the table, but being in haste she had not stopped to see what it was. Now, the stamp and the letter could hardly have come together without hands, for they lay a yard apart, and here, also, on the unwritten portion of the page, was the mark of a small green thumb. Jill had been winding wool for a stripe in her new afghan, and the green ball lay on her sofa. These signs suggested and confirmed what Mrs. Minot did not want to believe; so did the voice, attitude, and air of Jill, all very unlike her usual open, alert ways.

The kind lady could easily forgive the reading of her letter since the girl had found such sad news there, but the dangers of disobedience were serious in her case, and a glance showed that she was suffering either in mind or body,—perhaps both.

"I will wait for her to tell me. She is an honest child, and the truth will soon come out," thought Mrs. Minot, as she took a clean sheet, and Jill tried to study.

"Shall I hear your lesson, dear? Jack means to recite his like a good boy, so suppose you follow his example," she said, presently.

"I don't know as I can say it, but I'll try."

Jill did try, and got on bravely till she came to the

word "permanent;" there she hesitated, remembering where
she saw it last.

"Do you know what that means?" asked her teacher,
thinking to help her on by defining the word.

"Always—for a great while—or something like that;
doesn't it?" faltered Jill, with a tight feeling in her throat,
and the color coming up, as she tried to speak easily, yet felt
so shame-stricken she could not.

"Are you in pain, my child? Never mind the lesson;
tell me, and I'll do something for you."

The kind words, the soft hand on her hot cheek, and
the pity in the eyes that looked at her, were too much for
Jill. A sob came first, and then the truth, told with hidden
face and tears that washed the blush away, and set free the
honest little soul that could not hide its fault from such a
friend.

"I knew it all before, and was sure you would tell me,
else you would not be the child I love and like to help so
well."

Then, while she soothed Jill's trouble, Mrs. Minot
told her story and showed the letter, wishing to lessen, if
possible, some part of the pain it had given.

"Sly old stamp! to go and tell on me when I meant to
own up, and get some credit if I could, after being so mean
and bad," said Jill, smiling through her tears when she saw
the tell-tale witnesses against her.

"You had better stick it in your book to remind you
of the bad consequences of disobedience, then perhaps *this*
lesson will leave a 'permanent' impression on your mind
and memory," answered Mrs. Minot, glad to see her natural
gayety coming back, and hoping that she had forgotten the
contents of the unfortunate letter.

But she had not; and presently, when the sad affair had

been talked over and forgiven, Jill asked, slowly, as she tried to put on a brave look, —

"Please tell me about Lucinda Snow. If I am to be like her, I might as well know how she managed to bear it so long."

"I'm sorry you ever heard of her, and yet perhaps it may help you to bear your trial, dear, which I hope will never be as heavy a one as hers. This Lucinda I knew for years, and though at first I thought her fate the saddest that could be, I came at last to see how happy she was in spite of her affliction, how good and useful and beloved."

"Why, how could she be? What did she do?" cried Jill, forgetting her own troubles to look up with an open, eager face again.

"She was so patient, other people were ashamed to complain of their small worries; so cheerful, that her own great one grew lighter; so industrious, that she made both money and friends by pretty things she worked and sold to her many visitors. And, best of all, so wise and sweet that she seemed to get good out of everything, and make her poor room a sort of chapel where people went for comfort, counsel, and an example of a pious life. So, you see, Lucinda was not so very miserable after all."

"Well, if I could not be as I was, I'd like to be a woman like that. Only, I hope I shall not!" answered Jill, thoughtfully at first, then coming out so decidedly with the last words that it was evident the life of a bedridden saint was not at all to her mind.

"So do I; and I mean to believe that you will not. Meantime, we can try to make the waiting as useful and pleasant as possible. This painful little back will be a sort of conscience to remind you of what you ought to do and leave undone, and so you can be learning obedience. Then, when the body is strong, it will have formed a good habit to make duty easier; and my Lucinda can be a sweet example, even while lying here, if she chooses."

"Can I?" and Jill's eyes were full of softer tears as the comfortable, cheering words sank into her heart, to blossom slowly by and by into her life, for this was to be a long lesson, hard to learn, but very useful in the years to come.

When the boys returned, after the Latin was recited and peace restored, Jack showed her a recovered stamp promptly paid by Frank, who was as just as he was severe, and Jill asked for the old red one, though she did not tell why she wanted it, nor show it put away in the spelling-book, a little seal upon a promise made to be kept.

Merry and Molly
CHAPTER 8

Now let us see how the other missionaries got on with their tasks.

Farmer Grant was a thrifty, well-to-do man, anxious to give his children greater advantages than he had enjoyed, and to improve the fine place of which he was justly proud. Mrs. Grant was a notable housewife, as ambitious and industrious as her husband, but too busy to spend any time on the elegancies of life, though always ready to help the poor and sick like a good neighbor and Christian woman. The three sons—Tom, Dick, and Harry—were big fellows of seventeen, nineteen, and twenty-one; the first two on the farm, and the elder in a store just setting up for himself. Kind-hearted but rough-mannered youths, who loved Merry very much, but teased her sadly about her "fine lady airs," as they called her dainty ways and love of beauty.

Merry was a thoughtful girl, full of innocent fancies, refined tastes, and romantic dreams, in which no one sympathized at home, though she was the pet of the family. It did seem, to an outsider, as if the delicate little creature had got there by mistake, for she looked very like a tea-rose in a field of clover and dandelions, whose highest aim in life was to feed cows and help make root beer.

When the girls talked over the new society, it pleased Merry very much, and she decided not only to try and love work better, but to convert her family to a liking for pretty things, as she called her own more cultivated tastes.

"I will begin at once, and show them that I don't mean to shirk my duty, though I do want to be nice," thought she, as she sat at supper one night and looked about her, planning her first move.

Not a very cheering prospect for a lover of the beautiful, certainly, for the big kitchen, though as neat as wax, had nothing lovely in it, except a red geranium blooming at the window. Nor were the people all that could be desired, in some respects, as they sat about the table shovelling in pork and beans with their knives, drinking tea from their saucers, and laughing out with a hearty "Haw, haw," when anything amused them. Yet the boys were handsome, strong specimens, the farmer a hale, benevolent-looking man, the housewife a pleasant, sharp-eyed matron, who seemed to find comfort in looking often at the bright face at her elbow, with the broad forehead, clear eyes, sweet mouth, and quiet voice that came like music in among the loud masculine ones, or the quick, nervous tones of a woman always in a hurry.

Merry's face was so thoughtful that evening that her father observed it, for, when at home, he watched her as one watches a kitten, glad to see anything so pretty, young, and happy, at its play.

"Little daughter has got something on her mind, I mistrust. Come and tell father all about it," he said, with a sounding slap on his broad knee as he turned his chair from the table to the ugly stove, where three pairs of wet boots steamed underneath, and a great kettle of cider apple-sauce simmered above.

"When I've helped clear up, I'll come and talk. Now, mother, you sit down and rest; Roxy and I can do everything," answered Merry, patting the old rocking-chair so invitingly that the tired woman could not resist, especially as watching the kettle gave her an excuse for obeying.

"Well, I don't care if I do, for I've been on my feet since five o'clock. Be sure you cover things up, and shut the buttery door, and put the cat down cellar, and sift your meal. I'll see to the buckwheats last thing before I go to bed."

Mrs. Grant subsided with her knitting, for her hands were never idle; Tom tilted his chair back against the wall and picked his teeth with his penknife; Dick got out a little pot of grease, to make the boots water-tight; and Harry sat down at the small table to look over his accounts, with an important air,—for every one occupied this room, and the work was done in the out-kitchen behind.

Merry hated clearing up, but dutifully did every distasteful task, and kept her eye on careless Roxy till all was in order; then she gladly went to perch on her father's knee, seeing in all the faces about her the silent welcome they always wore for the "little one."

"Yes, I do want something, but I know you will say it is silly," she began, as her father pinched her blooming cheek, with the wish that his peaches would ever look half as well.

"Shouldn't wonder if it was a doll now;" and Mr.

Grant stroked her head with an indulgent smile, as if she was about six instead of fifteen.

"Why, father, you know I don't! I haven't played with dollies for years and years. No; I want to fix up my room pretty, like Jill's. I'll do it all myself, and only want a few things, for I don't expect it to look as nice as hers."

Indignation gave Merry courage to state her wishes boldly, though she knew the boys would laugh. They did, and her mother said in a tone of surprise,—

"Why, child, what more can you want? I'm sure your room is always as neat as a new pin, thanks to your bringing up, and I told you to have a fire there whenever you wanted to."

"Let me have some old things out of the garret, and I'll show you what I want. It *is* neat, but so bare and ugly I hate to be there. I do so love something pretty to look at!" and Merry gave a little shiver of disgust as she turned her eyes away from the large greasy boot Dick was holding up to be sure it was well lubricated all round.

"So do I, and that's a fact. I couldn't get on without my pretty girl here, any way. Why, she touches up the old place better than a dozen flower-pots in full blow," said the farmer, as his eye went from the scarlet geranium to the bright young face so near his own.

"I wish I had a dozen in the sitting-room window. Mother says they are not tidy, but I'd keep them neat, and I know you'd like it," broke in Merry, glad of the chance to get one of the long-desired wishes of her heart fulfilled.

"I'll fetch you some next time I go over to Ballad's. Tell me what you want, and we'll have a posy bed somewhere round, see if we don't," said her father, dimly understanding what she wanted.

"Now, if mother says I may fix my room, I shall be

satisfied, and I'll do my chores without a bit of fuss, to show how grateful I am," said the girl, thanking her father with a kiss, and smiling at her mother so wistfully that the good woman could not refuse.

"You may have anything you like out of the blue chest. There's a lot of things there that the moths got at after Grandma died, and I couldn't bear to throw or give 'em away. Trim up your room as you like, and mind you don't forget your part of the bargain," answered Mrs. Grant, seeing profit in the plan.

"I won't; I'll work all the morning to-morrow, and in the afternoon I'll get ready to show you what I call a nice, pretty room," answered Merry, looking so pleased it seemed as if another flower had blossomed in the large bare kitchen.

She kept her word, and the very stormy afternoon when Jill got into trouble, Merry was working busily at her little bower. In the blue chest she found a variety of treasures, and ignoring the moth holes, used them to the best advantage, trying to imitate the simple comfort with a touch of elegance which prevailed in Mrs. Minot's back bedroom.

Three faded red-moreen curtains went up at the windows over the chilly paper shades, giving a pleasant glow to the bare walls. A red quilt with white stars, rather the worse for many washings, covered the bed, and a gay cloth the table, where a judicious arrangement of books and baskets concealed the spots. The little air-tight stove was banished, and a pair of ancient andirons shone in the fire-light. Grandma's last and largest braided rug lay on the hearth, and her brass candlesticks adorned the bureau, over the mirror of which was festooned a white muslin skirt, tied up with Merry's red sash. This piece of elegance gave the last touch to her room, she thought, and she was very proud of it, setting forth all her small store of trinkets in a large shell, with an empty scent bottle, and a clean tidy over the pin-cushion. On the walls she hung three old-fashioned pictures, which she ventured to borrow from the garret till better could be found. One a mourning piece, with a very tall lady weeping on an urn in a grove of willows, and two small boys in knee breeches and funny little square tails to their coats, looking like cherubs in large frills. The other was as good as a bonfire, being an eruption of Vesuvius, and very lurid indeed, for the Bay of Naples was boiling like a pot, the red sky raining rocks, and a few distracted people lying flat upon the shore. The third was a really pretty scene of children dancing round a May-pole, for though nearly a hundred years old, the little maids smiled and the boys pranced as gayly as if the flowers they carried were still alive and sweet.

"Now I'll call them all to see, and say that it is pretty. Then I'll enjoy it, and come here when things look dismal and bare everywhere else," said Merry, when at last it was done. She had worked all the afternoon, and only finished at supper time, so the candles had to be lighted that the toilette might look its best, and impress the beholders with an idea of true elegance. Unfortunately, the fire smoked a little, and a window was set ajar to clear the room; an evil-disposed gust blew in, wafting the thin drapery within reach of the light, and when Merry threw open the door proudly thinking to display her success, she was horrified to find the room in a blaze, and half her labor all in vain.

The conflagration was over in a minute, however, for the boys tore down the muslin and stamped out the fire with much laughter, while Mrs. Grant bewailed the damage to her carpet, and poor Merry took refuge in her father's arms, refusing to be comforted in spite of his kind commendation of "Grandma's fixin's."

The third little missionary had the hardest time of all, and her first efforts were not much more satisfactory nor successful than the others. Her father was away from morning till night, and then had his paper to read, books to keep, or "a man to see down town," so that, after a hasty word at tea, he saw no more of the children till another evening, as they were seldom up at his early breakfast. He thought they were well taken care of, for Miss Bathsheba Dawes was an energetic, middle-aged spinster when she came into the family, and had been there fifteen years, so he did not observe, what a woman would have seen at once, that Miss Bat was getting old and careless, and everything about the house was at sixes and sevens. She took good care of him, and thought she had done her duty if she got three comfortable meals, nursed the children when they were ill, and saw that the house did not burn up. So Maria Louisa and Napoleon Bonaparte got on as they could, without the tender cares of a mother. Molly had been a happy-go-lucky child, contented with her pets, her freedom, and little Boo to love; but now she was just beginning to see that they were not like other children, and to feel ashamed of it.

"Papa is busy, but Miss Bat ought to see to us; she is paid for it, and goodness knows she has an easy time now, for if I ask her to do anything, she groans over her bones, and tells me young folks should wait on themselves. I take all the care of Boo off her hands, but I can't wash my own things, and he hasn't a decent trouser to his blessed little legs. I'd tell papa, but it wouldn't do any good; he'd only say, 'Yes, child, yes, I'll attend to it,' and never do a thing."

This used to be Molly's lament, when some especially trying event occurred, and if the girls were not there to condole with her, she would retire to the shed-chamber, call her nine cats about her, and, sitting in the old bushel

basket, pull her hair about her ears, and scold all alone. The
cats learned to understand this habit, and nobly did their
best to dispel the gloom which now and then obscured the
sunshine of their little mistress. Some of them would creep
into her lap and purr till the comfortable sound soothed her
irritation; the sedate elders sat at her feet blinking with such
wise and sympathetic faces, that she felt as if half-a-dozen
Solomons were giving her the sagest advice; while the kit-
tens frisked about, cutting up their drollest capers till she
laughed in spite of herself. When the laugh came, the worst
of the fit was over, and she soon cheered up, dismissing the
consolers with a pat all round, a feast of good things from
Miss Bat's larder, and the usual speech:—

"Well, dears, it's of no use to worry. I guess we shall
get along somehow, if we don't fret."

With which wise resolution, Molly would leave her
retreat and freshen up her spirits by a row on the river or a
romp with Boo, which always finished the case. Now, however, she was bound to try the new plan and do something
toward reforming not only the boy's condition, but the disorder and discomfort of home.

"I'll play it is Siam, and this the house of a native, and
I'm come to show the folks how to live nicely. Miss Bat
won't know what to make of it, and I can't tell her, so I
shall get some fun out of it, any way," thought Molly, as she
surveyed the dining-room the day her mission began.

The prospect was not cheering; and, if the natives of
Siam live in such confusion, it is high time they were attended to. The breakfast-table still stood as it was left, with
slops of coffee on the cloth; bits of bread, egg-shells, and
potato-skins lay about, and one lonely sausage was cast away
in the middle of a large platter. The furniture was dusty,
stove untidy, and the carpet looked as if crumbs had been

scattered to chickens who declined their breakfast. Boo was sitting on the sofa, with his arm through a hole in the cover, hunting for some lost treasure put away there for safe keeping, like a little magpie as he was. Molly fancied she washed and dressed him well enough; but to-day she seemed to see more clearly, and sighed as she thought of the hard job in store for her if she gave him the thorough washing he needed, and combed out that curly mop of hair.

"I'll clear up first and do that by and by. I ought to have a nice little tub and good towels, like Mrs. Minot, and I will, too, if I buy them myself," she said, piling up cups with an energy that threatened destruction to handles.

Miss Bat, who was trailing about the kitchen, with her head pinned up in a little plaid shawl, was so surprised by the demand for a pan of hot water and four clean towels, that she nearly dropped her snuff-box, chief comfort of her lazy soul.

"What new whimsey now? Generally, the dishes stand round till I have time to pick 'em up, and you are off coasting or careering somewhere. Well, this tidy fit won't last long, so I may as well make the most of it," said Miss Bat, as she handed out the required articles, and then pushed her spectacles from the tip of her sharp nose to her sharper black eyes for a good look at the girl who stood primly before her, with a clean apron on and her hair braided up instead of flying wildly about her shoulders.

"Umph!" was all the comment that Miss Bat made on this unusual neatness, and she went on scraping her saucepans, while Molly returned to her work, very well pleased with the effect of her first step, for she felt that the bewilderment of Miss Bat would be a constant inspiration to fresh efforts.

An hour of hard work produced an agreeable change

in the abode of the native, for the table was cleared, room swept and dusted, fire brightened, and the holes in the sofa-covering were pinned up till time could be found to mend them. To be sure, rolls of lint lay in corners, smears of ashes were on the stove hearth, and dust still lurked on chair rounds and table legs. But too much must not be expected of a new convert, so the young missionary sat down to rest, well pleased and ready for another attempt as soon as she could decide in what direction it should be made. She quailed before Boo as she looked at the unconscious inno-cent peacefully playing with the spotted dog, now bereft of his tail, and the lone sausage with which he was attempting to feed the hungry animal, whose red mouth always gaped for more.

"It will be an awful job, and he is so happy I won't plague him yet. Guess I'll go and put my room to rights first, and pick up some clean clothes to put on him, if he is alive after I get through with him," thought Molly, foresee-ing a stormy passage for the boy, who hated a bath as much as some people hate a trip across the Atlantic.

Up she went, and finding the fire out felt discouraged, thought she would rest a little more, so retired under the blankets to read one of the Christmas books. The dinner-bell rang while she was still wandering happily in "Nelly's Silver Mine," and she ran down to find that Boo had laid out a railroad all across her neat room, using bits of coal for sleepers and books for rails, over which he was dragging the yellow sled laden with a dismayed kitten, the tailless dog, and the remains of the sausage, evidently on its way to the tomb, for Boo took bites at it now and then, no other lunch being offered him.

"Oh, dear! why can't boys play without making such a mess?" sighed Molly, picking up the feathers from the duster with which Boo had been trying to make a "cocky-doo" of the hapless dog. "I'll wash him right after dinner, and that will keep him out of mischief for a while," she thought, as the young engineer unsuspiciously proceeded to ornament his already crocky countenance with squash, cranberry sauce, and gravy, till he looked more like a Fiji chief in full war-paint than a Christian boy.

"I want two pails of hot water, please, Miss Bat, and the big tub," said Molly, as the ancient handmaid emptied her fourth cup of tea, for she dined with the family, and enjoyed her own good cooking in its prime.

"What are you going to wash now?"

"Boo—I'm sure he needs it enough;" and Molly could not help laughing as the victim added to his brilliant appearance by smearing the colors all together with a rub of two grimy hands, making a fine "Turner," of himself.

"Now, Maria Louisa Bemis, you ain't going to cut up no capers with that child! The idea of a hot bath in the middle of the day, and him full of dinner, and croupy into the bargain! Wet a corner of a towel at the kettle-spout and polish him off if you like, but you won't risk his life in no bath-tubs this cold day."

Miss Bat's word was law in some things, so Molly had to submit, and took Boo away, saying, loftily, as she left the room,—

"I shall ask father, and do it to-night, for I will *not* have my brother look like a pig."

"My patience! how the Siamese do leave their things round," she exclaimed, as she surveyed her room after making up the fire and polishing off Boo. "I'll put things in order, and then mend up my rags, if I can find my thimble. Now, let me see;" and she went to exploring her closet, bureau, and table; finding such disorder everywhere that her courage nearly gave out.

She had clothes enough, but all needed care; even her best dress had two buttons off, and her Sunday hat but one string. Shoes, skirts, books, and toys lay about, and her drawers were a perfect chaos of soiled ruffles, odd gloves, old ribbons, boot lacings, and bits of paper.

"Oh, my heart, what a muddle! Mrs. Minot wouldn't think much of me if she could see that," said Molly, recalling how that lady once said she could judge a good deal of a little girl's character and habits by a peep at her top drawer, and went on, with great success, to guess how each of the schoolmates kept her drawer.

"Come, missionary, clear up, and don't let me find such a glory-hole again, or I'll report you to the society," said Molly, tipping the whole drawer-full out upon the bed, and beguiling the tiresome job by keeping up the new play.

Twilight came before it was done, and a great pile of things loomed up on her table, with no visible means of repair,— for Molly's work-basket was full of nuts, and her thimble down a hole in the shed-floor, where the cats had dropped it in their play.

"I'll ask Bat for hooks and tape, and papa for some money to buy scissors and things, for I don't know where mine are. Glad I can't do any more now! Being neat is such hard work!" and Molly threw herself down on the rug beside the old wooden cradle in which Boo was blissfully rocking, with a cargo of toys aboard.

She watched her time, and as soon as her father had done supper, she hastened to say, before he got to his desk,—

"Please, papa, I want a dollar to get some brass buttons

and things to fix Boo's clothes with. He wore a hole in his
new trousers coasting down the Kembles' steps. And can't
I wash him? He needs it, and Miss Bat won't let me have
a tub."

"Certainly, child, certainly; do what you like, only
don't keep me. I must be off, or I shall miss Jackson, and
he's the man I want;" and, throwing down two dollars instead of one, Mr. Bemis hurried away, with a vague impression that Boo had swallowed a dozen brass buttons, and Miss
Bat had been coasting somewhere in a bath-pan; but catching Jackson was important, so he did not stop to investigate.

Armed with the paternal permission, Molly carried
her point, and oh, what a dreadful evening poor Boo spent!
First, he was decoyed upstairs an hour too soon, then put in
a tub by main force and sternly scrubbed, in spite of shrieks
that brought Miss Bat to the locked door to condole with
the sufferer, scold the scrubber, and depart, darkly proph-
esying croup before morning.

"He always howls when he is washed; but I shall do it,
since you won't, and he must get used to it. I will not have
people tell me he's neglected, if I can help it," cried Molly,
working away with tears in her eyes—for it was as hard for
her as for Boo; but she meant to be thorough for once in her
life, no matter what happened.

When the worst was over, she coaxed him with candy
and stories till the long task of combing out the curls was
safely done; then, in the clean nightgown with a blue button
newly sewed on, she laid him in bed, worn out, but sweet
as a rose.

"Now, say your prayers, darling, and go to sleep with
the nice red blanket all tucked round so you won't
get cold," said Molly, rather doubtful of the effect of the
wet head.

"No, I won't! Going to sleep *now!*" and Boo shut his eyes wearily, feeling that his late trials had not left him in a prayerful mood.

"Then you'll be a real little heathen, as Mrs. Pecq called you, and I don't know what I shall do with you," said Molly, longing to cuddle rather than scold the little fellow, whose soul needed looking after as well as his body.

"No, no; I won't be a heevin! I don't want to be frowed to the trockindiles. I will say my prayers! oh, I will!" and, rising in his bed, Boo did so, with the devotion of an infant Samuel, for he remembered the talk when the society was formed.

Molly thought her labors were over for that night, and soon went to bed, tired with her first attempts. But toward morning she was wakened by the hoarse breathing of the boy, and was forced to patter away to Miss Bat's room, humbly asking for the squills, and confessing that the prophecy had come to pass.

"I knew it! Bring the child to me, and don't fret. I'll see to him, and next time you do as I say," was the consoling welcome she received as the old lady popped up a sleepy but anxious face in a large flannel cap, and shook the bottle with the air of a general who had routed the foe before and meant to do it again.

Leaving her little responsibility in Miss Bat's arms, Molly retired to wet her pillow with a few remorseful tears, and to fall asleep, wondering if real missionaries ever killed their pupils in the process of conversion.

So the girls all failed in the beginning; but they did not give up, and succeeded better next time, as we shall see.

The Debating Club
CHAPTER 9

"Look here, old man, we ought to have a meeting. Holidays are over, and we must brace up and attend to business," said Frank to Gus, as they strolled out of the school-yard one afternoon in January, apparently absorbed in conversation, but in reality waiting for a blue cloud and a scarlet feather to appear on the steps.

"All right. When, where, and what?" asked Gus, who was a man of few words.

"To-night, our house, subject, 'Shall girls go to college with us?' Mother said we had better be making up our minds, because every one is talking about it, and we shall have to be on one side or the other, so we may as well settle it now," answered Frank, for there was an impression among the members that all vexed questions would be much helped by the united eloquence and wisdom of the club.

"Very good; I'll pass the word and be there. Hullo, Neddy! The D. C. meets to-night, at Minot's, seven sharp. Co-ed, &c.," added Gus, losing no time, as a third boy came briskly round the corner, with a little bag in his hand.

"I'll come. Got home an hour earlier to-night, and thought I'd look you up as I went by," responded Ed Devlin, as he took possession of the third post, with a glance toward the schoolhouse to see if a seal-skin cap, with a long, yellow braid depending therefrom, was anywhere in sight.

"Very good of you, I'm sure," said Gus, ironically, not a bit deceived by this polite attention.

"The longest way round is sometimes the shortest way

home, hey, Ed?" and Frank gave him a playful poke that nearly sent him off his perch.

Then they all laughed at some joke of their own, and Gus added, "No girls coming to hear us to-night. Don't think it, my son."

"More's the pity," and Ed shook his head regretfully over the downfall of his hopes.

"Can't help it; the other fellows say they spoil the fun, so we have to give in, sometimes, for the sake of peace and quietness. Don't mind having them a bit myself," said Frank, in such a tone of cheerful resignation that they laughed again, for the "Triangle," as the three chums were called, always made merry music.

"We must have a game party next week. The girls like that, and so do I," candidly observed Gus, whose pleasant parlors were the scene of many such frolics.

"And so do your sisters and your cousins and your aunts," hummed Ed, for Gus was often called Admiral be-cause he really did possess three sisters, two cousins, and four aunts, besides mother and grandmother, all living in the big house together.

The boys promptly joined in the popular chorus, and other voices all about the yard took it up, for the "Pinafore" epidemic raged fearfully in Harmony Village that winter.

"How's business?" asked Gus, when the song ended, for Ed had not returned to school in the autumn, but had gone into a store in the city.

"Dull; things will look up toward spring, they say. I get on well enough, but I miss you fellows dreadfully;" and Ed put a hand on the broad shoulder of each friend, as if he longed to be a school-boy again.

"Better give it up and go to college with me next

year," said Frank, who was preparing for Boston University, while Gus fitted for Harvard.

"No; I've chosen business, and I mean to stick to it, so don't you unsettle my mind. Have you practised that March?" asked Ed, turning to a gayer subject, for he had his little troubles, but always looked on the bright side of things.

"Skating is so good, I don't get much time. Come early, and we'll have a turn at it."

"I will. Must run home now."

"Pretty cold loafing here."

"Mail is in by this time."

And with these artless excuses the three boys leaped off the posts, as if one spring moved them, as a group of girls came chattering down the path. The blue cloud floated away beside Frank, the scarlet feather marched off with the Admiral, while the fur cap nodded to the gray hat as two happy faces smiled at each other.

The same thing often happened, for twice a day the streets were full of young couples walking to and from school together, smiled at by the elders, and laughed at by the less susceptible boys and girls, who went alone or trooped along in noisy groups. The prudent mothers had tried to stop this guileless custom, but found it very difficult, as the fathers usually sympathized with their sons, and dismissed the matter with the comfortable phrase, "Never mind; boys will be boys." "Not forever," returned the anxious mammas, seeing the tall lads daily grow more manly, and the pretty daughters fast learning to look demure when certain names were mentioned.

It could not be stopped without great parental sternness and the danger of deceit, for co-education will go on outside of school if not inside, and the safest way is to let sentiment and study go hand in hand, with teachers and parents to direct and explain the great lesson all are the better for learning soon or late. So the elders had to give in, acknowledging that this sudden readiness to go to school was a comfort, that the new sort of gentle emulation worked wonders in lazy girls and boys, and that watching these "primrose friendships" bud, blossom, and die painless deaths, gave a little touch of romance to their own work-a-day lives.

"On the whole I'd rather have my sons walking, playing, and studying with bright, well-mannered girls, than always knocking about with rough boys," said Mrs. Minot at one of the Mothers' Meetings, where the good ladies met to talk over their children, and help one another to do their duty by them.

"I find that Gus is more gentle with his sisters since Juliet took him in hand, for he wants to stand well with her, and they report him if he troubles them. I really see no harm in the little friendship, though I never had any such when I was a girl," said Mrs. Burton, who adored her one boy and was his confidante.

"My Merry seems to be contented with her brothers so far, but I shouldn't wonder if I had my hands full by and by," added Mrs. Grant, who already foresaw that her sweet little daughter would be sought after as soon as she should lengthen her skirts and turn up her bonny brown hair.

Molly Loo had no mother to say a word for her, but she settled matters for herself by holding fast to Merry, and declaring that she would have no escort but faithful Boo.

It is necessary to dwell a moment upon this new amusement, because it was not peculiar to Harmony Village, but appears everywhere as naturally as the game parties and croquet which have taken the place of the husking frolics and apple-bees of olden times, and it is impossible to dodge the subject if one attempts to write of boys and girls as they really are nowadays.

"Here, my hero, see how you like this. If it suits, you will be ready to march as soon as the doctor gives the word," said Ralph, coming into the Bird Room that evening with a neat little crutch under his arm.

"Ha, ha, that looks fine! I'd like to try it right off, but I won't till I get leave. Did you make it yourself, Ral?" asked Jack, handling it with delight, as he sat bolt upright, with his leg on a rest, for he was getting on capitally now.

"Mostly. Rather a neat job, I flatter myself."

"I should say so. What a clever fellow you are! Any new inventions lately?" asked Frank, coming up to examine and admire.

"Only an anti-snoring machine and an elbow-pad," answered Ralph, with a twinkle in his eye, as if reminded of something funny.

"Go on, and tell about them. I never heard of an anti-snorer. Jack better have one," said Frank, interested at once.

"Well, a rich old lady kept her family awake with that lively music, so she sent to Shirtman and Codleff for something to stop it. They thought it was a good joke, and told me to see what I could do. I thought it over, and got up the nicest little affair you ever saw. It went over the mouth, and had a tube to fit the ear, so when the lady snored she woke herself up and stopped it. It suited exactly. I think of taking out a patent," concluded Ralph, joining in the boys' laugh at the droll idea.

"What was the pad?" asked Frank, returning to the small model of an engine he was making.

"Oh, that was a mere trifle for a man who had a tender elbow-joint and wanted something to protect it. I made a little pad to fit on, and his crazy-bone was safe."

"I planned to have you make me a new leg if this one was spoilt," said Jack, sure that his friend could invent anything under the sun.

"I'd do my best for you. I made a hand for a fellow once, and that got me my place, you know," answered Ralph, who thought little of such mechanical trifles, and longed to be painting portraits or modelling busts, being an artist as well as an inventor.

Here Gus, Ed, and several other boys came in, and the conversation became general. Grif, Chick, and Brickbat were three young gentlemen whose own respectable names were usually ignored, and they cheerfully answered to these nicknames.

As the clock struck seven, Frank, who ruled the club with a rod of iron when Chairman, took his place behind the study table. Seats stood about it, and a large, shabby book lay before Gus, who was Secretary, and kept the records with a lavish expenditure of ink, to judge by the blots. The members took their seats, and nearly all tilted back their chairs and put their hands in their pockets, to keep them out of mischief; for, as every one knows, it is impossible for two lads to be near each other and refrain from tickling or pinching. Frank gave three raps with an old croquet-mallet set on a short handle, and with much dignity opened the meeting.

"Gentlemen, the business of the club will be attended to, and then we will discuss the question, 'Shall girls go to our colleges?' The Secretary will now read the report of the last meeting."

Clearing his throat, Gus read the following brief and elegant report:—

"Club met, December 18th, at the house of G. Burton, Esq. Subject: 'Is summer or winter best fun?' A lively pow-wow. About evenly divided. J. Flint fined five cents for disrespect to the Chair. A collection of forty cents taken up to pay for breaking a pane of glass during a free fight of the members on the door-step. E. Devlin was chosen Secretary for the coming year, and a new book contributed by the Chairman."

"That's all."

"Is there any other business before the meeting?" asked Frank, as the reader closed the old book with a slam and shoved the new one across the table.

Ed rose, and glancing about him with an appealing look, said, as if sure his proposition would not be well received, "I wish to propose the name of a new member. Bob Walker wants to join, and *I* think we ought to let him. He is trying to behave well, and I am sure we could help him. Can't we?"

All the boys looked sober, and Joe, otherwise Brickbat, said, bluntly, "I won't. He's a bad lot, and we don't want any such here. Let him go with chaps of his own sort."

"That is just what I want to keep him from! He's a good-hearted boy enough, only no one looks after him; so he gets into scrapes, as we should, if we were in his place, I dare say. He wants to come here, and would be so proud if he was let in, I know he'd behave. Come now, let's give him a chance," and Ed looked at Gus and Frank, sure that if they stood by him he should carry his point.

But Gus shook his head, as if doubtful of the wisdom of the plan, and Frank said gravely: "You know we made the rule that the number should never be over eight, and we cannot break it."

"You needn't. I can't be here half the time, so I will resign and let Bob have my place," began Ed, but he was silenced by shouts of "No, no, you shan't!" "We won't let you off!" "Club would go to smash, if you back out!"

"Let him have my place; I'm the youngest, and you won't miss me," cried Jack, bound to stand by Ed at all costs.

"We might do that," said Frank, who did object to small boys, though willing to admit this particular one.

"Better make a new rule to have ten members, and admit both Bob and Tom Grant," said Ralph, whereat Grif grinned and Joe scowled, for one lad liked Merry's big brother and the other did not.

"That's a good idea! Put it to vote," said Gus, too kind-hearted to shut the door on any one.

"First I want to ask if all you fellows are ready to stand by Bob, out of the club as well as in, for it won't do much good to be kind to him here and cut him at school and in the street," said Ed, heartily in earnest about the matter.

"I will!" cried Jack, ready to follow where his beloved friend led, and the others nodded, unwilling to be outdone by the youngest member.

"Good! With all of us to lend a hand, we can do a great deal; and I tell you, boys, it is time, if we want to keep poor Bob straight. We all turn our backs on him, so he loafs round the tavern, and goes with fellows we don't care to know. But he isn't bad yet, and we can keep him up, I'm sure, if we just try. I hope to get him into the Lodge, and that will be half the battle, won't it, Frank?" added Ed, sure that this suggestion would have weight with the honorable Chairman.

"Bring him along; I'm with you!" answered Frank, making up his mind at once, for he had joined the Temperance Lodge four years ago, and already six boys had followed his example.

"He is learning to smoke, but we'll make him drop it before it leads to worse. You can help him there, Admiral, if you only will," added Ed, giving a grateful look at one friend, and turning to the other.

"I'm your man;" and Gus looked as if he knew what he promised, for he had given up smoking to oblige his father, and kept his word like a hero.

"You other fellows can do a good deal by just being kind and not twitting him with old scrapes, and I'll do anything I can for you all to pay for this;" and Ed sat down with a beaming smile, feeling that his cause was won.

The vote was taken, and all hands went up, for even surly Joe gave in; so Bob and Tom were duly elected, and proved their gratitude for the honor done them by becoming worthy members of the club. It was only boys' play now, but the kind heart and pure instincts of one lad showed the others how to lend a helping hand to a comrade in danger, and win him away from temptation to the safer pastimes of their more guarded lives.

Well pleased with themselves, — for every genuine act or word, no matter how trifling it seems, leaves a sweet and strengthening influence behind, — the members settled down to the debate, which was never very long, and often only an excuse for fun of all sorts.

"Ralph, Gus, and Ed are for, and Brickbat, Grif, and Chick against, I suppose?" said Frank, surveying his company like a general preparing for battle.

"No, sir! I believe in co-everything!" cried Chick, a mild youth, who loyally escorted a chosen damsel home from school every day.

A laugh greeted this bold declaration, and Chick sat down, red but firm.

"I'll speak for two since the Chairman can't, and Jack won't go against those who pet him most to death," said Joe, who, not being a favorite with the girls, considered them a nuisance and lost no opportunity of telling them so.

"Fire away, then, since you are up;" commanded Frank.

"Well," began Joe, feeling too late how much he had undertaken, "I don't know a great deal about it, and I don't care, but I do *not* believe in having girls at college. They don't belong there, nobody wants 'em, and they'd better be at home darning their stockings."

"Yours, too," put in Ralph, who had heard that argument so often he was tired of it.

"Of course; that's what girls are for. I don't mind 'em at school, but I'd just as soon they had a room to themselves. We should get on better."

"*You* would if Mabel wasn't in your class and always ahead of you," observed Ed, whose friend was a fine scholar, and he very proud of the fact.

"Look here, if you fellows keep interrupting, I won't sit down for half an hour," said Joe, well knowing that eloquence was not his gift, but bound to have his say out.

Deep silence reigned, for that threat quelled the most impatient member, and Joe prosed on, using all the arguments he had ever heard, and paying off several old scores by sly hits of a personal nature, as older orators often do.

"It is clear to my mind that boys would get on better without any girls fooling round. As for their being as smart as we are, it is all nonsense, for some of 'em cry over their lessons every day, or go home with headaches, or get mad and scold all recess, because something 'isn't fair.' No, *sir;* girls ain't meant to know much, and they can't. Wise folks say so and I believe 'em. Haven't got any sisters myself, and I don't want any, for they don't seem to amount to much, according to those who do have 'em."

Groans from Gus and Ed greeted the closing remarks of the ungallant Joe, who sat down, feeling that he had made somebody squirm. Up jumped Grif, the delight of whose life was practical jokes, which amiable weakness made him the terror of the girls, though they had no other fault to find with the merry lad.

"Mr. Chairman, the ground I take is this: girls have not the strength to go to college with us. They couldn't row a race, go on a lark, or take care of themselves, as we do. They are all well enough at home, and I like them at parties, but for real fun and go I wouldn't give a cent for them," began Grif, whose views of a collegiate life were confined to the enjoyments rather than the studies of that festive period. "I have tried them, and they can't stand anything. They scream if you tell them there is a mouse in the room, and run if they see a big dog. I just put a cockroach in Molly's desk one day, and when she opened it she jumped as if she was shot."

So did the gentlemen of the club, for at that moment half-a-dozen fire-crackers exploded under the chair Grif had left, and flew wildly about the room. Order was with difficulty restored, the mischievous party summarily chastised and commanded to hold his tongue, under penalty of ejectment from the room if he spoke again. Firmly grasping that red and unruly member, Grif composed himself to listen, with his nose in the air and his eyes shining like black beads.

Ed was always the peace-maker, and now, when he rose with his engaging smile, his voice fell like oil upon the troubled waters, and his bright face was full of the becoming bashfulness which afflicts youths of seventeen when touching upon such subjects of newly acquired interest as girls and their pleasant but perplexing ways.

"It seems to me we have hardly considered the matter enough to be able to say much. But I think that school would be awfully dry and dismal without—ahem!—any young ladies to make it nice. I wouldn't give a pin to go if there was only a crowd of fellows, though I like a good game as well as any man. I pity any boy who has no sisters," continued Ed, warming up as he thought of his own, who loved him dearly, as well they might, for a better brother never lived. "Home wouldn't be worth having without them to look after a fellow, to keep him out of scrapes, help him with his lessons, and make things jolly for his friends. I tell you we can't do without girls, and I'm not ashamed to say that I think the more we see of them, and try to be like them in many ways, the better men we shall be by and by."

"Hear! hear!" cried Frank, in his deepest tone, for he heartily agreed to that, having talked the matter over with his mother, and received much light upon things which should always be set right in young heads and hearts. And who can do this so wisely and well as mothers, if they only will?

Feeling that his sentiments had been approved, and he need not be ashamed of the honest color in his cheeks, Ed sat down amid the applause of his side, especially of Jack, who pounded so vigorously with his crutch that Mrs. Pecq popped in her head to see if anything was wanted.

"No, thank you, ma'am, we were only cheering Ed," said Gus, now upon his legs, and rather at a loss what to say till Mrs. Pecq's appearance suggested an idea, and he seized upon it.

"My honored friend has spoken so well that I have little to add. I agree with him, and if you want an example of

what girls *can* do, why, look at Jill. She's young, I know,
but a first-rate scholar for her age. As for pluck, she is
as brave as a boy, and almost as smart at running, rowing,
and so on. Of course, she can't play ball,—no girl can;
their arms are not made right to throw,—but she can catch
remarkably well. I'll say that for her. Now, if she and
Mabel—and—and—some others I could name, are so
clever and strong at the beginning, I don't see why they
shouldn't keep up and go along with us all through. I'm
willing, and will do what I can to help other fellows' sisters
as I'd like to have them help mine. And I'll punch their
heads if they don't;" and Gus subsided, assured, by a burst
of applause, that his manly way of stating the case met with
general approval.

"We shall be happy to hear from our senior member if
he will honor us with a few remarks," said Frank, with a
bow to Ralph.

No one ever knew whom he would choose to person-
ate, for he never spoke in his own character.

Now he rose slowly, put one hand in his bosom, and
fixing his eye sternly on Grif, who was doing something suspicious with a pin, gave them a touch of Sergeant Buzfuz,
from the Pickwick trial, thinking that the debate was not
likely to throw much light on the subject under discussion.
In the midst of this appeal to "Me lud and gentlemen of the
jury," he suddenly paused, smoothed his hair down upon his
forehead, rolled up his eyes, and folding his hands, droned
out Mr. Chadband's sermon on Peace, delivered over poor
Jo, and ending with the famous lines:—

> "Oh, running stream of sparkling joy,
>   To be a glorious human boy!"

Then, setting his hair erect with one comprehensive sweep, he caught up his coat-skirts over his arm, and, assuming a parliamentary attitude, burst into a comical medley, composed of extracts from Jefferson Brick's and Lafayette Kettle's speeches, and Elijah Pogram's Defiance, from "Martin Chuzzlewit." Gazing at Gus, who was convulsed with suppressed merriment, he thundered forth:—

"In the name of our common country, sir, in the name of that righteous cause in which we are jined, and in the name of the star-spangled banner, I thank you for your eloquent and categorical remarks. You, sir, are a model of a man fresh from Natur's mould. A true-born child of this free hemisphere, verdant as the mountains of our land; bright and flowin' as our mineral Licks; unspiled by fashion as air our boundless perearers. Rough you may be; so air our Barrs. Wild you may be; so air our Buffalers. But, sir, you air a Child of Freedom, and your proud answer to the Tyrant is, that your bright home is in the Settin' Sun. And, sir, if any man denies this fact, though it be the British Lion himself, I defy him. Let me have him here!"—smiting the table, and causing the inkstand to skip—"here, upon this sacred altar! Here, upon the ancestral ashes cemented with the glorious blood poured out like water on the plains of Chickabiddy Lick. Alone I dare that Lion, and tell him that Freedom's hand once twisted in his mane, he rolls a corse before me, and the Eagles of the Great Republic scream, Ha, ha!"

By this time the boys were rolling about in fits of laughter; even sober Frank was red and breathless; and Jack lay back, feebly squealing, as he could laugh no more. In a moment Ralph was as meek as a Quaker, and sat looking about him with a mildly astonished air, as if inquiring the cause of such unseemly mirth. A knock at the door produced a lull, and in came a maid with apples.

"Time's up; fall to and make yourselves comfortable," was the summary way in which the club was released from its sterner duties and permitted to unbend its mighty mind for a social half-hour, chiefly devoted to whist, with an Indian war-dance as a closing ceremony.

The Dramatic Club

CHAPTER 10

While Jack was hopping gayly about on his crutches, poor Jill was feeling the effects of her second fall, and instead of sitting up, as she hoped to do after six weeks of rest, she was ordered to lie on a board for two hours each day. Not an easy penance, by any means, for the board was very hard, and she could do nothing while she lay there, as it did not slope enough to permit her to read without great fatigue of both eyes and hands. So the little martyr spent her first hour of trial in sobbing, the second in singing, for just as her mother and Mrs. Minot were deciding in despair that neither she nor they could bear it, Jill suddenly broke out into a merry chorus she used to hear her father sing:—

> *"Faut jouer le mirliton,*
> *Faut jouer le mirlitir,*
> *Faut jouer le mirliter,*
> *Mir—li—ton."*

The sound of the brave little voice was very comforting to the two mothers hovering about her, and Jack said, with a look of mingled pity and admiration, as he brandished his crutch over the imaginary foes,—

"That's right! Sing away, and we'll play you are an Indian captive being tormented by your enemies, and too
proud to complain. I'll watch the clock, and the minute
time is up I'll rush in and rescue you."

Jill laughed, but the fancy pleased her, and she
straightened herself out under the gay afghan, while she
sang, in a plaintive voice, another little French song her
father taught her:—

> "J'avais une colombe blanche,
> J'avais un blanc petit pigeon,
> Tous deux volaient, de branche en branche,
> Jusqu'au faîte de mon dongeon:
> Mais comme un coup de vent d'automne,
> S'est abattu là, l'épervier,
> Et ma colombe si mignonne
> Ne revient plus au colombier."

"My poor Jean had a fine voice, and always hoped the
child would take after him. It would break his heart to see
her lying there trying to cheer her pain with the songs he
used to sing her to sleep with," said Mrs. Pecq, sadly.

"She really has a great deal of talent, and when she is
able she shall have some lessons, for music is a comfort and
a pleasure, sick or well," answered Mrs. Minot, who had
often admired the fresh voice, with its pretty accent.

Here Jill began the Canadian boat-song, with great
vigor, as if bound to play her part of Indian victim with
spirit, and not disgrace herself by any more crying. All
knew the air, and joined in, especially Jack, who came out
strong on the "Row, brothers, row," but ended in a squeak
on a high note, so drolly, that the rest broke down. So the
hour that began with tears ended with music and laughter,
and a new pleasure to think of for the future.

After that day Jill exerted all her fortitude, for she liked to have the boys call her brave and admire the cheerful way in which she endured two hours of discomfort. She found she could use her zither as it lay upon her breast, and every day the pretty music began at a certain hour, and all in the house soon learned to love and listen for it. Even the old cook set open her kitchen door, saying pitifully, "Poor darlint, hear how purty she's singin', wid the pain, on that crewel boord. It's a little saint, she is. May her bed above be aisy!"

Frank would lift her gently on and off, with a kind word that comforted her immensely, and gentle Ed would come and teach her new bits of music, while the other fellows were frolicking below. Ralph added his share to her amusement, for he asked leave to model her head in clay, and set up his work in a corner, coming to pat, scrape, and mould whenever he had a spare minute, amusing her by his lively chat, and showing her how to shape birds, rabbits, and queer faces in the soft clay, when the songs were all sung and her fingers tired of the zither.

The girls sympathized very heartily with her new trial, and brought all manner of gifts to cheer her captivity. Merry and Molly made a gay screen by pasting pictures on the black cambric which covered the folding frame that stood before her to keep the draughts from her as she lay on her board. Bright birds and flowers, figures and animals, covered one side, and on the other they put mottoes, bits of poetry, anecdotes, and short stories, so that Jill could lie and look or read without the trouble of holding a book. It was not all done at once, but grew slowly, and was a source of instruction as well as amusement to them all, as they read carefully, that they might make good selections.

But the thing that pleased Jill most was something Jack did, for he gave up going to school, and stayed at home nearly a fortnight after he might have gone, all for her sake. The day the doctor said he might try it if he would be very careful, he was in great spirits, and limped about, looking up his books, and planning how he would astonish his mates by the rapidity of his recovery. When he sat down to rest he remembered Jill, who had been lying quietly behind the screen, while he talked with his mother, busy putting fresh covers on the books.

"She is so still, I guess she is asleep," thought Jack, peeping round the corner.

No, not asleep, but lying with her eyes fixed on the sunny window, beyond which the bright winter world sparkled after a fresh snow-fall. The jingle of sleigh-bells could be heard, the laughter of boys and girls on their way to school, all the pleasant stir of a new day of happy work and play for the rest of the world, more lonely, quiet, and wearisome than ever to her since her friend and fellow-prisoner was set free and going to leave her.

Jack understood that patient, wistful look, and, without a word, went back to his seat, staring at the fire so soberly, that his mother presently asked: "What are you thinking of so busily, with that pucker in your forehead?"

"I've about made up my mind that I won't go to school just yet," answered Jack, slowly lifting his head, for it cost him something to give up the long-expected pleasure.

"Why not?" and Mrs. Minot looked much surprised, till Jack pointed to the screen, and, making a sad face to express Jill's anguish, answered in a cheerful tone, "Well, I'm not sure that it is best. Doctor did not want me to go, but said I might because I teased. I shall be sure to come to grief, and then every one will say, 'I told you so,' and that is so provoking. I'd rather keep still a week longer. Hadn't I better?"

His mother smiled and nodded as she said, sewing away at much-abused old Caesar, as if she loved him, "Do as you think best, dear. I always want you at home, but I don't wonder you are rather tired of it after this long confinement."

"I say, Jill, should I be in your way if I didn't go to school till the first of February?" called Jack, laughing to himself at the absurdity of the question.

"Not much!" answered a glad voice from behind the screen, and he knew the sorrowful eyes were shining with delight, though he could not see them.

"Well, I guess I may as well, and get quite firm on my legs before I start. Another week or so will bring me up if I study hard, so I shall not lose my time. I'll tackle my Latin as soon as it's ready, mother."

Jack got a hearty kiss with the neatly covered book, and Mamma loved him for the little sacrifice more than if he had won a prize at school. He did get a reward, for, in five minutes from the time he decided, Jill was singing like a bobolink, and such a medley of merry music came from behind the screen, that it was a regular morning concert. She did not know then that he stayed for her sake, but she found it out soon after, and when the time came did as much for him, as we shall see.

It proved a wise decision, for the last part of January was so stormy Jack could not have gone half the time. So, while the snow drifted, and bitter winds raged, he sat snugly at home amusing Jill, and getting on bravely with his lessons, for Frank took great pains with him to show his approbation of the little kindness, and, somehow, the memory of it seemed to make even the detested Latin easier.

With February fair weather set in, and Jack marched happily away to school, with Jill's new mittens on his hands, Mamma nodding from the door-step, and Frank ready to give him a lift on the new sled, if the way proved too long or too rough.

"I shall not have time to miss him now, for we are to be very busy getting ready for the Twenty-second. The Dramatic Club meets to-night, and would like to come here, if they may, so I can help?" said Jill, as Mrs. Minot came up, expecting to find her rather low in her mind.

"Certainly; and I have a basket of old finery I looked up for the club when I was rummaging out bits of silk for your blue quilt," answered the good lady, who had set up a new employment to beguile the hours of Jack's absence.

When the girls arrived, that evening, they found Mrs. Chairwoman surrounded by a strew of theatrical properties, enjoying herself very much. All brought such contributions as they could muster, and all were eager about a certain tableau which was to be the gem of the whole, they thought. Jill, of course, was not expected to take any part, but her taste was good, so all consulted her as they showed their old silks, laces, and flowers, asking who should be this, and who that. All wanted to be the "Sleeping Beauty," for that was the chosen scene, with the slumbering court about the princess, and the prince in the act of awakening her. Jack was to be the hero, brave in his mother's velvet cape, red boots, and a real sword, while the other boys were to have parts of more or less splendor.

"Mabel should be the Beauty, because her hair is so lovely," said Juliet, who was quite satisfied with her own part of the Queen.

"No, Merry ought to have it, as she is the prettiest, and has that splendid veil to wear," answered Molly, who was to be the maid of honor, cuffing the little page, Boo.

"I don't care a bit, but my feather would be fine for the Princess, and I don't know as Emma would like to have me lend it to any one else," said Annette, waving a long white plume over her head, with girlish delight in its grace.

"I should think the white silk dress, the veil, and the feather ought to go together, with the scarlet crape shawl and these pearls. That would be sweet, and just what princesses really wear," advised Jill, who was stringing a quantity of old Roman pearls.

"We all want to wear the nice things, so let us draw lots. Wouldn't that be the fairest way?" asked Merry, looking like a rosy little bride, under a great piece of illusion, which had done duty in many plays.

"The Prince is light, so the Princess must be darkish. We ought to choose the girl who will look best, as it is a picture. I heard Miss Delano say so, when the ladies got up the tableaux, last winter, and every one wanted to be Cleopatra," said Jill decidedly.

"You choose, and then if we can't agree we will draw lots," proposed Susy, who, being plain, knew there was little hope of her getting a chance in any other way.

So all stood in a row, and Jill, from her sofa, surveyed them critically, feeling that the one Jack would really prefer was not among the number.

"I choose that one, for Juliet wants to be Queen, Molly would make faces, and the others are too big or too light," pronounced Jill, pointing to Merry, who looked pleased, while Mabel's face darkened, and Susy gave a disdainful sniff.

"You'd better draw lots, and then there will be no fuss. Ju and I are out of the fight, but you three can try, and let this settle the matter," said Molly, handing Jill a long strip of paper.

All agreed to let it be so, and when the bits were ready drew in turn. This time fate was evidently on Merry's side, and no one grumbled when she showed the longest paper.

"Go and dress, then come back, and we'll plan how we are to be placed before we call up the boys," commanded Jill, who was manager, since she could be nothing else.

The girls retired to the bedroom and began to "rig up," as they called it; but discontent still lurked among them, and showed itself in sharp words, envious looks, and disobliging acts.

"Am I to have the white silk and the feather?" asked Merry, delighted with the silvery shimmer of the one and the graceful droop of the other, though both were rather shabby.

"You can use your own dress. I don't see why you should have everything," answered Susy, who was at the mirror, putting a wreath of scarlet flowers on her red head, bound to be gay since she could not be pretty.

"I think I'd better keep the plume, as I haven't anything else that is nice, and I'm afraid Emma wouldn't like me to lend it," added Annette, who was disappointed that Mabel was not to be the Beauty.

"*I* don't intend to act at all!" declared Mabel, beginning to braid up her hair with a jerk, out of humor with the whole affair.

"*I* think you are a set of cross, selfish girls to back out and keep your nice things just because you can't *all* have the

best part. I'm ashamed of you!" scolded Molly, standing by
Merry, who was sadly surveying her mother's old purple
silk, which looked like brown in the evening.

"I'm going to have Miss Delano's red brocade for the
Queen, and I shall ask her for the yellow-satin dress for
Merry when I go to get mine, and tell her how mean you
are," said Juliet, frowning under her gilt-paper crown as
she swept about in a red table-cloth for train till the brocade
arrived.

"Perhaps you'd like to have Mabel cut her hair off, so
Merry can have that, too?" cried Susy, with whom hair was
a tender point.

"Light hair isn't wanted, so Ju will have to give hers,
or you'd better borrow Miss Bat's frisette," added Mabel,
with a scornful laugh.

"I just wish Miss Bat was here to give you girls a good
shaking. Do let some one else have a chance at the glass, you
peacock!" exclaimed Molly Loo, pushing Susy aside to
arrange her own blue turban, out of which she plucked the
pink pompon to give Merry.

"Don't quarrel about me. I shall do well enough, and
the scarlet shawl will hide my ugly dress," said Merry, from
the corner, where she sat waiting for her turn at the mirror.

As she spoke of the shawl her eye went in search of it,
and something that she saw in the other room put her own
disappointment out of her head. Jill lay there all alone,
rather tired with the lively chatter, and the effort it cost her
not to repine at being shut out from the great delight of
dressing up and acting. Her eyes were closed, her net was
off, and all the pretty black curls lay about her shoulders as
one hand idly pulled them out, while the other rested on the
red shawl, as if she loved its glowing color and soft texture.
She was humming to herself the little song of the dove and

the donjon, and something in the plaintive voice, the solitary figure, went straight to Merry's gentle heart.

"Poor Jilly can't have any of the fun," was the first thought; then came a second, that made Merry start and smile, and in a minute whisper so that all but Jill could hear her, "Girls, I'm not going to be the Princess. But I've thought of a splendid one!"

"Who?" asked the rest, staring at one another, surprised by this sudden announcement.

"Hush! Speak low, or you will spoil it all. Look in the Bird Room, and tell me if that isn't a prettier Princess than I could make?"

They all looked, but no one spoke, and Merry added, with sweet eagerness, "It is the only thing poor Jill *can* be, and it would make her so happy; Jack would like it, and it would please every one, I know. Perhaps she will never walk again, so we ought to be very good to her, poor dear."

The last words, whispered with a little quiver in the voice, settled the matter better than hours of talking, for girls are tender-hearted creatures, and not one of these but would have gladly given all the pretty things she owned to see Jill dancing about well and strong again. Like a ray of sunshine the kind thought touched and brightened every face; envy, impatience, vanity, and discontent flew away like imps at the coming of the good fairy, and with one accord they all cried, —

"It will be lovely; let us go and tell her!"

Forgetting their own adornment, out they trooped after Merry, who ran to the sofa, saying, with a smile which was reflected in all the other faces, "Jill, dear, we have chosen another Princess, and I know you'll like her."

"Who is it?" asked Jill, languidly, opening her eyes without the least suspicion of the truth.

"I'll show you;" and taking the cherished veil from her own head, Merry dropped it like a soft cloud over Jill; Annette added the long plume, Susy laid the white silk dress about her, while Juliet and Mabel lifted the scarlet shawl to spread it over the foot of the sofa, and Molly tore the last ornament from her turban, a silver star, to shine on Jill's breast. Then they all took hands and danced round the couch, singing, as they laughed at her astonishment, "There she is! There she is! Princess Jill as fine as you please!"

"Do you really mean it? But can I? Is it fair? How sweet of you! Come here and let me hug you all!" cried Jill, in a rapture at the surprise, and the pretty way in which it was done.

The grand scene on the Twenty-second was very fine, indeed; but the little tableau of that minute was infinitely better, though no one saw it, as Jill tried to gather them all in her arms, for that nosegay of girlish faces was the sweeter, because each one had sacrificed her own little vanity to please a friend, and her joy was reflected in the eyes that sparkled round the happy Princess.

"Oh, you dear, kind things, to think of me and give me all your best clothes! I never shall forget it, and I'll do anything for you. Yes! I'll write and ask Mrs. Piper to lend us her ermine cloak for the king. See if I don't!"

Shrieks of delight hailed this noble offer, for no one had dared to borrow the much-coveted mantle, but all agreed that the old lady would not refuse Jill. It was astonishing how smoothly everything went after this, for each was eager to help, admire, and suggest, in the friendliest way; and when all were dressed, the boys found a party of very gay ladies waiting for them round the couch, where lay the brightest little Princess ever seen.

"Oh, Jack, I'm to act! Wasn't it dear of the girls to

choose me? Don't they look lovely? Aren't you glad?" cried
Jill, as the lads stared and the lasses blushed and smiled, well
pleased at the frank admiration the boyish faces showed.

"I guess I am! You are a set of trumps, and we'll give
you a first-class spread after the play to pay for it. Won't
we, fellows?" answered Jack, much gratified, and feeling
that now he could act his own part capitally.

"We will. It was a handsome thing to do, and we think
well of you for it. Hey, Gus?" and Frank nodded approvingly at all, though he looked only at Annette.

"As king of this crowd, I call it to order," said Gus, retiring to the throne, where Juliet sat laughing in her red
table-cloth.

"We'll have 'The Fair One with Golden Locks' next
time; I promise you that," whispered Ed to Mabel, whose
shining hair streamed over her blue dress like a mantle of
gold-colored silk.

"Girls are pretty nice things, aren't they? Kind of 'em
to take Jill in. Don't Molly look fine, though?" and Grif's
black eyes twinkled as he planned to pin her skirts to
Merry's at the first opportunity.

"Susy looks as gay as a feather-duster. I like her. She
never snubs a fellow," said Joe, much impressed with the
splendor of the court ladies.

The boys' costumes were not yet ready, but they
posed well, and all had a merry time, ending with a game of
blind-man's-buff, in which every one caught the right person in the most singular way, and all agreed as they went
home in the moonlight that it had been an unusually jolly
meeting.

So the fairy play woke the sleeping beauty that lies in
all of us, and makes us lovely when we rouse it with a kiss of
unselfish good-will, for, though the girls did not know it

then, they had adorned themselves with pearls more precious than the waxen ones they decked their Princess in.

"Down Brakes"

CHAPTER 11

*T*he greatest people have their weak points, and the
best-behaved boys now and then yield to temptation and get
into trouble, as everybody knows. Frank was considered a
remarkably well-bred and proper lad, and rather prided
himself on his good reputation, for he never got into scrapes
like the other fellows. Well, hardly ever, for we must
confess that at rare intervals his besetting sin overcame his
prudence, and he proved himself an erring, human boy.
Steam-engines had been his idols for years, and they alone
could lure him from the path of virtue. Once, in trying to investigate the mechanism of a toy specimen, which had its
little boiler and ran about whistling and puffing in the most
delightful way, he nearly set the house afire by the sparks
that dropped on the straw carpet. Another time, in trying
experiments with the kitchen tea-kettle, he blew himself up,
and the scars of that explosion he still carried on his hands.

He was long past such childish amusements now, but
his favorite haunt was the engine-house of the new railroad,
where he observed the habits of his pets with never-failing
interest, and cultivated the good-will of stokers and brake-
men till they allowed him many liberties, and were rather
flattered by the admiration expressed for their iron horses
by a young gentleman who liked them better even than his
Greek and Latin.

There was not much business doing on this road as
yet, and the two cars of the passenger-trains were often

ting his heart's desire and astonishing his friend at the same
time by his skill and coolness.

"Go ahead. I'll jump when you do;" and Gus calmly sat
down again, bound in honor to stand by his mate till the
smash came, though rather dismayed at the audacity of the
prank.

"Don't you call this just splendid?" exclaimed Frank,
as they rolled along over the crossing, past the bridge, toward the curve, a mile from the station.

"Not bad. They are yelling like mad after us. Better go
back, if you can," said Gus, who was anxiously peering out,
and, in spite of his efforts to seem at ease, not enjoying the
trip a particle.

"Let them yell. I started to go to the curve, and I'll do
it if it costs me a hundred dollars. No danger; there's no
train under twenty minutes, I tell you," and Frank pulled
out his watch. But the sun was in his eyes, and he did not see
clearly, or he would have discovered that it was later than
he thought.

On they went, and were just rounding the bend when
a shrill whistle in front startled both boys, and drove the
color out of their cheeks.

"It's the factory train!" cried Gus, in a husky tone, as
he sprang to his feet.

"No; it's the five-forty on the other road," answered
Frank, with a queer thrill all through him at the thought of
what might happen if it was not. Both looked straight ahead
as the last tree glided by, and the long track lay before
them, with the freight-train slowly coming down. For an instant, the boys stood as if paralyzed.

"Jump!" said Gus, looking at the steep bank on one
side and the river on the other, undecided which to try.

"Sit still!" commanded Frank, collecting his wits, as he

gave a warning whistle to retard the on-coming train, while he reversed the engine and went back faster than he came.

A crowd of angry men was waiting for them, and Bill stood at the open switch in a towering passion as No. 11 returned to her place unharmed, but bearing two pale and frightened boys, who stepped slowly and silently down, without a word to say for themselves while the freight-train rumbled by on the main track.

Frank and Gus never had a very clear idea as to what occurred during the next few minutes, but vaguely remembered being well shaken, sworn at, questioned, threatened with direful penalties, and finally ordered off the premises forever by the wrathful depot-master. Joe was nowhere to be seen, and as the two culprits walked away, trying to go steadily, while their heads spun round, and all the strength seemed to have departed from their legs, Frank said, in an exhausted tone,—

"Come down to the boat-house and rest a minute."

Both were glad to get out of sight, and dropped upon the steps red, rumpled, and breathless, after the late exciting scene. Gus generously forebore to speak, though he felt that he was the least to blame; and Frank, after eating a bit of snow to moisten his dry lips, said, handsomely,—

"Now, don't you worry, old man. I'll pay the damages, for it was my fault. Joe will dodge, but I won't, so make your mind easy."

"We sha'n't hear the last of this in a hurry," responded Gus, relieved, yet anxious, as he thought of the reprimand his father would give him.

"I hope mother won't hear of it till I tell her quietly myself. She will be so frightened, and think I'm surely smashed up, if she is told in a hurry;" and Frank gave a shiver, as all the danger he had run came over him suddenly. "I thought we were done for when we saw that train. Guess we should have been if you had not had your wits about you. I always said you were a cool one;" and Gus patted Frank's back with a look of great admiration, for, now that it was all over, he considered it a very remarkable performance.

"Which do you suppose it will be, fine or imprisonment?" asked Frank, after sitting in a despondent attitude for a moment.

"Shouldn't wonder if it was both. Running off with an engine is no joke, you know."

"What did possess me to be such a fool?" groaned Frank, repenting, all too late, of yielding to the temptation which assailed him.

"Bear up, old fellow, I'll stand by you; and if the worst comes, I'll call as often as the rules of the prison allow," said Gus, consolingly, as he gave his afflicted friend an arm, and they walked away, both feeling that they were marked men from that day forth.

Meantime, Joe, as soon as he recovered from the shock of seeing the boys actually go off, ran away, as fast as his legs could carry him, to prepare Mrs. Minot for the loss of her son; for the idea of their coming safely back never occurred to him, his knowledge of engines being limited. A loud ring at the bell brought Mrs. Pecq, who was guarding the house, while Mrs. Minot entertained a parlor full of company.

"Frank's run off with No. 11, and he'll be killed sure. Thought I'd come up and tell you," stammered Joe, all out of breath and looking wild.

He got no further, for Mrs. Pecq clapped one hand over his mouth, caught him by the collar with the other, and hustled him into the ante-room before any one else could hear the bad news.

"Tell me all about it, and don't shout. What's come to the boy?" she demanded, in a tone that reduced Joe to a whisper at once.

"Go right back and see what has happened to him, then come and tell me quietly. I'll wait for you here. I wouldn't have his mother startled for the world," said the good soul, when she knew all.

"Oh, I dar'sn't! I opened the switch as they told me to, and Bill will half kill me when he knows it!" cried Joe, in a panic, as the awful consequences of his deed rose before him, showing both boys mortally injured and several trains wrecked.

"Then take yourself off home and hold your tongue. I'll watch the door, for I won't have any more ridiculous boys tearing in to disturb my lady."

Mrs. Pecq often called this good neighbor "my lady" when speaking of her, for Mrs. Minot was a true gentle-woman, and much pleasanter to live with than the titled mistress had been.

Joe scudded away as if the constable was after him, and presently Frank was seen slowly approaching with an unusually sober face and a pair of very dirty hands.

"Thank heaven, he's safe!" and, softly opening the door, Mrs. Pecq actually hustled the young master into the ante-room as unceremoniously as she had hustled Joe.

"I beg pardon, but the parlor is full of company, and that fool of a Joe came roaring in with a cock-and-bull story that gave me quite a turn. What is it, Mr. Frank?" she asked eagerly, seeing that something was amiss.

He told her in a few words, and she was much relieved to find that no harm had been done.

"Ah, the danger is to come," said Frank, darkly, as he went away to wash his hands and prepare to relate his misdeeds.

It was a very bad quarter of an hour for the poor fellow, who so seldom had any grave faults to confess; but he did it manfully, and his mother was so grateful for the safety of her boy that she found it difficult to be severe enough, and contented herself with forbidding any more visits to the too charming No. 11.

"What do you suppose will be done to me?" asked Frank, on whom the idea of imprisonment had made a deep impression.

"I don't know, dear, but I shall go over to see Mr. Burton right after tea. He will tell us what to do and what to expect. Gus must not suffer for your fault."

"He'll come off clear enough, but Joe must take his share, for if he hadn't opened that confounded switch, no harm would have been done. But when I saw the way clear, I actually couldn't resist going ahead," said Frank, getting excited again at the memory of that blissful moment when he started the engine.

Here Jack came hurrying in, having heard the news, and refused to believe it from any lips but Frank's. When he could no longer doubt, he was so much impressed with the daring of the deed that he had nothing but admiration for his brother, till a sudden thought made him clap his hands and exclaim exultingly,—

"His runaway beats mine all hollow, and now he can't crow over me! Won't that be a comfort? The good boy has got into a scrape. Hooray!"

This was such a droll way of taking it, that they had to

laugh; and Frank took his humiliation so meekly that Jack soon fell to comforting him, instead of crowing over him.

Jill thought it a most interesting event; and, when Frank and his mother went over to consult Mr. Burton, she and Jack planned out for the dear culprit a dramatic trial which would have convulsed the soberest of judges. His sentence was ten years' imprisonment, and such heavy fines that the family would have been reduced to beggary but for the sums made by Jill's fancy work and Jack's success as a champion pedestrian.

They found such comfort and amusement in this sensational programme that they were rather disappointed when Frank returned, reporting that a fine would probably be all the penalty exacted, as no harm had been done, and he and Gus were such respectable boys. What would happen to Joe, he could not tell, but he thought a good whipping ought to be added to his share.

Of course, the affair made a stir in the little world of children; and when Frank went to school, feeling that his character for good behavior was forever damaged, he found himself a lion, and was in danger of being spoiled by the admiration of his comrades, who pointed him out with pride as "the fellow who ran off with a steam-engine."

But an interview with Judge Kemble, a fine of twenty-five dollars, and lectures from all the grown people of his acquaintance, prevented him from regarding his escapade as a feat to boast of. He discovered, also, how fickle a thing is public favor, for very soon those who had praised began to tease, and it took all his courage, patience, and pride to carry him through the next week or two. The lads were never tired of alluding to No. 11, giving shrill whistles in his ear, asking if his watch was right, and drawing locomotives on the blackboard whenever they got a chance.

The girls, too, had sly nods and smiles, hints and jokes of a milder sort, which made him color and fume, and once lose his dignity entirely. Molly Loo, who dearly loved to torment the big boys, and dared attack even solemn Frank, left one of Boo's old tin trains on the door-step, directed to "Conductor Minot," who, I regret to say, could not refrain from kicking it into the street, and slamming the door with a bang that shook the house. Shrieks of laughter from wicked Molly and her coadjutor, Grif, greeted this explosion of wrath, which did no good, however, for half an hour later the same cars, all in a heap, were on the steps again, with two headless dolls tumbling out of the cab, and the dilapidated engine labelled, "No. 11 after the collision."

No one ever saw that ruin again, and for days Frank was utterly unconscious of Molly's existence, as propriety forbade his having it out with her as he had with Grif. Then Annette made peace between them, and the approach of the Twenty-second gave the wags something else to think of.

But it was long before Frank forgot that costly prank; for he was a thoughtful boy, who honestly wanted to be good; so he remembered this episode humbly, and whenever he felt the approach of temptation he made the strong will master it, saying to himself "Down brakes!" thus saving the precious freight he carried from many of the accidents which befall us when we try to run our trains without orders, and so often wreck ourselves as well as others.

The Twenty-Second of February
CHAPTER 12

*O*f course, the young ladies and gentlemen had a ball on the evening of that day, but the boys and girls were full of excitement about their "Scenes from the Life of Washington and other brilliant tableaux," as the programme announced. The Bird Room was the theatre, being very large, with four doors conveniently placed. Ralph was in his element, putting up a little stage, drilling boys, arranging groups, and uniting in himself carpenter, scene-painter, manager, and gas man. Mrs. Minot permitted the house to be turned topsy-turvy, and Mrs. Pecq flew about, lending a hand everywhere. Jill was costumer, with help from Miss Delano, who did not care for balls, and kindly took charge of the girls. Jack printed tickets, programmes, and placards of the most imposing sort, and the work went gayly on till all was ready.

When the evening came, the Bird Room presented a fine appearance. One end was curtained off with red drapery; and real footlights, with tin shades, gave a truly theatrical air to the little stage. Rows of chairs, filled with mammas and little people, occupied the rest of the space. The hall and Frank's room were full of amused papas, uncles, and old gentlemen whose patriotism brought them out in spite of rheumatism. There was a great rustling of skirts, fluttering of fans, and much lively chat, till a bell rang and the orchestra struck up.

Yes, there really was an orchestra, for Ed declared that the national airs *must* be played, or the whole thing would be a failure. So he had exerted himself to collect all the musical talent he could find, a horn, a fiddle, and a flute, with drum and fife for the martial scenes. Ed looked more beaming than ever, as he waved his baton and led off with Yankee Doodle as a safe beginning, for every one knew that. It was fun to see little Johnny Cooper bang away on a big drum, and old Mr. Munson, who had been a fifer all his days, blow till he was as red as a lobster, while every one kept time to the music which put them all in good spirits for the opening scene.

Up went the curtain and several trees in tubs appeared, then a stately gentleman in small clothes, cocked hat, gray wig, and an imposing cane, came slowly walking in. It was Gus, who had been unanimously chosen not only for Washington but for the father of the hero also, that the family traits of long legs and a somewhat massive nose might be preserved.

"Ahem! My trees are doing finely," observed Mr. W., senior, strolling along with his hands behind him, casting satisfied glances at the dwarf orange, oleander, abutilon, and little pine that represented his orchard.

Suddenly he starts, pauses, frowns, and, after examining the latter shrub, which displayed several hacks in its stem and a broken limb with six red-velvet cherries hanging on it, he gave a thump with his cane that made the little ones jump, and cried out,—

"Can it have been my son?"

He evidently thought it *was,* for he called, in tones of thunder,—

"George! George Washington, come hither this moment!"

Great suspense on the part of the audience, then a general burst of laughter as Boo trotted in, a perfect miniature of his honored parent, knee breeches, cocked hat, shoe buckles and all. He was so fat that the little tails of his coat stuck out in the drollest way, his chubby legs could hardly carry the big buckles, and the rosy face displayed, when he took his hat off with a dutiful bow, was so solemn, the real George could not have looked more anxious when he gave the immortal answer.

"Sirrah, did you cut that tree?" demanded the papa,

with another rap of the cane, and such a frown that poor
Boo looked dismayed, till Molly whispered, "Put your hand
up, dear." Then he remembered his part, and, putting one
finger in his mouth, looked down at his square-toed shoes,
the image of a shame-stricken boy.

"My son, do not deceive me. If you have done this
deed I shall chastise you, for it is my duty not to spare the
rod, lest I spoil the child. But if you lie about it you disgrace
the name of Washington forever."

This appeal seemed to convulse George with inward
agony, for he squirmed most effectively as he drew from his
pocket a toy hatchet, which would not have cut a straw,
then looking straight up into the awe-inspiring countenance
of his parent, he bravely lisped, —

"Papa, I tannot tell a lie. I did tut it with my little
hanchet."

"Noble boy, — come to my arms! I had rather you
spoilt *all* my cherry trees than tell one lie!" cried the delighted gentleman, catching his son in an embrace so close
that the fat legs kicked convulsively, and the little coat-tails
waved in the breeze, while cane and hatchet fell with a dramatic bang.

The curtain descended on this affecting tableau; but
the audience called out both Washingtons, and they came,
hand in hand, bowing with the cocked hats pressed to their
breasts, the elder smiling blandly, while the younger, still
flushed by his exertions, nodded to his friends, asking, with
engaging frankness, "Wasn't it nice?"

The next was a marine piece, for a boat was seen, surrounded by tumultuous waves of blue cambric, and rowed
by a party of stalwart men in regimentals, who with difficulty kept their seats, for the boat was only a painted board,

and they sat on boxes or stools behind it. But few marked the rowers, for in their midst, tall, straight, and steadfast as a mast, stood one figure in a cloak, with folded arms, high boots, and, under the turned-up hat, a noble countenance, stern with indomitable courage. A sword glittered at his side, and a banner waved over him, but his eye was fixed on the distant shore, and he was evidently unconscious of the roaring billows, the blocks of ice, the discouragement of his men, or the danger and death that might await him. Napoleon crossing the Alps was not half so sublime, and with one voice the audience cried, "Washington crossing the Delaware!" while the band burst forth with, "See, the conquering hero comes!" all out of tune, but bound to play it or die in the attempt.

It would have been very successful if, all of a sudden, one of the rowers had not "caught a crab" with disastrous consequences. The oars were not moving, but a veteran, who looked very much like Joe, dropped the one he held, and in trying to turn and pummel the black-eyed warrior behind him, he tumbled off his seat, upsetting two other men, and pulling the painted boat upon them as they lay kicking in the cambric deep. Shouts of laughter greeted this mishap, but George Washington never stirred. Grasping the banner, he stood firm when all else went down in the general wreck, and the icy waves engulfed his gallant crew, leaving him erect amid a chaos of wildly tossing boots, entangled oars, and red-faced victims. Such god-like dignity could not fail to impress the frivolous crowd of laughers, and the curtain fell amid a round of applause for him alone.

"Quite exciting, wasn't it? Didn't know Gus had so much presence of mind," said Mr. Burton, well pleased with his boy.

"If we did not know that Washington died in his bed, December 14, 1799, I should fear that we'd seen the last of him in that shipwreck," laughed an old gentleman, proud of his memory for dates.

Much confusion reigned behind the scenes; Ralph was heard scolding, and Joe set every one off again by explaining, audibly, that Grif tickled him, and he couldn't stand it. A pretty, old-fashioned picture of the "Daughters of Liberty" followed, for the girls were determined to do honor to the brave and patient women who so nobly bore their part in the struggle, yet are usually forgotten when those days are celebrated. The damsels were charming in the big caps, flowered gowns, and high-heeled shoes of their great-grandmothers, as they sat about a spider-legged table talking over the tax, and pledging themselves to drink no more tea till it was taken off. Molly was on her feet proposing, "Liberty forever, and down with all tyrants," to judge from her flashing eyes as she held her egg-shell cup aloft, while the others lifted theirs to drink the toast, and Merry, as hostess, sat with her hand on an antique teapot, labelled "Sage," ready to fill again when the patriotic ladies were ready for a second "dish."

This was much applauded, and the curtain went up again, for the proud parents enjoyed seeing their pretty girls in the faded finery of a hundred years ago. The band played "Auld Lang Syne," as a gentle hint that our fore-mothers should be remembered as well as the fore-fathers.

It was evident that something very martial was to follow, for a great tramping, clashing, and flying about took place behind the scenes while the tea-party was going on. After some delay, "The Surrender of Cornwallis" was presented in the most superb manner, as you can believe when

I tell you that the stage was actually lined with a glittering array of Washington and his generals, Lafayette, Kosciusko, Rochambeau and the rest, all in astonishing uniforms, with swords which were evidently the pride of their lives. Fife and drum struck up a march, and in came Cornwallis, much cast down but full of manly resignation, as he surrendered his sword, and stood aside with averted eyes while his army marched past, piling their arms at the hero's feet.

This scene was the delight of the boys, for the rifles of Company F had been secured, and at least a dozen soldiers kept filing in and out in British uniform till Washington's august legs were hidden by the heaps of arms rattled down before him. The martial music, the steady tramp, and the patriotic memories awakened, caused this scene to be enthusiastically encored, and the boys would have gone on marching till midnight if Ralph had not peremptorily ordered down the curtain and cleared the stage for the next tableau.

This had been artfully slipped in between two brilliant ones, to show that the Father of his Country had to pay a high price for his glory. The darkened stage represented what seemed to be a camp in a snow-storm, and a very forlorn camp, too; for on "the cold, cold ground" (a reckless display of cotton batting) lay ragged soldiers, sleeping without blankets, their worn-out boots turned up pathetically, and no sign of food or fire to be seen. A very shabby sentinel, with feet bound in bloody cloths, and his face as pale as chalk could make it, gnawed a dry crust as he kept his watch in the wintry night.

A tent at the back of the stage showed a solitary figure sitting on a log of wood, poring over the map spread upon his knee, by the light of one candle stuck in a bottle. There could be no doubt who this was, for the buff-and-blue coat, the legs, the nose, the attitude, all betrayed the great George laboring to save his country, in spite of privations, discouragements, and dangers which would have daunted any other man.

"Valley Forge," said some one, and the room was very still as old and young looked silently at this little picture of a great and noble struggle in one of its dark hours. The crust, the wounded feet, the rags, the snow, the loneliness, the indomitable courage and endurance of these men touched the hearts of all, for the mimic scene grew real for a moment; and, when a child's voice broke the silence, asking pitifully, "Oh, mamma, was it truly as dreadful as that?" a general outburst answered, as if every one wanted to cheer up the brave fellows and bid them fight on, for victory was surely coming.

In the next scene it did come, and "Washington at Trenton" was prettily done. An arch of flowers crossed the stage, with the motto, "The Defender of the Mothers will be the Preserver of the Daughters;" and, as the hero with his generals advanced on one side, a troop of girls, in old-fashioned muslin frocks, came to scatter flowers before him, singing the song of long ago:—

> "Welcome, mighty chief, once more
> Welcome to this grateful shore;
> Now no mercenary foe
> Aims again the fatal blow,—
> Aims at thee the fatal blow.
>
> "Virgins fair and matrons grave,
> Those thy conquering arm did save,
> Build for thee triumphal bowers;
> Strew, ye fair, his way with flowers,—
> Strew your hero's way with flowers."

And they did, singing with all their hearts as they flung
artificial roses and lilies at the feet of the great men, who
bowed with benign grace. Jack, who did Lafayette with a
limp, covered himself with glory by picking up one of the
bouquets and pressing it to his heart with all the gallantry of
a Frenchman; and when Washington lifted the smallest of
the maids and kissed her, the audience cheered. Couldn't
help it, you know, it was so pretty and inspiring.

The Washington Family, after the famous picture,
came next, with Annette as the serene and sensible Martha,
in a very becoming cap. The General was in uniform, there
being no time to change, but his attitude was quite correct,
and the Custis boy and girl displayed the wide sash and
ruffled collar with historic fidelity. The band played
"Home," and every one agreed that it was "Sweet!"

"Now I don't see what more they can have except the
death-bed, and that would be rather out of place in this gay
company," said the old gentleman to Mr. Burton, as he
mopped his heated face after pounding so heartily he nearly
knocked the ferule off his cane.

"No; they gave that up, for my boy wouldn't wear a
night-gown in public. I can't tell secrets, but I think they
have got a very clever little finale for the first part, — a
pretty compliment to one person and a pleasant surprise to
all," answered Mr. Burton, who was in great spirits, being
fond of theatricals and very justly proud of his children, for
the little girls had been among the Trenton maids, and the
mimic General had kissed his own small sister, Nelly, very
tenderly.

A great deal of interest was felt as to what this surprise
was to be, and a general "Oh!" greeted the "Minute Man,"
standing motionless upon his pedestal. It was Frank, and
Ralph had done his best to have the figure as perfect as

possible, for the maker of the original had been a good friend to him; and, while the young sculptor was dancing gayly at the ball, this copy of his work was doing him honor among the children. Frank looked it very well, for his firm-set mouth was full of resolution, his eyes shone keen and courageous under the three-cornered hat, and the muscles stood out upon the bare arm that clutched the old gun. Even the buttons on the gaiters seemed to flash defiance, as the sturdy legs took the first step from the furrow toward the bridge where the young farmer became a hero when he "fired the shot heard 'round the world."

"That *is* splendid!" "As like to the original as flesh can be to bronze." "How still he stands!" "He'll fight when the time comes, and die hard, won't he?" "Hush! You make the statue blush!" These very audible remarks certainly did, for the color rose visibly as the modest lad heard himself praised, though he saw but one face in all the crowd, his mother's, far back, but full of love and pride, as she looked up at her young minute man waiting for the battle which often calls us when we least expect it, and for which she had done her best to make him ready.

If there had been any danger of Frank being puffed up by the success of his statue, it was counteracted by irre-pressible Grif, who, just at the most interesting moment, when all were gazing silently, gave a whistle, followed by a "Choo, choo, choo!" and "All aboard!" so naturally that no one could mistake the joke, especially as another laughing voice added, "Now, then, No. 11!" which brought down the house and the curtain too.

Frank was so angry, it was very difficult to keep him on his perch for the last scene of all. He submitted, how-ever, rather than spoil the grand finale, hoping that its beauty would efface that ill-timed pleasantry from the public mind. So, when the agreeable clamor of hands and voices called for a repetition, the Minute Man reappeared, grimmer than before. But not alone, for grouped all about his pedestal were Washington and his generals, the matrons and maids, with a background of troops shouldering arms, Grif and Joe doing such rash things with their muskets, that more than one hero received a poke in his august back. Before the full richness of this picture had been taken in, Ed gave a rap, and all burst out with "Hail Columbia," in such an inspiring style that it was impossible for the audience to refrain from joining, which they did, all standing and all singing with a heartiness that made the walls ring. The fife shrilled, the horn blew sweet and clear, the fiddle was nearly drowned by the energetic boom of the drum, and out into the starry night, through open windows, rolled the song that stirs the coldest heart with patriotic warmth and tunes every voice to music.

" 'America!' We must have 'America!' Pipe up, Ed, this is too good to end without one song more," cried Mr. Burton, who had been singing like a trumpet; and, hardly waiting to get their breath, off they all went again with the national hymn, singing as they never had sung it before, for somehow the little scenes they had just acted or beheld seemed to show how much this dear America of ours had cost in more than one revolution, how full of courage, energy, and virtue it was in spite of all its faults, and what a privilege, as well as duty, it was for each to do his part toward its safety and its honor in the present, as did those brave men and women in the past.

So the "Scenes from the Life of Washington" were a great success, and, when the songs were over, people were glad of a brief recess while they had raptures, and refreshed themselves with lemonade.

The girls had kept the secret of who the "Princess" was to be, and, when the curtain rose, a hum of surprise and pleasure greeted the pretty group. Jill lay asleep in all her splendor, the bonny "Prince" just lifting the veil to wake her with a kiss, and all about them the court in its nap of a hundred years: the "King" and "Queen" dozing comfortably on the throne; the maids of honor, like a garland of nodding flowers, about the couch; the little page, unconscious of the blow about to fall, and the fool dreaming, with his mouth wide open.

It was so pretty, people did not tire of looking, till Jack's lame leg began to tremble, and he whispered: "Drop her or I shall pitch." Down went the curtain; but it rose in a moment, and there was the court after the awakening: the "King" and "Queen" looking about them with sleepy dignity, the maids in various attitudes of surprise, the fool grinning from ear to ear, and the "Princess" holding out her hand to the "Prince," as if glad to welcome the right lover when he came at last.

Molly got the laugh this time, for she could not resist giving poor Boo the cuff which had been hanging over him so long. She gave it with unconscious energy, and Boo cried "Ow!" so naturally that all the children were delighted and wanted it repeated. But Boo declined, and the scenes which followed were found quite as much to their taste, having been expressly prepared for the little people.

Mother Goose's Reception was really very funny, for Ralph was the old lady, and had hired a representation of the immortal bird from a real theatre for this occasion. There they stood, the dame in her pointed hat, red petticoat, cap, and cane, with the noble fowl, a good deal larger than life, beside her, and Grif inside, enjoying himself immensely as he flapped the wings, moved the yellow legs, and waved the long neck about, while unearthly quacks issued from the bill. That was a great surprise for the children, and they got up in their seats to gaze their fill, many of them firmly believing that they actually beheld the blessed old woman who wrote the nursery songs they loved so well.

Then in came, one after another, the best of the characters she has made famous, while a voice behind the scenes sang the proper rhyme as each made their manners to the interesting pair. "Mistress Mary," and her "pretty maids all in a row," passed by to their places in the background; "King Cole" and his "fiddlers three" made a goodly show; so did the royal couple, who followed the great pie borne before them, with the "four-and-twenty blackbirds" popping their heads out in the most delightful way. Little "Bo-peep" led a woolly lamb and wept over its lost tail, for not a sign of one appeared on the poor thing. "Simple Simon" followed the pie-man, gloating over his wares with the drollest antics. The little wife came trundling by in a wheelbarrow and was not upset; neither was the lady with "rings on her fingers and bells on her toes," as she cantered along on a rocking-horse. "Bobby Shafto's" yellow hair shone finely as he led in the maid whom he came back from sea to marry. "Miss Muffet," bowl in hand, ran away from an immense black spider, which waggled its long legs in a way so life-like that some of the children shook in their little shoes. The beggars who came to town were out in full force, "rags, tags, and velvet gowns," quite true to life. "Boy Blue" rubbed his eyes, with hay sticking in his hair, and tooted on a tin horn, as if bound to get the cows out of the corn. Molly, with a long-handled frying-pan, made a capital "Queen," in a tucked-up gown, checked apron, and high crown, to good "King Arthur," who, very properly, did not appear after stealing the barley-meal, which might be seen in the pan tied up in a pudding, like a cannon-ball, ready to fry.

But Tobias, Molly's black cat, covered himself with glory by the spirit with which he acted his part in

"Sing, sing, what shall I sing?
The cat's run away with the pudding-bag string."

First he was led across the stage on his hind legs, looking very fierce and indignant, with a long tape trailing behind him; and, being set free at the proper moment, he gave one bound over the four-and-twenty blackbirds who happened to be in the way, and dashed off as if an enraged cook had actually been after him, straight downstairs to the coalbin, where he sat glaring in the dark, till the fun was over.

When all the characters had filed in and stood in two long rows, music struck up and they danced, "All the way to Boston," a simple but lively affair, which gave each a chance to show his or her costume as they pranced down the middle and up outside.

Such a funny medley as it was, for there went fat "King Cole" with the most ragged of the beggar-maids. "Mistress Mary," in her pretty blue dress, tripped along with "Simple Simon" staring about him like a blockhead. The fine lady left her horse to dance with "Bobby Shafto" till every bell on her slippers tinkled its tongue out. "Bo-Peep" and a jolly fiddler skipped gayly up and down. "Miss Muffet" took the big spider for her partner, and made his many legs fly about in the wildest way. The little wife got out of the wheelbarrow to help "Boy Blue" along, and Molly, with the frying-pan over her shoulder, led off splendidly when it was "Grand right and left."

But the old lady and her goose were the best of all, for the dame's shoe-buckles cut the most astonishing pigeon wings, and to see that mammoth bird waddle down the middle with its wings half open, its long neck bridling, and its yellow legs in the first position as it curtsied to its partner, was a sight to remember, it was so intensely funny.

The merry old gentleman laughed till he cried; Mr. Burton split his gloves, he applauded so enthusiastically; while the children beat the dust out of the carpet hopping up and down, as they cried: "Do it again!" "We want it all over!" when the curtain went down at last on the flushed and panting party, Mother G ———— bowing, with her hat all awry, and the goose doing a double shuffle as if it did not know how to leave off.

But they could not "do it all over again," for it was growing late, and the people felt that they certainly had received their money's worth that evening.

So it all ended merrily, and when the guests departed the boys cleared the room like magic, and the promised supper to the actors was served in handsome style. Jack and Jill were at one end, Mrs. Goose and her bird at the other, and all between was a comical collection of military heroes, fairy characters, and nursery celebrities. All felt the need of refreshment after their labors, and swept over the table like a flight of locusts, leaving devastation behind. But they had earned their fun: and much innocent jollity prevailed, while a few lingering papas and mammas watched the revel from afar, and had not the heart to order these noble beings home till even the Father of his Country declared "that he'd had a perfectly splendid time, but couldn't keep his eyes open another minute," and very wisely retired to replace the immortal cocked hat with a night-cap.

Jack Has a Mystery
CHAPTER 13

"What is the matter? Does your head ache?" asked Jill, one evening in March, observing that Jack sat with his head in his hands, an attitude which, with him, meant either pain or perplexity.

"No; but I'm bothered. I want some money, and I don't see how I can earn it," he answered, tumbling his hair about, and frowning darkly at the fire.

"How much?" and Jill's ready hand went to the pocket where her little purse lay, for she felt rich with several presents lately made her.

"Two seventy-five. No, thank you, I won't borrow."

"What is it for?"

"Can't tell."

"Why, I thought you told me everything."

"Sorry, but I can't this time. Don't you worry; I shall think of something."

"Couldn't your mother help?"

"Don't wish to ask her."

"Why! can't *she* know?"

"Nobody can."

"How queer! Is it a scrape, Jack?" asked Jill, looking as curious as a magpie."

"It is likely to be, if I can't get out of it this week, somehow."

"Well, I don't see how I can help if I'm not to know anything;" and Jill seemed rather hurt.

"You can just stop asking questions, and tell me how a fellow can earn some money. That would help. I've got one dollar, but I must have some more;" and Jack looked worried as he fingered the little gold dollar on his watch-guard.

"Oh, do you mean to use that?"

"Yes, I do; a man must pay his debts if he sells all he has to do it," said Jack sternly.

"Dear me; it must be something very serious." And Jill lay quite still for five minutes, thinking over all the ways in which Jack ever did earn money, for Mrs. Minot liked to have her boys work, and paid them in some way for all they did.

"Is there any wood to saw?" she asked presently, being very anxious to help.

"All done."

"Paths to shovel?"

"No snow."

"Lawn to rake, then?"

"Not time for that yet."

"Catalogue of books?"

"Frank got that job."

"Copy those letters for your mother?"

"Take me too long. Must have my money Friday, if possible."

"I don't see what we can do, then. It is too early or too late for everything, and you won't borrow."

"Not of you. No, nor of any one else, if I can possibly help it. I've promised to do this myself, and I will;" and Jack wagged his head resolutely.

"Couldn't you do something with the printing press? Do me some cards, and then, perhaps, the other girls will want some," said Jill, as a forlorn hope.

"Just the thing! What a goose I was not to think of it. I'll rig the old machine up at once." And, starting from his seat, Jack dived into the big closet, dragged out the little press, and fell to oiling, dusting, and putting it in order, like one relieved of a great anxiety.

"Give me the types; I'll sort them and set up my name, so you can begin as soon as you are ready. You know what a help I was when we did the programmes. I'm almost sure the girls *will* want cards, and I know your mother would like some more tags," said Jill, briskly rattling the letters into the different compartments, while Jack inked the rollers and hunted up his big apron, whistling the while with recovered spirits.

A dozen neat cards were soon printed, and Jill insisted on paying six cents for them, as earning was not borrowing. A few odd tags were found and done for Mamma, who immediately ordered four dozen at six cents a dozen, though she was not told why there was such a pressing call for money.

Jack's monthly half-dollar had been spent the first week,—twenty-five cents for a concert, ten paid a fine for keeping a book too long from the library, ten more to have his knife ground, and five in candy, for he dearly loved sweeties, and was under bonds to Mamma not to spend more than five cents a month on these unwholesome temptations. She never asked the boys what they did with their money, but expected them to keep account in the little books she gave them; and, now and then, they showed the neat pages with pardonable pride, though she often laughed at the queer items.

All that evening Jack & Co. worked busily, for when Frank came in he good-naturedly ordered some pale-pink cards for Annette, and ran to the store to choose the right shade, and buy some packages for the young printer also.

"What *do* you suppose he is in such a pucker for?"

whispered Jill, as she set up the new name, to Frank, who sat close by, with one eye on his book and one on her.

"Oh, some notion. He's a queer chap; but I guess it isn't much of a scrape, or I should know it. He's so good-natured he's always promising to do things for people, and has too much pluck to give up when he finds he can't. Let him alone, and it will all come out soon enough," answered Frank, who laughed at his brother, but loved him none the less for the tender heart that often got the better of his young head.

But for once Frank was mistaken; the mystery did not come out, and Jack worked like a beaver all that week, as orders poured in when Jill and Annette showed their elegant cards; for, as everybody knows, if one girl has a new thing all the rest must, whether it is a bow on the top of her head, a peculiar sort of pencil, or the latest kind of chewing-gum. Little play did the poor fellow get, for every spare minute was spent at the press, and no invitation could tempt him away, so much in earnest was our honest little Franklin about paying his debt. Jill helped all she could, and cheered his labors with her encouragement, remembering how he stayed at home for her.

"It is real good of you to lend a hand, and I'm ever so much obliged," said Jack, as the last order was struck off, and the drawer of the type-box held a pile of shining five and ten cent pieces, with two or three quarters.

"I love to; only it would be nicer if I knew what we were working for," she said demurely, as she scattered type for the last time; and seeing that Jack was both tired and grateful, hoped to get a hint of the secret.

"I want to tell you, dreadfully; but I can't, because I've promised."

"What, never?"

"Never!" and Jack looked as firm as a rock.

"Then I shall find out, for *I* haven't promised."

"You can't."

"See if I don't!"

"You are sharp, but you won't guess this. It's a tremendous secret, and nobody will tell it."

"You'll tell it yourself. You always do."

"I won't tell this. It would be mean."

"Wait and see; I can get anything out of you if I try;" and Jill laughed, knowing her power well, for Jack found it very hard to keep a secret from her.

"Don't try; please don't! It wouldn't be right, and you don't want to make me do a dishonorable thing for your sake, I know."

Jack looked so distressed that Jill promised not to *make* him tell, though she held herself free to find out in other ways, if she could.

Thus relieved, Jack trudged off to school on Friday with the two dollars and seventy-five cents jingling in his pocket, though the dear gold coin had to be sacrificed to make up the sum. He did his lessons badly that day, was late at recess in the afternoon, and, as soon as school was over, departed in his rubber-boots "to take a walk," he said, though the roads were in a bad state with a spring thaw. Nothing was seen of him till after tea-time, when he came limping in, very dirty and tired, but with a reposeful expression, which betrayed that a load was off his mind. Frank was busy about his own affairs and paid little attention to him, but Jill was on tenter-hooks to know where he had been, yet dared not ask the question.

"Merry's brother wants some cards. He liked hers so much he wishes to make his lady-love a present. Here's the name;" and Jill held up the order from Harry Grant, who was to be married in the autumn.

"Must wait till next week. I'm too tired to do a thing to-night, and I hate the sight of that old press," answered Jack, laying himself down upon the rug as if every joint ached.

"What made you take such a long walk? You look as tired as if you'd been ten miles," said Jill, hoping to discover the length of the trip.

"Had to. Four or five miles isn't much, only my leg bothered me;" and Jack gave the ailing member a slap, as if he had found it much in his way that day; for, though he had given up the crutches long ago, he rather missed their support sometimes. Then, with a great yawn, he stretched himself out to bask in the blaze, pillowing his head on his arms.

"Dear old thing, he looks all used up; I won't plague him with talking;" and Jill began to sing, as she often did in the twilight.

By the time the first song ended a gentle snore was heard, and Jack lay fast asleep, worn out with the busy week and the walk, which had been longer and harder than any one guessed. Jill took up her knitting and worked quietly by fire-light, still wondering and guessing what the secret could be; for she had not much to amuse her, and little things were very interesting if connected with her friends. Presently Jack rolled over and began to mutter in his sleep, as he often did when too weary for sound slumber. Jill paid no attention till he uttered a name which made her prick up her ears and listen to the broken sentences which followed. Only a few words, but she dropped her work, saying to herself,—

"I do believe he is talking about the secret. Now I shall find out, and he *will* tell me himself, as I said he would."

Much pleased, she leaned and listened, but could make no sense of the confused babble about "heavy boots;" "All right, old fellow;" "Jerry's off;" and "The ink is too thick."

The slam of the front door woke Jack, and he pulled himself up, declaring that he believed he had been having a nap.

"I wish you'd have another," said Jill, greatly disappointed at the loss of the intelligence she seemed to be so near getting.

"Floor is too hard for tired bones. Guess I'll go to bed and get rested up for Monday. I've worked like fury this week, so next I'm going in for fun;" and, little dreaming what hard times were in store for him, Jack went off to enjoy his warm bath and welcome bed, where he was soon sleeping with the serene look of one whose dreams were happy, whose conscience was at rest.

"I have a few words to say to you before you go," said Mr. Acton, pausing with his hand on the bell, Monday afternoon, when the hour came for dismissing school.

The bustle of putting away books and preparing for as rapid a departure as propriety allowed, subsided suddenly, and the boys and girls sat as still as mice, while the hearts of such as had been guilty of any small sins began to beat fast.

"You remember that we had some trouble last winter about keeping the boys away from the saloon, and that a rule was made forbidding any pupil to go to town during recess?" began Mr. Acton, who, being a conscientious man as well as an excellent teacher, felt that he was responsible for the children in school hours, and did his best to aid parents in guarding them from the few temptations which beset them in a country town. A certain attractive little shop, where confectionery, base-balls, stationery, and picture papers were sold, was a favorite loafing place for some of the boys till the rule forbidding it was made, because in the rear of the shop was a beer and billiard saloon. A wise rule, for the picture papers were not always of the best sort; cigars were to be had; idle fellows hung about there, and some of the lads, who wanted to be thought manly, ventured to pass the green baize door "just to look on."

A murmur answered the teacher's question, and he continued,—

"You all know that the rule was broken several times, and I told you the next offender would be publicly reprimanded, as private punishments had no effect. I am sorry to say that the time has come and the offender is a boy whom I trusted entirely. It grieves me to do this, but I must keep my promise, and hope the example will have a good effect."

Mr. Acton paused, as if he found it hard to go on, and the boys looked at one another with inquiring eyes, for their teacher seldom punished, and when he did, it was a very solemn thing. Several of these anxious glances fell upon Joe, who was very red and sat whittling a pencil as if he dared not lift his eyes.

"He's the chap. Won't he catch it!" whispered Gus to Frank, for both owed him a grudge.

"The boy who broke the rule last Friday, at afternoon recess, will come to the desk," said Mr. Acton in his most impressive manner.

If a thunderbolt had fallen through the roof it would hardly have caused a greater surprise than the sight of Jack Minot walking slowly down the aisle, with a wrathful flash in the eyes he turned on Joe as he passed him.

"Now, Minot, let us have this over as soon as possible,

for I do not like it any better than you do, and I am sure there is some mistake. I'm told you went to the shop on Friday. Is it true?" asked Mr. Acton very gently, for he liked Jack and seldom had to correct him in any way.

"Yes, sir;" and Jack looked up as if proud to show that he was not afraid to tell the truth as far as he could.

"To buy something?"

"No, sir."

"To meet some one?"

"Yes, sir."

"Was it Jerry Shannon?"

No answer, but Jack's fists doubled up of themselves as he shot another fiery glance at Joe, whose face burned as if it scorched him.

"I am told it was; also that you were seen to go into the saloon with him. Did you?" and Mr. Acton looked so sure that it was a mistake that it cost Jack a great effort to say, slowly,—

"Yes, sir."

Quite a thrill pervaded the school at this confession, for Jerry was one of the wild fellows the boys all shunned, and to have any dealings with him was considered a very disgraceful thing.

"Did you play?"

"No, sir. I can't."

"Drink beer?"

"I belong to the Lodge;" and Jack stood as erect as any little soldier who ever marched under a temperance banner, and fought for the cause none are too young nor too old to help along.

"I was sure of that. Then what took you there, my boy?"

The question was so kindly put that Jack forgot himself an instant, and blurted out,—

"I only went to pay him some money, sir."

"Ah, how much?"

"Two seventy-five," muttered Jack, as red as a cherry at not being able to keep a secret better.

"Too much for a lad like you to owe such a fellow as Jerry. How came it?" And Mr. Acton looked disturbed.

Jack opened his lips to speak, but shut them again, and stood looking down with a little quiver about the mouth that showed how much it cost him to be silent.

"Does any one beside Jerry know of this?"

"One other fellow," after a pause.

"Yes, I understand;" and Mr. Acton's eye glanced at Joe with a look that seemed to say, "I wish he'd held his tongue."

A queer smile flitted over Jack's face, for Joe was not the "other fellow," and knew very little about it, excepting what he had seen when he was sent on an errand by Mr. Acton on Friday.

"I wish you would explain the matter, John, for I am sure it is better than it seems, and it would be very hard to punish you when you don't deserve it."

"But I do deserve it; I've broken the rule, and I ought to be punished," said Jack, as if a good whipping would be easier to bear than this public cross-examination.

"And you can't explain, or even say you are sorry or ashamed?" asked Mr. Acton, hoping to surprise another fact out of the boy.

"No, sir; I can't; I'm not ashamed; I'm not sorry, and I'd do it again to-morrow if I had to," cried Jack, losing patience, and looking as if he would not bear much more.

A groan from the boys greeted this bare-faced declaration, and Susy quite shivered at the idea of having taken two bites out of the apple of such a hardened desperado.

"Think it over till to-morrow, and perhaps you will change your mind. Remember that this is the last week of the month, and reports are given out next Friday," said Mr. Acton, knowing how much the boy prided himself on always having good ones to show his mother.

Poor Jack turned scarlet and bit his lips to keep them still, for he had forgotten this when he plunged into the affair which was likely to cost him dear. Then the color faded away, the boyish face grew steady, and the honest eyes looked up at his teacher as he said very low, but all heard him, the room was so still,—

"It isn't as bad as it looks, sir, but I can't say any more. No one is to blame but me; and I couldn't help breaking the rule, for Jerry was going away, I had only that time, and I'd promised to pay up, so I did."

Mr. Acton believed every word he said, and regretted that they had not been able to have it out privately, but he, too, must keep his promise and punish the offender, whoever he was.

"Very well, you will lose your recess for a week, and this month's report will be the first one in which behavior does not get the highest mark. You may go; and I wish it understood that Master Minot is not to be troubled with questions till he chooses to set this matter right."

Then the bell rang, the children trooped out, Mr. Acton went off without another word, and Jack was left alone to put up his books and hide a few tears that would come because Frank turned his eyes away from the imploring look cast upon him as the culprit came down from the platform, a disgraced boy.

Elder brothers are apt to be a little hard on younger ones, so it is not surprising that Frank, who was an eminently proper boy, was much cut up when Jack publicly confessed to dealings with Jerry, leaving it to be supposed that the worst half of the story remained untold. He felt it his duty, therefore, to collar poor Jack when he came out, and talk to him all the way home, like a judge bent on getting at the truth by main force. A kind word would have been very comforting, but the scolding was too much for Jack's temper, so he turned dogged and would not say a word, though Frank threatened not to speak to him for a week.

At tea-time both boys were very silent, one looking grim, the other excited. Frank stared sternly at his brother across the table, and no amount of marmalade sweetened or softened that reproachful look. Jack defiantly crunched his toast, with occasional slashes at the butter, as if he must vent the pent-up emotions which half distracted him. Of course, their mother saw that something was amiss, but did not allude to it, hoping that the cloud would blow over as so many did if left alone. But this one did not, and when both refused cake, this sure sign of unusual perturbation made her anxious to know the cause. As soon as tea was over, Jack retired with gloomy dignity to his own room, and Frank, casting away the paper he had been pretending to read, burst out with the whole story. Mrs. Minot was as much surprised as he, but not angry, because, like most mothers, she was sure that her sons could not do anything very bad.

"I will speak to him; my boy won't refuse to give *me* some explanation," she said, when Frank had freed his mind with as much warmth as if Jack had broken all the ten commandments.

"He will. You often call me obstinate, but he is as

pig-headed as a mule; Joe only knows what he saw, old tell-tale! and Jerry has left town, or I'd have it out of him. Make Jack own up, whether he can or not. Little donkey!" stormed Frank, who hated rowdies and could not forgive his brother for being seen with one.

"My dear, all boys do foolish things sometimes, even the wisest and best behaved, so don't be hard on the poor child. He has got into trouble, I've no doubt, but it cannot be very bad, and he earned the money to pay for his prank, whatever it was."

Mrs. Minot left the room as she spoke, and Frank cooled down as if her words had been a shower-bath, for he remembered his own costly escapade, and how kindly both his mother and Jack had stood by him on that trying occasion. So, feeling rather remorseful, he went off to talk it over with Gus, leaving Jill in a fever of curiosity, for Merry and Molly had dropped in on their way home to break the blow to her, and Frank declined to discuss it with her, after mildly stating that Jack was a "ninny," in his opinion.

"Well, I know one thing," said Jill confidentially to Snow-ball, when they were left alone together, "if every one else is scolding him I won't say a word. It's so mean to crow over people when they are down, and I'm sure he hasn't done anything to be ashamed of, though he won't tell."

Snow-ball seemed to agree to this, for he went and sat down by Jack's slippers waiting for him on the hearth, and Jill thought that a very touching proof of affectionate fidelity to the little master who ruled them both.

When he came, it was evident that he had found it harder to refuse his mother than all the rest. But she trusted him in spite of appearances, and that was such a comfort! for poor Jack's heart was very full, and he longed to tell the whole story, but he would not break his promise, and so kept silence bravely. Jill asked no questions, affecting to be anxious for the games they always played together in the evening, but while they played, though the lips were sealed, the bright eyes said as plainly as words, "I trust you," and Jack was very grateful.

It was well he had something to cheer him up at home, for he got little peace at school. He bore the grave looks of Mr. Acton meekly, took the boys' jokes good-naturedly, and withstood the artful teasing of the girls with patient silence. But it was very hard for the social, affectionate fellow to bear the general distrust, for he had been such a favorite he felt the change keenly.

But the thing that tried him most was the knowledge that his report would not be what it usually was. It was always a happy moment when he showed it to his mother, and saw her eye brighten as it fell on the 99 or 100, for she cared more for good behavior than for perfect lessons. Mr. Acton once said that Frank Minot's moral influence in the school was unusual, and Jack never forgot her pride and delight as she told them what Frank himself had not known till then. It was Jack's ambition to have the same said of him, for he was not much of a scholar, and he had tried hard since he went back to school to get good records in that respect at least. Now here was a dreadful downfall, tardy marks, bad company, broken rules, and something too wrong to tell, apparently.

"Well, I deserve a good report, and that's a comfort, though nobody believes it," he said to himself, trying to keep up his spirits, as the slow week went by, and no word from him had cleared up the mystery.

And Jill Finds It Out
CHAPTER 14

*J*ill worried about it more than he did, for she was a faithful little friend, and it was a great trial to have Jack even suspected of doing anything wrong. School is a child's world while he is there, and its small affairs are very important to him, so Jill felt that the one thing to be done was to clear away the cloud about her dear boy, and restore him to public favor.

"Ed will be here Saturday night and may be he will find out, for Jack tells him everything. I do hate to have him hectored so, for I know he is, though he's too proud to complain," she said, on Thursday evening, when Frank told her some joke played upon his brother that day.

"I let him alone, but I see that he isn't badgered too much. That's all I can do. If Ed had only come home last Saturday it might have done some good, but now it will be too late; for the reports are given out to-morrow, you know," answered Frank, feeling a little jealous of Ed's influence over Jack, though his own would have been as great if he had been as gentle.

"Has Jerry come back?" asked Jill, who kept all her questions for Frank, because she seldom alluded to the tender subject when with Jack.

"No, he's off for the summer. Got a place somewhere. Hope he'll stay there and let Bob alone."

"Where is Bob now? I don't hear much about him lately," said Jill, who was constantly on the lookout for "the other fellow," since it was not Joe.

"Oh, he went to Captain Skinner's the first of March, chores round, and goes to school up there. Captain is strict,

and won't let Bob come to town, except Sundays; but he
don't mind it much, for he likes horses, has nice grub, and
the Hill fellows are good chaps for him to be with. So he's
all right, if he only behaves."

"How far is it to Captain Skinner's?" asked Jill suddenly, having listened, with her sharp eyes on Frank, as he
tinkered away at his model, since he was forbidden all other
indulgence in his beloved pastime.

"It's four miles to Hill District, but the Captain lives
this side of the school-house. About three from here, I
should say."

"How long would it take a boy to walk up there?"
went on the questioner, with a new idea in her head.

"Depends on how much of a walkist he is."

"Suppose he was lame and it was sloshy, and he made a
call and came back. How long would that take?" asked Jill
impatiently.

"Well, in that case, I should say two or three hours.
But it's impossible to tell exactly, unless you know how
lame the fellow was, and how long a call he made," said
Frank, who liked to be accurate.

"Jack couldn't do it in less, could he?"

"He used to run up that hilly road for a breather, and
think nothing of it. It would be a long job for him now, poor
little chap, for his leg often troubles him, though he hates to
own it."

Jill lay back and laughed, a happy little laugh, as if she
was pleased about something, and Frank looked over his
shoulder to ask questions in his turn.

"What are you laughing at?"

"Can't tell."

"Why do you want to know about Hill District? Are
you going there?"

"Wish I could! I'd soon have it out of him."

"Who?"

"Never mind. Please push up my table. I must write a letter, and I want you to post it for me tonight, and never say a word till I give you leave."

"Oh, now *you* are going to have secrets and be mysterious, and get into a mess, are you?" and Frank looked down at her with a suspicious air, though he was intensely curious to know what she was about.

"Go away till I'm done. You will have to see the outside, but you can't know the inside till the answer comes;" and propping herself up, Jill wrote the following note, with some hesitation at the beginning and end, for she did not know the gentleman she was addressing, except by sight, and it was rather awkward:—

ROBERT WALKER.

DEAR SIR,—I want to ask if Jack Minot came to see you last Friday afternoon. He got into trouble being seen with Jerry Shannon. He paid him some money. Jack won't tell, and Mr. Acton talked to him about it before all the school. We feel bad, because we think Jack did not do wrong. I don't know as you have anything to do with it, but I thought I'd ask. Please answer quick.—Respectfully yours,

JANE PECQ.

To make sure that her despatch was not tampered with, Jill put a great splash of red sealing-wax on it, which gave it a very official look, and much impressed Bob when he received it.

"There! Go and post it, and don't let any one see or know about it," she said, handing it over to Frank, who left his work with unusual alacrity to do her errand. When his eye fell on the address, he laughed, and said in a teasing way,—

"Are you and Bob such good friends that you correspond? What will Jack say?"

"Don't know, and don't care! Be good, now, and let's have a little secret as well as other folks. I'll tell you all about it when he answers," said Jill in her most coaxing tone.

"Suppose he doesn't?"

"Then I shall send you up to see him. I *must* know something, and I want to do it myself, if I can."

"Look here; what are you after? I do believe you think" —Frank got no farther, for Jill gave a little scream, and stopped him by crying eagerly, "Don't say it out loud! I really do believe it may be, and I'm going to find out."

"What made you think of him?" and Frank looked thoughtfully at the letter, as if turning carefully over in his mind the idea that Jill's quick wits had jumped at.

"Come here and I'll tell you."

Holding him by one button, she whispered something in his ear that made him exclaim, with a look at the rug,—

"No! did he? I declare I shouldn't wonder! It would be just like the dear old blunder-head."

"I never thought of it till you told me where Bob was, and then it all sort of burst upon me in one minute!" cried Jill, waving her arms about to express the intellectual explosion which had thrown light upon the mystery, like sky-rockets in a dark night.

"You are as bright as a button. No time to lose; I'm off;" and off he was, splashing through the mud to post the letter, on the back of which he added, to make the thing sure, "Hurry up. F. M."

Both felt rather guilty next day, but enjoyed themselves very much nevertheless, and kept chuckling over the mine they were making under Jack's unconscious feet. They hardly expected an answer at noon, as the Hill people were not very eager for their mail, but at night Jill was sure of a letter, and to her great delight it came. Jack brought it himself, which added to the fun, and while she eagerly read it he sat calmly poring over the latest number of his own private and particular "Youth's Companion."

Bob was not a "complete letter-writer" by any means, and with great labor and much ink had produced the following brief but highly satisfactory epistle. Not knowing how to address his fair correspondent he let it alone, and went at once to the point in the frankest possible way:—

Jack did come up Friday. Sorry he got into a mess. It was real kind of him, and I shall pay him back soon. Jack paid Jerry for me and I made him promise not to tell. Jerry said he'd come here and make a row if I didn't cash up. I was afraid I'd lose the place if he did, for the Capt. is awful strict. If Jack don't tell now, I will. I ain't mean. Glad you wrote.

R. O. W.

"Hurrah!" cried Jill, waving the letter over her head in great triumph. "Call everybody and read it out," she added, as Frank snatched it, and ran for his mother, seeing at a glance that the news was good. Jill was so afraid she should tell before the others came that she burst out singing "Pretty Bobby Shafto" at the top of her voice, to Jack's great disgust, for he considered the song very personal, as he *was* rather fond of "combing down his yellow hair," and Jill often plagued him by singing it when he came in with the golden quirls very smooth and nice to hide the scar on his forehead.

In about five minutes the door flew open and in came Mamma, making straight for bewildered Jack, who thought the family had gone crazy when his parent caught him in her arms, saying tenderly, —

"My good, generous boy! I knew he was right all the time!" while Frank worked his hand up and down like a pump-handle, exclaiming heartily, —

"You're a trump, sir, and I'm proud of you!" Jill meantime calling out, in wild delight, —

"I told you so! I told you so! I did find out; ha, ha, I did!"

"Come, I say! What's the matter? I'm all right. Don't squeeze the breath out of me, please," expostulated Jack, looking so startled and innocent, as he struggled feebly, that they all laughed, and this plaintive protest caused him to be released. But the next proceeding did not enlighten him much, for Frank kept waving a very inky paper before him and ordering him to read it, while Mamma made a charge at Jill, as if it was absolutely necessary to hug somebody.

"Hullo!" said Jack, when he got the letter into his own hand and read it. "Now who put Bob up to this? Nobody had any business to interfere—but it's mighty good of him, anyway," he added, as the anxious lines in his round face smoothed themselves away, while a smile of relief told how hard it had been for him to keep his word.

"I did!" cried Jill, clapping her hands, and looking so happy that he could not have scolded her if he had wanted to.

"Who told you he was in the scrape?" demanded Jack, in a hurry to know all about it now the seal was taken off his own lips.

"You did;" and Jill's face twinkled with naughty satisfaction, for this was the best fun of all.

"I didn't! When? Where? It's a joke!"

"You did," cried Jill, pointing to the rug. "You went to
sleep there after the long walk, and talked in your sleep
about 'Bob' and 'All right, old boy,' and ever so much gib-
berish. I didn't think about it then, but when I heard that
Bob was up there I thought may be he knew something
about it, and last night I wrote and asked him, and that's the
answer, and now it *is* all right, and you are the best boy that
ever was, and I'm so glad!"

Here Jill paused, all out of breath, and Frank said,
with an approving pat on the head, —

"It won't do to have such a sharp young person round
if we are going to have secrets. You'd make a good detec-
tive, miss."

"Catch me taking naps before people again;" and Jack
looked rather crestfallen that his own words had set "Fine
Ear" on the track. "Never mind, I didn't *mean* to tell, though
I just ached to do it all the time, so I haven't broken
my word. I'm glad you all know, but you needn't let it get
out, for Bob is a good fellow, and it might make trouble
for him," added Jack, anxious lest his gain should be the
other's loss.

"I shall tell Mr. Acton myself, and the Captain, also,
for I'm not going to have my son suspected of wrong-doing
when he has only tried to help a friend, and borne enough
for his sake," said Mamma, much excited by this discovery
of generous fidelity in her boy; though when one came to
look at it calmly, one saw that it might have been done in a
wiser way.

"Now, please, don't make a fuss about it; that would
be most as bad as having every one down on me. I can stand

your praising me, but I won't be patted on the head by anybody else;" and Jack assumed a manly air, though his face
was full of genuine boyish pleasure at being set right in the
eyes of those he loved.

"I'll be discreet, dear, but you owe it to yourself, as
well as Bob, to have the truth known. Both have behaved
well, and no harm will come to him, I am sure. I'll see to
that myself," said Mrs. Minot, in a tone that set Jack's mind
at rest on that point.

"Now do tell all about it," cried Jill, who was pining to
know the whole story, and felt as if she had earned the right
to hear it.

"Oh, it wasn't much. We promised Ed to stand by
Bob, so I did as well as I knew how;" and Jack seemed to
think that was about all there was to say.

"I never saw such a fellow for keeping a promise! You
stick to it through thick and thin, no matter how silly or
hard it is. You remember, mother, last summer, how you
told him not to go in a boat and he promised, the day we
went on the picnic. We rode up, but the horse ran off
home, so we had to come back by way of the river, all but
Jack, and he walked every step of five miles because he
wouldn't go near a boat, though Mr. Burton was there to
take care of him. I call that rather overdoing the matter;"
and Frank looked as if he thought moderation even in virtue
a good thing.

"And I call it a fine sample of entire obedience. He
obeyed orders, and that is what we all must do, without always seeing why, or daring to use our own judgment. It is a
great safeguard to Jack, and a very great comfort to me; for
I know that if he promises he will keep his word, no matter
what it costs him," said Mamma warmly, as she tumbled up
the quirls with an irrepressible caress, remembering how

the boy came wearily in after all the others, without seeming for a moment to think that he could have done anything else.

"Like Casablanca!" cried Jill, much impressed, for obedience was her hardest trial.

"I think he was a fool to burn up," said Frank, bound not to give in.

"I don't. It's a splendid piece, and every one likes to speak it, and it was true, and it wouldn't be in all the books if he was a fool. Grown people know what is good," declared Jill, who liked heroic actions, and was always hoping for a chance to distinguish herself in that way.

"You admire 'The Charge of the Light Brigade,' and glow all over as you thunder it out. Yet they went gallantly to their death rather than disobey orders. A mistake, perhaps, but it makes us thrill to hear of it; and the same spirit keeps my Jack true as steel when once his word is passed, or he thinks it is his duty. Don't be laughed out of it, my son, for faithfulness in little things fits one for heroism when the great trials come. One's conscience can hardly be *too* tender when honor and honesty are concerned."

"You are right, mother, and I am wrong. I beg your pardon, Jack, and you sha'n't get ahead of me next time."

Frank made his mother a little bow, gave his brother a shake of the hand, and nodded to Jill, as if anxious to show that he was not too proud to own up when he made a mistake.

"Please tell on, Jack. This is very nice, but I do want to know all about the other," said Jill, after a short pause.

"Let me see. Oh, I saw Bob at church, and he looked rather blue; so, after Sunday School, I asked what the matter was. He said Jerry bothered him for some money he lent him at different times when they were loafing round together, before we took him up. He wouldn't get any wages for some time. The Captain keeps him short on purpose, I guess, and won't let him come down town except on Sundays. He didn't want any one to know about it, for fear he'd lose his place. So I promised I wouldn't tell. Then I was afraid Jerry would go and make a fuss, and Bob would run off, or do something desperate, being worried, and I said I'd pay it for him, if I could. So he went home pretty jolly, and I scratched 'round for the money. Got it, too, and wasn't I glad?"

Jack paused to rub his hands, and Frank said, with more than usual respect,—

"Couldn't you get hold of Jerry in any other place, and out of school time? That did the mischief, thanks to Joe. I thrashed him, Jill,—did I mention it?"

"I couldn't get all my money till Friday morning, and I knew Jerry was off at night. I looked for him before school, and at noon, but couldn't find him, so afternoon recess was my last chance. I was bound to do it, and I didn't mean to break the rule, but Jerry was just going into the shop, so I pelted after him, and as it was private business we went to the billiard-room. I declare I never was so relieved as when I handed over that money, and made him say it was all right, and he wouldn't go near Bob. He's off, so my mind is easy, and Bob will be so grateful I can keep him steady, perhaps. That will be worth two seventy-five, I think," said Jack heartily.

"You should have come to me," began Frank.

"And got laughed at,—no, thank you," interrupted Jack, recollecting several philanthropic little enterprises which were nipped in the bud for want of co-operation.

"To me, then," said his mother. "It would have saved so much trouble."

"I thought of it, but Bob didn't want the big fellows to know for fear they'd be down on him, so I thought he might not like me to tell grown people. I don't mind the fuss now, and Bob is as kind as he can be. Wanted to give me his big knife, but I wouldn't take it. I'd rather have this," and Jack put the letter in his pocket with a slap outside, as if it warmed the cockles of his heart to have it there.

"Well, it seems rather like a tempest in a teapot, now it is all over, but I do admire your pluck, little boy, in holding out so well when every one was scolding at you, and you in the right all the time," said Frank, glad to praise, now that he honestly could, after his wholesale condemnation.

"That is what pulled me through, I suppose. I used to think if I *had* done anything wrong, that I couldn't stand the snubbing a day. I should have told right off, and had it over. Now, I guess I'll have a good report if you do tell Mr. Acton," said Jack, looking at his mother so wistfully, that she resolved to slip away that very evening, and make sure that the thing was done.

"That will make you happier than anything else, won't it?" asked Jill, eager to have him rewarded after his trials.

"There's one thing I like better, though I'd be very sorry to lose my report. It's the fun of telling Ed I tried to do as he wanted us to, and seeing how pleased he'll be," added Jack, rather bashfully, for the boys laughed at him sometimes for his love of this friend.

"I know he won't be any happier about it than some one else, who stood by you all through, and set her bright wits to work till the trouble was all cleared away," said Mrs. Minot, looking at Jill's contented face, as she lay smiling on them all.

Jack understood, and, hopping across the room, gave both the thin hands a hearty shake; then, not finding any words quite cordial enough in which to thank this faithful little sister, he stooped down and kissed her gratefully.

Saint Lucy
CHAPTER 15

Saturday was a busy and a happy time to Jack, for in the morning Mr. Acton came to see him, having heard the story overnight, and promised to keep Bob's secret while giving Jack an acquittal as public as the reprimand had been. Then he asked for the report which Jack had bravely received the day before and put away without showing to anybody.

"There is one mistake here which we must rectify," said Mr. Acton, as he crossed out the low figures under the word "Behavior," and put the much-desired 100 there.

"But I did break the rule, sir," said Jack, though his face glowed with pleasure, for Mamma was looking on.

"I overlook that as I should your breaking into my house if you saw it was on fire. You ran to save a friend, and I wish I could tell those fellows why you were there. It would do them good. I am not going to praise you, John, but I did believe you in spite of appearances, and I am glad to have for a pupil a boy who loves his neighbor better than himself."

Then, having shaken hands heartily, Mr. Acton went away, and Jack flew off to have rejoicings with Jill, who sat up on her sofa, without knowing it, so eager was she to hear all about the call.

In the afternoon Jack drove his mother to the Captain's, confiding to her on the way what a hard time he had when he went before, and how nothing but the thought of cheering Bob kept him up when he slipped and hurt his knee, and his boot sprung a leak, and the wind came up very cold, and the hill seemed an endless mountain of mud and snow.

Mrs. Minot had such a gentle way of putting things that she would have won over a much harder man than the strict old Captain, who heard the story with interest, and was much pleased with the boys' efforts to keep Bob straight. That young person dodged away into the barn with Jack, and only appeared at the last minute to shove a bag of chestnuts into the chaise. But he got a few kind words that did him good, from Mrs. Minot and the Captain, and from that day felt himself under bonds to behave well if he would keep their confidence.

"I shall give Jill the nuts; and I wish I had something she wanted very, very much, for I do think she ought to be rewarded for getting me out of the mess," said Jack, as they drove happily home again.

"I hope to have something in a day or two that *will* delight her very much. I will say no more now, but keep my little secret and let it be a surprise to all by and by," answered his mother, looking as if she had not much doubt about the matter.

"That will be jolly. You are welcome to your secret, Mamma. I've had enough of them for one while;" and Jack shrugged his broad shoulders as if a burden had been taken off.

In the evening Ed came, and Jack was quite satisfied when he saw how pleased his friend was at what he had done.

"I never meant you should take so much trouble, only be kind to Bob," said Ed, who did not know how strong his influence was, nor what a sweet example of quiet well-doing his own life was to all his mates.

"I wished to be really useful; not just to talk about it and do nothing. That isn't your way, and I want to be like you," answered Jack, with such affectionate sincerity that Ed could not help believing him, though he modestly declined the compliment by saying, as he began to play softly, "Better than I am, I hope. I don't amount to much."

"Yes, you do! and if any one says you don't I'll shake him. I can't tell what it is, only you always look so happy and contented—sort of sweet and shiny," said Jack, as he stroked the smooth brown head, rather at a loss to describe the unusually fresh and sunny expression of Ed's face, which was always cheerful, yet had a certain thoughtfulness that made it very attractive to both young and old.

"Soap makes him shiny; I never saw such a fellow to wash and brush," put in Frank, as he came up with one of the pieces of music he and Ed were fond of practising together.

"I don't mean that!" said Jack indignantly. "I wash and brush till you call me a dandy, but I don't have the same look—it seems to come from the inside, somehow, as if he was always jolly and clean and good in his mind, you know."

"Born so," said Frank, rumbling away in the bass with a pair of hands that would have been the better for some of the above-mentioned soap, for he did not love to do much in the washing and brushing line.

"I suppose that's it. Well, I like it, and I shall keep on trying, for being loved by every one is about the nicest thing in the world. Isn't it, Ed?" asked Jack, with a gentle tweak of the ear as he put a question which he knew would get no answer, for Ed was so modest he could not see wherein he differed from other boys, nor believe that the sunshine he saw in other faces was only the reflection from his own.

Sunday evening Mrs. Minot sat by the fire, planning how she should tell some good news she had been saving up all day. Mrs. Pecq knew it, and seemed so delighted that she went about smiling as if she did not know what trouble meant, and could not do enough for the family. She was downstairs now, seeing that the clothes were properly prepared for the wash, so there was no one in the Bird Room but Mamma and the children. Frank was reading up all he could find about some Biblical hero mentioned in the day's sermon; Jill lay where she had lain for nearly four long months, and though her face was pale and thin with the confinement, there was an expression on it now sweeter even than health. Jack sat on the rug beside her, looking at a white carnation through the magnifying glass, while she was enjoying the perfume of a red one as she talked to him.

"If you look at the white petals you'll see that they sparkle like marble, and go winding a long way down to the middle of the flower where it grows sort of rosy; and in among the small, curly leaves, like fringed curtains, you can see the little green fairy sitting all alone. Your mother showed me that, and I think it is very pretty. I call it a 'fairy,' but it is really where the seeds are hidden and the sweet smell comes from."

Jill spoke softly lest she should disturb the others, and, as she turned to push up her pillow, she saw Mrs. Minot looking at her with a smile she did not understand.

"Did you speak, 'm?" she asked, smiling back again, without in the least knowing why.

"No, dear. I was listening and thinking what a pretty little story one could make out of your fairy living alone down there, and only known by her perfume."

"Tell it, Mamma. It is time for our story, and that would be a nice one, I guess," said Jack, who was as fond of stories as when he sat in his mother's lap and chuckled over the hero of the bean-stalk.

"We don't have fairy tales on Sunday, you know," began Jill regretfully.

"Call it a parable, and have a moral to it, then it will be all right," put in Frank, as he shut his big book, having found what he wanted.

"I like stories about saints, and the good and wonderful things they did," said Jill, who enjoyed the wise and interesting bits Mrs. Minot often found for her in grown-up books, for Jill had thoughtful times, and asked questions which showed that she was growing fast in mind if not in body.

"This is a true story; but I will disguise it a little, and call it 'The Miracle of St. Lucy,' " began Mrs. Minot, seeing a way to tell her good news and amuse the children likewise.

Frank retired to the easy-chair, that he might sleep if the tale should prove too childish for him. Jill settled herself among her cushions, and Jack lay flat upon the rug, with his feet up, so that he could admire his red slippers and rest his knee, which ached.

"Once upon a time there was a queen who had two princes"—

"Wasn't there a princess?" asked Jack, interested at once.

"No; and it was a great sorrow to the queen that she had no little daughter, for the sons were growing up, and she was often very lonely."

"Like Snowdrop's mother," whispered Jill.

"Now, don't keep interrupting, children, or we never

shall get on," said Frank, more anxious to hear about the
boys that were than the girl that was not.

"One day, when the princes were out,—ahem! we'll
say hunting,—they found a little damsel lying on the snow,
half dead with cold, they thought She was the child of a poor
woman who lived in the forest,—a wild little thing, always
dancing and singing about; as hard to catch as a squirrel, and
so fearless she would climb the highest trees, leap broad
brooks, or jump off the steep rocks to show her courage.
The boys carried her home to the palace, and the queen was
glad to have her. She had fallen and hurt herself, so she lay
in bed week after week, with her mother to take care of
her"—

"That's you," whispered Jack, throwing the white carnation at Jill, and she threw back the red one, with her
finger on her lips, for the tale was *very* interesting now.

"She did not suffer much after a time, but she scolded
and cried, and could not be resigned, because she was a
prisoner. The queen tried to help her, but she could not do
much; the princes were kind, but they had their books and
plays, and were away a good deal. Some friends she had
came often to see her, but still she beat her wings against the
bars, like a wild bird in a cage, and soon her spirits were all
gone, and it was sad to see her."

"Where was your St. Lucy? I thought it was about
her," asked Jack, who did not like to have Jill's past troubles
dwelt upon, since his were not.

"She is coming. Saints are not born—they are made
after many trials and tribulations," answered his mother,
looking at the fire as if it helped her to spin her little story.
"Well, the poor child used to sing sometimes to while away
the long hours—sad songs mostly, and one among them
which the queen taught her was 'Sweet Patience, Come.'

"This she used to sing a great deal after a while, never dreaming that Patience was an angel who could hear and obey. But it was so; and one night, when the girl had lulled herself to sleep with that song, the angel came. Nobody saw the lovely spirit with tender eyes, and a voice that was like balm. No one heard the rustle of wings as she hovered over the little bed and touched the lips, the eyes, the hands of the sleeper, and then flew away, leaving three gifts behind. The girl did not know why, but after that night the songs grew gayer, there seemed to be more sunshine every where her eyes looked, and her hands were never tired of helping others in various pretty, useful, or pleasant ways. Slowly the wild bird ceased to beat against the bars, but sat in its cage and made music for all in the palace, till the queen could not do without it, the poor mother cheered up, and the princes called the girl their nightingale."

"Was that the miracle?" asked Jack, forgetting all about his slippers, as he watched Jill's eyes brighten and the color come up in her white cheeks.

"That was the miracle, and Patience can work far greater ones if you will let her."

"And the girl's name was Lucy?"

"Yes; they did not call her a saint then, but she was trying to be as cheerful as a certain good woman she had heard of, and so the queen had that name for her, though she did not let her know it for a long time."

"That's not bad for a Sunday story, but there might have been more about the princes, seems to me," was Frank's criticism, as Jill lay very still, trying to hide her face behind the carnation, for she had no words to tell how touched and pleased she was to find that her little efforts to be good had been seen, remembered, and now rewarded in this way.

"There is more."

"Then the story isn't done?" cried Jack.

"Oh dear, no; the most interesting things are to come, if you can wait for them."

"Yes, I see, this is the moral part. Now keep still, and let us have the rest," commanded Frank, while the others composed themselves for the sequel, suspecting that it was rather nice, because Mamma's sober face changed, and her eyes laughed as they looked at the fire.

"The elder prince was very fond of driving dragons, for the people of that country used these fiery monsters as horses."

"And got run away with, didn't he?" laughed Jack, adding, with great interest, "What did the other fellow do?"

"He went about fighting other people's battles, helping the poor, and trying to do good. But he lacked judgment, so he often got into trouble, and was in such a hurry that he did not always stop to find out the wisest way. As when he gave away his best coat to a beggar boy, instead of the old one which he intended to give."

"I say, that isn't fair, mother! Neither of them was new, and the boy needed the best more than I did, and I wore the old one all winter, didn't I?" asked Jack, who had rather exulted over Frank, and was now taken down himself.

"Yes, you did, my dear; and it was not an easy thing for my dandiprat to do. Now listen, and I'll tell you how they both learned to be wiser. The elder prince soon found that the big dragons were too much for him, and set about training his own little one, who now and then ran away with him. Its name was Will, a good servant, but a bad master; so he learned to control it, and in time this gave him great power over himself, and fitted him to be a king over others."

"Thank you, mother; I'll remember my part of the moral. Now give Jack his," said Frank, who liked the dragon episode, as he had been wrestling with his own of late, and found it hard to manage.

"He had a fine example before him in a friend, and he followed it more reasonably till he grew able to use wisely one of the best and noblest gifts of God,—benevolence."

"Now tell about the girl. Was there more to that part of the story?" asked Jack, well pleased with his moral, as it took Ed in likewise.

"That is the best of all, but it seems as if I never should get to it. After Patience made Lucy sweet and cheerful, she began to have a curious power over those about her, and to work little miracles herself, though she did not know it. The queen learned to love her so dearly she could not let her go; she cheered up all her friends when they came with their small troubles; the princes found bright eyes, willing hands, and a kind heart always at their service, and felt, without quite knowing why, that it was good for them to have a gentle little creature to care for; so they softened their rough manners, loud voices, and careless ways, for her sake, and when it was proposed to take her away to her own home they could not give her up, but said she must stay longer, didn't they?"

"I'd like to see them saying anything else," said Frank, while Jack sat up to demand fiercely,—

"Who talks about taking Jill away?"

"Lucy's mother thought she ought to go, and said so, but the queen told her how much good it did them all to have her there, and begged the dear woman to let her little cottage and come and be housekeeper in the palace, for the queen was getting lazy, and liked to sit and read, and talk and sew with Lucy, better than to look after things."

"And she said she would?" cried Jill, clasping her hands in her anxiety, for she had learned to love her cage now.

"Yes." Mrs. Minot had no time to say more, for one of the red slippers flew up in the air, and Jack had to clap both hands over his mouth to suppress the "hurrah!" that nearly escaped. Frank said, "That's good!" and nodded with his most cordial smile at Jill who pulled herself up with cheeks now as rosy as the red carnation, and a little catch in her breath as she said to herself,—

"It's too lovely to be true."

"That's a first-rate end to a very good story," began Jack, with grave decision, as he put on his slipper and sat up to pat Jill's hand, wishing it was not quite so like a little claw.

"That's not the end;" and Mamma's eyes laughed more than ever as three astonished faces turned to her, and three voices cried out,—

"Still more?"

"The very best of all. You must know that, while Lucy was busy for others, she was not forgotten, and when she was expecting to lie on her bed through the summer, plans were being made for all sorts of pleasant changes. First of all, she was to have a nice little brace to support the back which was growing better every day; then, as the warm weather came on, she was to go out, or lie on the piazza; and by and by, when school was done, she was to go with the queen and the princes for a month or two down to the sea-side, where fresh air and salt water were to build her up in the most delightful way. There, now! isn't that the best ending of all?" and Mamma paused to read her answer in the bright faces of two of the listeners, for Jill hid hers in the pillow, and lay quite still, as if it was too much for her.

"That will be regularly splendid! I'll row you all

about—boating is so much easier than riding, and I like it on salt water," said Frank, going to sit on the arm of the sofa, quite excited by the charms of the new plan.

"And I'll teach you to swim, and roll you over the beach, and get sea-weed and shells, and no end of nice things, and we'll all come home as strong as lions," added Jack, scrambling up as if about to set off at once.

"The doctor says you have been doing finely of late, and the brace will come to-morrow, and the first really mild day you are to have a breath of fresh air. Won't that be good?" asked Mrs. Minot, hoping her story had not been too interesting.

"Is she crying?" said Jack, much concerned as he patted the pillow in his most soothing way, while Frank lifted one curl after another to see what was hidden underneath.

Not tears, for two eyes sparkled behind the fingers, then the hands came down like clouds from before the sun, and Jill's face shone out so bright and happy it did one's heart good to see it.

"I'm not crying," she said with a laugh which was fuller of blithe music than any song she sung. "But it was so splendid, it sort of took my breath away for a minute. I thought I wasn't any better, and never should be, and I made up my mind I wouldn't ask, it would be so hard for any one to tell me so. Now I see why the doctor made me stand up, and told me to get my baskets ready to go a-Maying. I thought he was in fun; did he really mean I could go?" asked Jill, expecting too much, for a word of encouragement made her as hopeful as she had been despondent before.

"No, dear, not so soon as that. It will be months, probably, before you can walk and run, as you used to; but they will soon pass. You needn't mind about May-day; it is

always too cold for flowers, and you will find more here
among your own plants, than on the hills, to fill your baskets," answered Mrs. Minot, hastening to suggest something pleasant to beguile the time of probation.

"I can wait. Months are not years, and if I'm truly getting well, everything will seem beautiful and easy to me,"
said Jill, laying herself down again, with the patient look she
had learned to wear, and gathering up the scattered carna-
tions to enjoy their spicy breath, as if the fairies hidden
there had taught her some of their sweet secrets.

"Dear little girl, it has been a long, hard trial for you,
but it is coming to an end, and I think you will find that it
has not been time wasted. I don't want you to be a saint
quite yet, but I am sure a gentler Jill will rise up from that
sofa than the one who lay down there in December."

"How could I help growing better, when you were so
good to me?" cried Jill, putting up both arms, as Mrs. Minot
went to take Frank's place, and he retired to the fire, there
to stand surveying the scene with calm approval.

"You have done quite as much for us; so we are even.
I proved that to your mother, and she is going to let the
little house and take care of the big one for me, while I bor-
row you to keep me happy and make the boys gentle and
kind. That is the bargain, and we get the best of it," said
Mrs. Minot, looking well pleased, while Jack added,
"That's so!" and Frank observed with an air of conviction,
"We couldn't get on without Jill, possibly."

"Can I do all that? I didn't know I was of any use. I
only tried to be good and grateful, for there didn't seem to
be anything else I could do," said Jill, wondering why they
were all so fond of her.

"No real trying is ever in vain. It is like the spring rain,
and flowers are sure to follow in good time. The three gifts

Patience gave St. Lucy were courage, cheerfulness, and love, and with these one can work the sweetest miracles in the world, as you see," and Mrs. Minot pointed to the pretty room and its happy inmates.

"Am I really the least bit like that good Lucinda? I tried to be, but I didn't think I was," asked Jill softly.

"You are very like her in all ways but one. *She* did not get well, and *you* will."

A short answer, but it satisfied Jill to her heart's core, and that night, when she lay in bed, she thought to herself: "How curious it is that I've been a sort of missionary without knowing it! They all love and thank me, and won't let me go, so I suppose I must have done something, but I don't know what, except trying to be good and pleasant."

That was the secret, and Jill found it out just when it was most grateful as a reward for past efforts, most helpful as an encouragement toward the constant well-doing which can make even a little girl a joy and comfort to all who know and love her.

Up at Merry's
CHAPTER 16

"Now fly round, child, and get your sweeping done up smart and early."

"Yes, mother."

"I shall want you to help me about the baking, by and by."

"Yes, mother."

"Roxy is cleaning the cellar-closets, so you'll have to get the vegetables ready for dinner. Father wants a boiled dish, and I shall be so busy I can't see to it."

"Yes, mother."

A cheerful voice gave the three answers, but it cost Merry an effort to keep it so, for she had certain little plans of her own which made the work before her unusually distasteful. Saturday always was a trying day, for, though she liked to see rooms in order, she hated to sweep, as no speck escaped Mrs. Grant's eye, and only the good old-fashioned broom, wielded by a pair of strong arms, was allowed. Baking was another trial: she loved good bread and delicate pastry, but did not enjoy burning her face over a hot stove, daubing her hands with dough, or spending hours rolling out cookies for the boys; while a "boiled dinner" was her especial horror, as it was not elegant, and the washing of vegetables was a job she always shirked when she could.

However, having made up her mind to do her work without complaint, she ran upstairs to put on her dust-cap, trying to look as if sweeping was the joy of her life.

"It is such a lovely day, I did want to rake my garden, and have a walk with Molly, and finish my book so I can get another," she said with a sigh, as she leaned out of the open window for a breath of the unusually mild air.

Down in the ten-acre lot the boys were carting and spreading loam; out in the barn her father was getting his plows ready; over the hill rose the smoke of the distant factory, and the river that turned the wheels was gliding through the meadows, where soon the blackbirds would be singing. Old Bess pawed the ground, eager to be off; the gray hens were scratching busily all about the yard; even the green things in the garden were pushing through the brown earth, softened by April rains, and there was a shimmer of sunshine over the wide landscape that made every familiar object beautiful with hints of spring, and the activity it brings.

Something made the old nursery hymn come into Merry's head, and humming to herself,—

"In works of labor or of skill
I would be busy too,"—

she tied on her cap, shouldered her broom, and fell to work so energetically that she soon swept her way through the chambers, down the front stairs to the parlor door, leaving freshness and order behind her as she went.

She always groaned when she entered that apartment, and got out of it again as soon as possible, for it was, like most country parlors, a prim and chilly place, with little beauty and no comfort. Black horse-hair furniture, very slippery and hard, stood against the wall; the table had its gift books, albums, worsted mat and ugly lamp; the mantel-piece its china vases, pink shells, and clock that never went; the gay carpet was kept distressingly bright by closed shut-ters six days out of the seven, and a general air of go-to-meeting solemnity pervaded the room. Merry longed to make it pretty and pleasant, but her mother would allow of no change there, so the girl gave up her dreams of rugs and hangings, fine pictures and tasteful ornaments, and dutifully aired, dusted, and shut up this awful apartment once a week, privately resolving that, if she ever had a parlor of her own, it should not be as dismal as a tomb.

The dining-room was a very different place, for here Merry had been allowed to do as she liked, yet so gradual had been the change, that she would have found it difficult to tell how it came about. It seemed to begin with the flow-ers, for her father kept his word about the "posy pots," and got enough to make quite a little conservatory in the bay-window, which was sufficiently large for three rows all round, and hanging-baskets overhead. Being discouraged by her first failure, Merry gave up trying to have things nice everywhere, and contented herself with making that one nook so pretty that the boys called it her "bower." Even busy Mrs. Grant owned that plants were not so messy as she expected, and the farmer was never tired of watching "little daughter" as she sat at work there, with her low chair and table full of books.

The lamp helped, also, for Merry set up her own, and kept it so well trimmed that it burned clear and bright, shining on the green arch of ivy overhead, and on the nasturtium vines framing the old glass, and peeping at their gay little faces, and at the pretty young girl, so pleasantly that first her father came to read his paper by it, then her mother slipped in to rest on the lounge in the corner, and finally the boys hovered about the door as if the "settin'-room" had grown more attractive than the kitchen.

But the open fire did more than anything else to win and hold them all, as it seldom fails to do when the black demon of an air-tight stove is banished from the hearth. After the room was cleaned till it shone, Merry begged to have the brass andirons put in, and offered to keep them as bright as gold if her mother would consent. So the great logs were kindled, and the flames went dancing up the chimney as if glad to be set free from their prison. It changed the whole room like magic, and no one could resist the desire to enjoy its cheery comfort. The farmer's three-cornered leathern chair soon stood on one side, and mother's rocker on the other, as they toasted their feet and dozed or chatted in the pleasant warmth.

The boys' slippers were always ready on the hearth; and when the big boots were once off, they naturally settled down about the table, where the tall lamp, with its pretty shade of pressed autumn leaves, burned brightly, and the books and papers lay ready to their hands instead of being tucked out of sight in the closet. They were beginning to see that "Merry's notions" had some sense in them, since they were made comfortable, and good-naturedly took some pains to please her in various ways. Tom brushed his hair and washed his hands nicely before he came to table. Dick tried to lower his boisterous laughter, and Harry never smoked in the sitting-room. Even Roxy expressed her pleasure in seeing "things kind of spruced up," and Merry's gentle treatment of the hard-working drudge won her heart entirely.

The girl was thinking of these changes as she watered her flowers, dusted the furniture, and laid the fire ready for kindling; and, when all was done, she stood a minute to enjoy the pleasant room, full of spring sunshine, fresh air, and exquisite order. It seemed to give her heart for more distasteful labors, and she fell to work at the pies as cheerfully as if she liked it.

Mrs. Grant was flying about the kitchen, getting the loaves of brown and white bread ready for the big oven. Roxy's voice came up from the cellar singing "Bounding Billows," with a swashing and scrubbing accompaniment which suggested that she was actually enjoying a "life on the ocean wave." Merry, in her neat cap and apron, stood smiling over her work as she deftly rolled and clipped, filled and covered, finding a certain sort of pleasure in doing it well, and adding interest to it by crimping the crust, making pretty devices with strips of paste and star-shaped prickings of the fork.

"Good-will giveth skill," says the proverb, and even particular Mrs. Grant was satisfied when she paused to examine the pastry with her experienced eye.

"You are a handy child and a credit to your bringing

up, though I do say it. Those are as pretty pies as I'd wish to
eat, if they bake well, and there's no reason why they
shouldn't."

"May I make some tarts or rabbits of these bits? The
boys like them, and I enjoy modelling this sort of thing,"
said Merry, who was trying to mould a bird, as she had seen
Ralph do with clay to amuse Jill while the bust was going on.

"No, dear; there's no time for knick-knacks today.
The beets ought to be on this minute. Run and get 'em, and
be sure you scrape the carrots well."

Poor Merry put away the delicate task she was just beginning to like, and taking a pan went down cellar, wishing
vegetables could be grown without earth, for she hated to
put her hands in dirty water. A word of praise to Roxy
made that grateful scrubber leave her work to poke about in
the root-cellar, choosing "sech as was pretty much of a
muchness, else they wouldn't bile even;" so Merry was
spared that part of the job, and went up to scrape and wash
without complaint, since it was for father. She was repaid at
noon by the relish with which he enjoyed his dinner, for
Merry tried to make even a boiled dish pretty by arranging
the beets, carrots, turnips, and potatoes in contrasting colors, with the beef hidden under the cabbage leaves.

"Now, I'll rest and read for an hour, then I'll rake my
garden, or run down town to see Molly and get some
seeds," she thought to herself, as she put away the spoons
and glasses, which she liked to wash, that they might always
be clear and bright.

"If you've done all your own mending, there's a heap
of socks to be looked over. Then I'll show you about darning the table-cloths. I do hate to have a stitch of work left
over till Monday," said Mrs. Grant, who never took naps,

and prided herself on sitting down to her needle at 3 P.M. every day.

"Yes, mother;" and Merry went slowly upstairs, feeling that a part of Saturday ought to be a holiday after books and work all the week. As she braided up her hair, her eye fell upon the reflection of her own face in the glass. Not a happy nor a pretty one just then, and Merry was so unaccustomed to seeing any other, that involuntarily the frown smoothed itself out, the eyes lost their weary look, the drooping lips curved into a smile, and, leaning her elbows on the bureau, she shook her head at herself, saying, half aloud, as she glanced at Ivanhoe lying near, —

"You needn't look so cross and ugly just because you can't have what you want. Sweeping, baking, and darning are not so bad as being plagued with lovers and carried off and burnt at the stake, so I won't envy poor Rebecca her jewels and curls and romantic times, but make the best of my own."

Then she laughed, and the bright face came back into the mirror, looking like an old friend, and Merry went on dressing with care, for she took pleasure in her own little charms, and felt a sense of comfort in knowing that she could always have one pretty thing to look at if she kept her own face serene and sweet. It certainly looked so as it bent over the pile of big socks half an hour later, and brightened with each that was laid aside. Her mother saw it, and, guessing why such wistful glances went from clock to window, kindly shortened the task of table-cloth darning by doing a good bit herself, before putting it into Merry's hands.

She was a good and loving mother in spite of her strict ways, and knew that it was better for her romantic daughter to be learning all the housewifery lessons she could teach

her, than to be reading novels, writing verses, or philander-
ing about with her head full of girlish fancies, quite innocent
in themselves, but not the stuff to live on. So she wisely
taught the hands that preferred to pick flowers, trim up
rooms and mould birds, to work well with needle, broom,
and rolling-pin; put a receipt-book before the eyes that
loved to laugh and weep over tender tales, and kept the
young head and heart safe and happy with wholesome duties, useful studies, and such harmless pleasures as girls
should love, instead of letting them waste their freshness in
vague longings, idle dreams, and frivolous pastimes.

But it was often hard to thwart the docile child, and
lately she had seemed to be growing up so fast that her
mother began to feel a new sort of tenderness for this sweet
daughter, who was almost ready to take upon herself the
cares, as well as triumphs and delights, of maidenhood.
Something in the droop of the brown head, and the quick
motion of the busy hand with a little burn on it, made it difficult for Mrs. Grant to keep Merry at work that day, and
her eye watched the clock almost as impatiently as the
girl's, for she liked to see the young face brighten when the
hour of release came.

"What next?" asked Merry, as the last stitch was set,
and she stifled a sigh on hearing the clock strike four, for the
sun was getting low, and the lovely afternoon going fast.

"One more job, if you are not too tired for it. I want
the receipt for diet drink Miss Dawes promised me; would
you like to run down and get it for me, dear?"

"Yes, mother," and that answer was as blithe as a
robin's chirp, for that was just where Merry wanted to go.

Away went thimble and scissors, and in five minutes
away went Merry, skipping down the hill without a care in

the world, for a happy heart sat singing within, and everything seemed full of beauty.

She had a capital time with Molly, called on Jill, did
her shopping in the village, and had just turned to walk up
the hill, when Ralph Evans came tramping along behind
her, looking so pleased and proud about something that she
could not help asking what it was, for they were great
friends, and Merry thought that to be an artist was the most
glorious career a man could choose.

"I know you've got some good news," she said, looking up at him as he touched his hat and fell into step with
her, seeming more contented than before.

"I have, and was just coming up to tell you, for I was
sure you would be glad. It is only a hope, a chance, but it is
so splendid I feel as if I must shout and dance, or fly over a
fence or two, to let off steam."

"Do tell me, quick; have you got an order?" asked
Merry, full of interest at once, for artistic vicissitudes were
very romantic, and she liked to hear about them.

"I may go abroad in the autumn."

"Oh, how lovely!"

"Isn't it? David German is going to spend a year
in Rome, to finish a statue, and wants me to go along.
Grandma is willing, as cousin Maria wants her for a long
visit, so everything looks promising and I really think I
may go."

"Won't it cost a great deal?" asked Merry, who, in
spite of her little elegancies, had a good deal of her thrifty
mother's common-sense.

"Yes; and I've got to earn it. But I can—I know I can,
for I've saved some, and I shall work like ten beavers all
summer. I won't borrow if I can help it, but I know some

one who would lend me five hundred if I wanted it;" and
Ralph looked as eager and secure as if the earning of twice
that sum was a mere trifle when all the longing of his life
was put into his daily tasks.

"I wish I had it to give you. It must be so splendid to
feel that you can do great things if you only have the chance.
And to travel, and see all the lovely pictures and statues,
and people and places in Italy. How happy you must be!"
and Merry's eyes had the wistful look they always wore
when she dreamed dreams of the world she loved to live in.

"I am—so happy that I'm afraid it never will happen.
If I do go, I'll write and tell you all about the fine sights, and
how I get on. Would you like me to?" asked Ralph, beginning enthusiastically and ending rather bashfully, for he admired Merry very much, and was not quite sure how this
proposal would be received.

"Indeed I should! I'd feel so grand to have letters from
Paris and Rome, and you'd have so much to tell it would be
almost as good as going myself," she said, looking off into
the daffodil sky, as they paused a minute on the hill-top to
get breath, for both had walked as fast as they talked.

"And will you answer the letters?" asked Ralph,
watching the innocent face, which looked unusually kind
and beautiful to him in that soft light.

"Why, yes; I'd love to, only I shall not have anything
interesting to say. What can I write about?" and Merry
smiled as she thought how dull her letters would sound
after the exciting details his would doubtless give.

"Write about yourself, and all the rest of the people I
know. Grandma will be gone, and I shall want to hear how
you get on." Ralph looked very anxious indeed to hear, and
Merry promised she would tell all about the other people,

adding, as she turned from the evening peace and loveliness to the house, whence came the clatter of milk-pans and the smell of cooking,—

"I never should have anything very nice to tell about myself, for I don't do interesting things as you do, and you wouldn't care to hear about school, and sewing, and messing round at home."

Merry gave a disdainful little sniff at the savory perfume of ham which saluted them, and paused with her hand on the gate, as if she found it pleasanter out there than in the house. Ralph seemed to agree with her, for, leaning on the gate, he lingered to say, with real sympathy in his tone and something else in his face,—

"Yes, I should; so you write and tell me all about it. I didn't know you had any worries, for you always seemed like one of the happiest people in the world, with so many to pet and care for you, and plenty of money, and nothing very hard or hateful to do. You'd think you were well off if you knew as much about poverty and work and never getting what you want, as I do."

"You bear your worries so well that nobody knows you have them. I ought not to complain, and I won't, for I do have all I need. I'm so glad you are going to get what you want at last;" and Merry held out her hand to say goodnight, with so much pleasure in her face that Ralph could not make up his mind to go just yet.

"I shall have to scratch round in a lively way before I do get it, for David says a fellow can't live on less than four or five hundred a year, even living as poor artists have to, in garrets and on crusts. I don't mind as long as Grandma is all right. She is away to-night, or I should not be here," he added, as if some excuse was necessary.

Merry needed no hint, for her tender heart was touched by the vision of her friend in a garret, and she suddenly rejoiced that there was ham and eggs for supper, so that he might be well fed once, at least, before he went away to feed on artistic crusts.

"Being here, come in and spend the evening. The boys will like to hear the news, and so will father. Do, now."

It was impossible to refuse the invitation he had been longing for, and in they went to the great delight of Roxy, who instantly retired to the pantry, smiling significantly, and brought out the most elaborate pie in honor of the occasion. Merry touched up the table, and put a little vase of flowers in the middle to redeem the vulgarity of doughnuts. Of course the boys upset it, but as there was company nothing was said, and Ralph devoured his supper with the appetite of a hungry boy, while watching Merry eat bread and cream out of an old-fashioned silver porringer, and thinking it the sweetest sight he ever beheld.

Then the young people gathered about the table, full of the new plans, and the elders listened as they rested after the week's work. A pleasant evening, for they all liked Ralph, but as the parents watched Merry sitting among the great lads like a little queen among her subjects, half unconscious as yet of the power in her hands, they nodded to one another, and then shook their heads as if they said,—

"I'm afraid the time is coming, mother."

"No danger as long as she don't know it, father."

At nine the boys went off to the barn, the farmer to wind up the eight-day clock, and the housewife to see how the baked beans and Indian pudding for to-morrow were getting on in the oven. Ralph took up his hat to go, saying as he looked at the shade on the tall student lamp,—

"What a good light that gives! I can see it as I go home

every night, and it burns up here like a beacon. I always look for it, and it hardly ever fails to be burning. Sort of cheers up the way, you know, when I'm tired or low in my mind."

"Then I'm very glad I got it. I liked the shape, but the boys laughed at it as they did at my bulrushes in a ginger-jar over there. I'd been reading about 'household art,' and I thought I'd try a little," answered Merry, laughing at her own whims.

"You've got a better sort of household art, I think, for you make people happy and places pretty, without fussing over it. This room is ever so much improved every time I come, though I hardly see what it is except the flowers," said Ralph, looking from the girl to the tall calla that bent its white cup above her as if to pour its dew upon her head.

"Isn't that lovely? I tried to draw it—the shape was so graceful I wanted to keep it. But I couldn't. Isn't it a pity such beautiful things won't last forever?" and Merry looked regretfully at the half-faded one that grew beside the fresh blossom.

"I can keep it for you. It would look well in plaster. May I?" asked Ralph.

"Thank you, I should like that very much. Take the real one as a model—please do; there are more coming, and this will brighten up your room for a day or two."

As she spoke, Merry cut the stem, and, adding two or three of the great green leaves, put the handsome flower in his hand with so much good-will that he felt as if he had received a very precious gift. Then he said good-night so gratefully that Merry's hand quite tingled with the grasp of his, and went away, often looking backward through the darkness to where the light burned brightly on the hill-top,—the beacon kindled by an unconscious Hero for a young Leander swimming gallantly against wind and tide toward the goal of his ambition.

Down at Molly's

CHAPTER 17 ॐ

"*N*ow, my dears, I've something very curious to tell you, so listen quietly and then I'll give you your dinners," said Molly, addressing the nine cats who came trooping after her as she went into the shed chamber with a bowl of milk and a plate of scraps in her hands. She had taught them to behave well at meals, so, though their eyes glared and their tails quivered with impatience, they obeyed; and when she put the food on a high shelf and retired to the big basket, the four old cats sat demurely down before her, while the five kits scrambled after her and tumbled into her lap, as if hoping to hasten the desired feast by their innocent gambols.

Granny, Tobias, Mortification, and Molasses were the elders. Granny, a gray old puss, was the mother and grandmother of all the rest. Tobias was her eldest son, and Mortification his brother, so named because he had lost his tail, which affliction depressed his spirits and cast a blight over his young life. Molasses was a yellow cat, the mamma of four of the kits, the fifth being Granny's latest darling. Toddlekins, the little aunt, was the image of her mother, and very sedate even at that early age; Miss Muffet, so called from her dread of spiders, was a timid black and white kit; Beauty, a pretty Maltese, with a serene little face and pink nose; Ragbag, a funny thing, every color that a cat could be; and Scamp, who well deserved his name, for he was the plague of Miss Bat's life, and Molly's especial pet.

He was now perched on her shoulder, and, as she talked, kept peeping into her face or biting her ear in the most impertinent way, while the others sprawled in her lap or promenaded round the basket rim.

"My friends, something very remarkable has happened: Miss Bat is cleaning house!" and, having made this announcement, Molly leaned back to see how the cats received it, for she insisted that they understood all she said to them.

Tobias stared, Mortification lay down as if it was too much for him, Molasses beat her tail on the floor as if whipping a dusty carpet, and Granny began to purr approvingly. The giddy kits paid no attention, as they did not know what house-cleaning meant, happy little dears!

"I thought you'd like it, Granny, for you are a decent cat, and know what is proper," continued Molly, leaning down to stroke the old puss, who blinked affectionately at her. "I can't imagine what put it into Miss Bat's head. I never said a word, and gave up groaning over the clutter, as I couldn't mend it. I just took care of Boo and myself, and left her to be as untidy as she pleased, and she is a regular old"—

Here Scamp put his paw on her lips because he saw them moving, but it seemed as if it was to check the disrespectful word just coming out.

"Well, I won't call names; but what *shall* I do when I see everything in confusion, and she won't let me clear up?" asked Molly, looking round at Scamp, who promptly put the little paw on her eyelid, as if the roll of the blue ball underneath amused him.

"Shut my eyes to it, you mean? I do all I can, but it is hard, when I wish to be nice, and do try; don't I?" asked Molly. But Scamp was ready for her, and began to comb her hair with both paws as he stood on his hind legs to work so busily that Molly laughed and pulled him down, saying, as she cuddled the sly kit, —

"You sharp little thing! I know my hair is not neat now, for I've been chasing Boo round the garden to wash him for school. Then Miss Bat threw the parlor carpet out of the window, and I was so surprised I had to run and tell you. Now, what had we better do about it?"

The cats all winked at her, but no one had any advice to offer, except Tobias, who walked to the shelf, and, looking up, uttered a deep, suggestive yowl, which said as plainly as words, "Dinner first and discussion afterward."

"Very well, don't scramble," said Molly, getting up to feed her pets. First the kits, who rushed at the bowl and thrust their heads in, lapping as if for a wager; then the cats, who each went to one of the four piles of scraps laid round at intervals and placidly ate their meat; while Molly retired to the basket, to ponder over the phenomena taking place in the house.

She could not imagine what had started the old lady. It was not the example of her neighbors, who had beaten carpets and scrubbed paint every spring for years without exciting her to any greater exertion than cleaning a few windows and having a man to clear away the rubbish displayed when the snow melted. Molly never guessed that her own efforts were at the bottom of the change, or knew that a few words not meant for her ear had shamed Miss Bat into action. Coming home from prayer-meeting one dark night, she trotted along behind two old ladies who were gossiping in loud voices, as one was rather deaf, and Miss Bat was both pleased and troubled to hear herself unduly praised.

"I always said Sister Dawes meant well; but she's getting into years, and the care of two children is a good deal for her, with her cooking and her rheumatiz. I don't deny she did neglect 'em for a spell, but she does well by 'em now, and I wouldn't wish to see better-appearing children."

"You've no idee how improved Molly is. She came in to see my girls, and brought her sewing-work, shirts for the boy, and done it as neat and capable as you'd wish to see. She always was a smart child, but dreadful careless," said the other old lady, evidently much impressed by the change in harum-scarum Molly Loo.

"Being over to Mis Minot's so much has been good for her, and up to Mis Grant's. Girls catch neat ways as quick as they do untidy ones, and them wild little tykes often turn out smart women."

"Sister Dawes *has* done well by them children, and I hope Mr. Bemis sees it. He ought to give her something comfortable to live on when she can't do for him any longer. He can well afford it."

"I haven't a doubt he will. He's a lavish man when he starts to do a thing, but dreadful unobserving, else he'd have seen to matters long ago. Them children was town-talk last fall, and I used to feel as if it was my bounden duty to speak to Miss Dawes. But I never did, fearing I might speak too plain, and hurt her feelings."

"You've spoken plain enough now, and I'm beholden to you, though you'll never know it," said Miss Bat to herself, as she slipped into her own gate, while the gossips trudged on quite unconscious of the listener behind them.

Miss Bat was a worthy old soul in the main, only, like so many of us, she needed rousing up to her duty. She had got the rousing now, and it did her good, for she could not bear to be praised when she had not deserved it. She had watched Molly's efforts with lazy interest, and when the girl gave up meddling with her affairs, as she called the

housekeeping, Miss Bat ceased to oppose her, and let her
scrub Boo, mend clothes, and brush her hair as much as she
liked. So Molly had worked along without any help from
her, running in to Mrs. Pecq for advice, to Merry for comfort, or Mrs. Minot for the higher kind of help one often
needs so much. Now Miss Bat found that she was getting the
credit and the praise belonging to other people, and it
stirred her up to try and deserve a part at least.

"Molly don't want any help about her work or the
boy: it's too late for that; but if this house don't get a spring
cleaning that will make it shine, my name ain't Bathsheba
Dawes," said the old lady, as she put away her bonnet that
night and laid energetic plans for a grand revolution, inspired thereto not only by shame, but by the hint that "Mr.
Bemis was a lavish man," as no one knew better than she.

Molly's amazement next day at seeing carpets fly
out of window, ancient cobwebs come down, and long-
undisturbed closets routed out to the great dismay of moths
and mice, has been already confided to the cats, and as she sat
there watching them lap and gnaw, she said to herself, —

"I don't understand it, but as she never says much to
me about my affairs, I won't take any notice till she gets
through, then I'll admire everything all I can. It is so pleasant to be praised after you've been trying hard."

She might well say that, for she got very little herself,
and her trials had been many, her efforts not always successful, and her reward seemed a long way off. Poor Boo could
have sympathized with her, for he had suffered much perse-
cution from his small schoolmates when he appeared with
large gray patches on the little brown trousers, where he
had worn them out coasting down those too fascinating
steps. As he could not see the patches himself, he fancied
them invisible, and came home much afflicted by the jeers

of his friends. Then Molly tried to make him a new pair out of a sack of her own; but she cut both sides for the same leg, so one was wrong side out. Fondly hoping no one would observe it, she sewed bright buttons wherever they could be put, and sent confiding Boo away in a pair of blue trousers, which were absurdly hunchy behind and buttony before. He came home heart-broken and muddy, having been accidentally dipped into a mud-puddle by two bad boys who felt that such tailoring was an insult to mankind. That roused Molly's spirit, and she begged her father to take the boy and have him properly fitted out, as he was old enough now to be well dressed, and she wouldn't have him tormented. His attention being called to the trousers, Mr. Bemis had a good laugh over them, and then got Boo a suit which caused him to be the admired of all observers, and to feel as proud as a little peacock.

Cheered by this success, Molly undertook a set of small shirts, and stitched away bravely, though her own summer clothes were in a sad state, and for the first time in her life she cared about what she should wear.

"I must ask Merry, and maybe father will let me go with her and her mother when they do their shopping, instead of leaving it to Miss Bat, who dresses me like an old woman. Merry knows what is pretty and becoming: I don't," thought Molly, meditating in the bushel basket, with her eyes on her snuff-colored gown and the dark purple bow at the end of the long braid Muffet had been playing with.

Molly was beginning to see that even so small a matter as the choice of colors made a difference in one's appearance, and to wonder why Merry always took such pains to have a blue tie for the gray dress, a rosy one for the brown, and gloves that matched her bonnet ribbons. Merry never wore a locket outside her sack, a gay bow in her hair and soiled cuffs, a smart hat and the braid worn off her skirts. She was exquisitely neat and simple, yet always looked well-dressed and pretty; for her love of beauty taught her what all girls should learn as soon as they begin to care for appearances, —that neatness and simplicity are their best ornaments, that good habits are better than fine clothes, and the most elegant manners are the kindest.

All these thoughts were dancing through Molly's head, and when she left her cats, after a general romp in which even decorous Granny allowed her family to play leap-frog over her respectable back, she had made up her mind not to have yellow ribbons on her summer hat if she got a pink muslin as she had planned, but to finish off Boo's last shirt before she went shopping with Merry.

It rained that evening, and Mr. Bemis had a headache, so he threw himself down upon the lounge after tea for a nap, with his silk handkerchief spread over his face. He did get a nap, and when he waked he lay for a time drowsily listening to the patter of the rain, and another sound which was even more soothing. Putting back a corner of the handkerchief to learn what it was, he saw Molly sitting by the fire with Boo in her lap, rocking and humming as she warmed his little bare feet, having learned to guard against croup by attending to the damp shoes and socks before going to bed. Boo lay with his round face turned up to hers, stroking her cheek while the sleepy blue eyes blinked lovingly at her as she sang her lullaby with a motherly patience sweet to see. They made a pretty little picture, and Mr. Bemis looked at it with pleasure, having a leisure moment in which to discover, as all parents do sooner or later, that his children were growing up.

"Molly is getting to be quite a woman, and very like

her mother," thought papa, wiping the eye that peeped, for he had been fond of the pretty wife who died when Boo was born. "Sad loss to them, poor things! but Miss Bat seems to have done well by them. Molly is much improved, and the boy looks finely. She's a good soul, after all;" and Mr. Bemis began to think he had been hasty when he half made up his mind to get a new housekeeper, feeling that burnt steak, weak coffee, and ragged wristbands were sure signs that Miss Bat's days of usefulness were over.

Molly was singing the lullaby her mother used to sing to her, and her father listened to it silently till Boo was carried away too sleepy for anything but bed. When she came back she sat down to her work, fancying her father still asleep. She had a crimson bow at her throat and one on the newly braided hair, her cuffs were clean, and a white apron hid the shabbiness of the old dress. She looked like a thrifty little housewife as she sat with her basket beside her full of neat white rolls, her spools set forth, and a new pair of scissors shining on the table. There was a sort of charm in watching the busy needle flash to and fro, the anxious pucker of the forehead as she looked to see if the stitches were even, and the expression of intense relief upon her face as she surveyed the finished button-hole with girlish satisfaction. Her father was wide awake and looking at her, thinking, as he did so, —

"Really the old lady has worked well to change my tomboy into that nice little girl: I wonder how she did it." Then he gave a yawn, pulled off the handkerchief, and said aloud, "What are you making, Molly?" for it struck him that sewing was a new amusement.

"Shirts for Boo, sir. Four, and this is the last," she answered, with pardonable pride, as she held it up and nodded toward the pile in her basket.

"Isn't that a new notion? I thought Miss Bat did the
sewing," said Mr. Bemis, as he smiled at the funny little gar-
ment, it looked so like Boo himself.

"No, sir; only yours. I do mine and Boo's. At least,
I'm learning how, and Mrs. Pecq says I get on nicely," answered Molly, threading her needle and making a knot in
her most capable way.

"I suppose it is time you did learn, for you are getting
to be a great girl, and all women should know how to make
and mend. You must take a stitch for me now and then:
Miss Bat's eyes are not what they were, I find;" and Mr.
Bemis looked at his frayed wristband, as if he particularly
felt the need of a stitch just then.

"I'd love to, and I guess I could. I can mend gloves;
Merry taught me, so I'd better begin on them, if you have
any," said Molly, much pleased at being able to do anything
for her father, and still more so at being asked.

"There's something to start with;" and he threw her a
pair, with nearly every finger ripped.

Molly shook her head over them, but got out her gray
silk and fell to work, glad to show how well she could sew.

"What are you smiling about?" asked her father, after a
little pause, for his head felt better, and it amused him to
question Molly.

"I was thinking about my summer clothes. I must get
them before long, and I'd like to go with Mrs. Grant and
learn how to shop, if you are willing."

"I thought Miss Bat did that for you."

"She always has, but she gets ugly, cheap things that I
don't like. I think I am old enough to choose myself, if there
is some one to tell me about prices and the goodness of the
stuff. Merry does; and she is only a few months older than
I am."

"How old are you, child?" asked her father, feeling as if he had lost his reckoning.

"Fifteen in August;" and Molly looked very proud of the fact.

"So you are! Bless my heart, how the time goes! Well, get what you please; if I'm to have a young lady here, I'd like to have her prettily dressed. It won't offend Miss Bat, will it?"

Molly's eyes sparkled, but she gave a little shrug as she answered, "She won't care. She never troubles herself about me if I let her alone."

"Hey? what? Not trouble herself? If *she* doesn't, who does?" and Mr. Bemis sat up as if this discovery was more surprising than the other.

"I take care of myself and Boo, and she looks after you. The house goes any way."

"I should think so! I nearly broke my neck over the parlor sofa in the hall to-night. What is it there for?"

Molly laughed. "That's the joke, sir; Miss Bat is cleaning house, and I'm sure it needs cleaning, for it is years since it was properly done. I thought you might have told her to."

"I've said nothing. Don't like house-cleaning well enough to suggest it. I did think the hall was rather dirty when I dropped my coat and took it up covered with lint. Is she going to upset the whole place?" asked Mr. Bemis, looking alarmed at the prospect.

"I hope so, for I really am ashamed when people come, to have them see the dust and cobwebs, and old carpets and dirty windows," said Molly, with a sigh, though she never had cared a bit till lately.

"Why don't you dust round a little, then? No time to spare from the books and play?"

"I tried, father, but Miss Bat didn't like it, and it was

too hard for me alone. If things were once in nice order, I think I could keep them so; for I do want to be neat, and I'm learning as fast as I can."

"It is high time some one took hold, if matters are left as you say. I've just been thinking what a clever woman Miss Bat was, to make such a tidy little girl out of what I used to hear called the greatest tomboy in town, and wondering what I could give the old lady. Now I find *you* are the one to be thanked, and it is a very pleasant surprise to me."

"Give her the present, please; I'm satisfied, if you like what I've done. It isn't much, and I didn't know as you would ever observe any difference. But I did try, and now I guess I'm really getting on," said Molly, sewing away with a bright color in her cheeks, for she, too, found it a pleasant surprise to be praised after many failures and few successes.

"You certainly are, my dear. I'll wait till the house-cleaning is over, and then, if we are all alive, I'll see about Miss Bat's reward. Meantime, you go with Mrs. Grant and get whatever you and the boy need, and send the bills to me;" and Mr. Bemis lighted a cigar, as if that matter was settled.

"Oh, thank you, sir! That will be splendid. Merry always has pretty things, and I know you will like me when I get fixed," said Molly, smoothing down her apron, with a little air.

"Seems to me you look very well as you are. Isn't that a pretty enough frock?" asked Mr. Bemis, quite unconscious that his own unusual interest in his daughter's affairs made her look so bright and winsome.

"This? Why, father, I've worn it all winter, and it's *frightfully* ugly, and almost in rags. I asked you for a new one a month ago, and you said you'd 'see about it;' but you didn't, so I patched this up as well as I could;" and Molly showed her elbows, feeling that such masculine blindness as this deserved a mild reproof.

"Too bad! Well, go and get half a dozen pretty muslin and gingham things, and be as gay as a butterfly, to make up for it," laughed her father, really touched by the patches and Molly's resignation to the unreliable "I'll see about it," which he recognized as a household word.

Molly clapped her hands, old gloves and all, exclaiming, with girlish delight, "How nice it will seem to have a plenty of new, neat dresses all at once, and be like other girls! Miss Bat always talks about economy, and has no more taste than a—caterpillar." Molly meant to say "cat," but remembering her pets, spared them the insult.

"I think I can afford to dress my girl as well as Grant does his. Get a new hat and coat, child, and any little notions you fancy. Miss Bat's economy isn't the sort I like;" and Mr. Bemis looked at his wristbands again, as if he could sympathize with Molly's elbows.

"At this rate, I shall have more clothes than I know what to do with, after being a rag-bag," thought the girl, in great glee, as she bravely stitched away at the worst glove, while her father smoked silently for a while, feeling that several little matters had escaped his eye which he really ought to "see about."

Presently he went to his desk, but not to bury himself in business papers, as usual, for, after rummaging in several drawers, he took out a small bunch of keys, and sat looking at them with an expression only seen on his face when he looked up at the portrait of a dark-eyed woman hanging in his room. He was a very busy man, but he had a tender place in his heart for his children; and when a look, a few words, a moment's reflection, called his attention to the fact that his little girl was growing up, he found both pride and pleasure in the thought that this young daughter was trying to fill her mother's place, and be a comfort to him, if he would let her.

"Molly, my dear, here is something for you," he said; and when she stood beside him, added, as he put the keys into her hand, keeping both in his own for a minute, —

"Those are the keys to your mother's things. I always meant you to have them, when you were old enough to use or care for them. I think you'll fancy this better than any other present, for you are a good child, and very like her."

Something seemed to get into his throat there, and Molly put her arm round his neck, saying, with a little choke in her own voice, "Thank you, father, I'd rather have this than anything else in the world, and I'll try to be more like her every day, for your sake."

He kissed her, then said, as he began to stir his papers about, "I must write some letters. Run off to bed, child. Good-night, my dear, good-night."

Seeing that he wanted to be alone, Molly slipped away, feeling that she had received a very precious gift; for she remembered the dear, dead mother, and had often longed to possess the relics laid away in the one room where order reigned and Miss Bat had no power to meddle. As she slowly undressed, she was not thinking of the pretty new gowns in which she was to be "as gay as a butterfly," but of the half-worn garments waiting for her hands to unfold with a tender touch; and when she fell asleep, with the keys under her pillow and her arms round Boo, a few happy tears on her cheeks seemed to show that, in trying to do the duty which lay nearest her, she had earned a very sweet reward.

So the little missionaries succeeded better in their second attempt than in their first; for, though still very far from being perfect girls, each was slowly learning, in her own way, one of the three lessons all are the better for knowing,—that cheerfulness can change misfortune into love and friends; that in ordering one's self aright one helps others to do the same; and that the power of finding beauty in the humblest things makes home happy and life lovely.

May Baskets

CHAPTER 18

Spring was late that year, but to Jill it seemed the loveliest she had ever known, for hope was growing green and strong in her own little heart, and all the world looked beautiful. With the help of the brace she could sit up for a short time every day, and when the air was mild enough she was warmly wrapped and allowed to look out at the open window into the garden, where the gold and purple cro-cuses were coming bravely up, and the snowdrops nodded their delicate heads as if calling to her,—

"Good day, little sister, come out and play with us, for winter is over and spring is here."

"I wish I could!" thought Jill, as the soft wind kissed a tinge of color into her pale cheeks. "Never mind, they have been shut up in a darker place than I for months, and had no fun at all; I won't fret, but think about July and the seashore while I work."

The job now in hand was May baskets, for it was the custom of the children to hang them on the doors of their friends the night before May-day; and the girls had agreed to supply baskets if the boys would hunt for flowers, much the harder task of the two. Jill had more leisure as well as taste and skill than the other girls, so she amused herself with making a goodly store of pretty baskets of all shapes, sizes, and colors, quite confident that they would be filled, though not a flower had shown its head except a few hardy dandelions, and here and there a small cluster of saxifrage.

The violets would not open their blue eyes till the sunshine was warmer, the columbines refused to dance with the boisterous east wind, the ferns kept themselves rolled up in their brown flannel jackets, and little Hepatica, with many another spring beauty, hid away in the woods, afraid to venture out, in spite of the eager welcome awaiting them. But the birds had come, punctual as ever, and the bluejays were screaming in the orchard, robins were perking up their heads and tails as they went house-hunting, purple finches in their little red hoods were feasting on the spruce buds, and the faithful chip birds chirped gayly on the grape-vine trellis where they had lived all winter, warming their little gray breasts against the southern side of the house when the sun shone, and hiding under the evergreen boughs when the snow fell.

"That tree is a sort of bird's hotel," said Jill, looking out at the tall spruce before her window, every spray now tipped with a soft green. "They all go there to sleep and eat, and it has room for every one. It is green when other trees die, the wind can't break it, and the snow only makes it look prettier. It sings to me, and nods as if it knew I loved it."

"We might call it 'The Holly Tree Inn,' as some of the cheap eating-houses for poor people are called in the city, as my holly bush grows at its foot for a sign. You can be the landlady, and feed your feathery customers every day, till the hard times are over," said Mrs. Minot, glad to see the child's enjoyment of the outer world from which she had been shut so long.

Jill liked the fancy, and gladly strewed crumbs on the

window-ledge for the chippies, who came confidingly to eat
almost from her hand. She threw out grain for the handsome jays, the jaunty robins, and the neighbors' doves, who
came with soft flight to trip about on their pink feet, arching
their shining necks as they cooed and pecked. Carrots and
cabbage-leaves also flew out of the window for the maraud-
ing gray rabbit, last of all Jack's half-dozen, who led him a
weary life of it because they would *not* stay in the Bunny-
house, but undermined the garden with their burrows, ate
the neighbors' plants, and refused to be caught till all but
one ran away, to Jack's great relief. This old fellow camped
out for the winter, and seemed to get on very well among
the cats and the hens, who shared their stores with him, and
he might be seen at all hours of the day and night scampering about the place, or kicking up his heels by moonlight,
for he was a desperate poacher.

Jill took great delight in her pretty pensioners, who
soon learned to love "The Holly Tree Inn," and to feel that
the Bird Room held a caged comrade; for, when it was too
cold or wet to open the windows, the doves came and
tapped at the pane, the chippies sat on the ledge in plump
little bunches as if she were their sunshine, the jays called
her in their shrill voices to ring the dinner-bell, and the
robins tilted on the spruce boughs where lunch was always
to be had.

The first of May came on Sunday, so all the celebrating
must be done on Saturday, which happily proved fair,
though too chilly for muslin gowns, paper garlands, and picnics on damp grass. Being a holiday, the boys decided to devote the morning to ball and the afternoon to the flower
hunt, while the girls finished the baskets; and in the evening
our particular seven were to meet at the Minots to fill them,

ready for the closing frolic of hanging on door-handles,
ringing bells, and running away.

"Now I must do my Maying, for there will be no more
sunshine, and I want to pick my flowers before it is dark.
Come, Mammy, you go too," said Jill, as the last sunbeams
shone in at the western window where her hyacinths stood
that no fostering ray might be lost.

It was rather pathetic to see the once merry girl who
used to be the life of the wood-parties now carefully lifting
herself from the couch, and, leaning on her mother's strong
arm, slowly take the half-dozen steps that made up her little
expedition. But she was happy, and stood smiling out at old
Bun skipping down the walk, the gold-edged clouds that
drew apart so that a sunbeam might give her a good-night
kiss as she gathered her long-cherished daisies, primroses,
and hyacinths to fill the pretty basket in her hand.

"Who is it for, my dearie?" asked her mother, standing
behind her as a prop, while the thin fingers did their work so
willingly that not a flower was left.

"For My Lady, of course. Who else would I give my
posies to, when I love them so well?" answered Jill, who
thought no name too fine for their best friend.

"I fancied it would be for Master Jack," said her
mother, wishing the excursion to be a cheerful one.

"I've another for him, but *she* must have the prettiest.
He is going to hang it for me, and ring and run away, and
she won't know who it's from till she sees this. She will remember it, for I've been turning and tending it ever so
long, to make it bloom to-day. Isn't it a beauty?" and Jill
held up her finest hyacinth, which seemed to ring its pale
pink bells as if glad to carry its sweet message from a grateful little heart.

"Indeed it is; and you are right to give your best to

her. Come away now, you must not stand any longer. Come and rest while I fetch a dish to put the flowers in it till you want them;" and Mrs. Pecq turned her round with her small Maying safely done.

"I didn't think I'd ever be able to do even so much, and here I am walking and sitting up, and going to drive some day. Isn't it nice that I'm not to be a poor Lucinda after all?" and Jill drew a long sigh of relief that six months instead of twenty years would probably be the end of her captivity.

"Yes, thank Heaven! I don't think I *could* have borne that;" and the mother took Jill in her arms as if she were a baby, holding her close for a minute, and laying her down with a tender kiss that made the arms cling about her neck as her little girl returned it heartily, for all sorts of new, sweet feelings seemed to be budding in both, born of great joy and thankfulness.

Then Mrs. Pecq hurried away to see about tea for the hungry boys, and Jill watched the pleasant twilight deepen as she lay singing to herself one of the songs her friend taught her because it fitted her so well.

> "A little bird I am,
>   Shut from the fields of air,
> And in my cage I sit and sing
>   To Him who placed me there:
> Well pleased a prisoner to be,
> Because, my God, it pleases Thee!
>
> "Naught have I else to do;
>   I sing the whole day long;
> And He whom most I love to please
>   Doth listen to my song;
> He caught and bound my wandering wing,
> But still He bends to hear me sing."

"Now we are ready for you, so bring on your flowers," said Molly to the boys, as she and Merry added their store of baskets to the gay show Jill had set forth on the long table ready for the evening's work.

"They wouldn't let me see one, but I guess they have had good luck, they look so jolly," answered Jill, looking at Gus, Frank, and Jack, who stood laughing, each with a large basket in his hands.

"Fair to middling. Just look in and see;" with which cheerful remark Gus tipped up his basket and displayed a few bits of green at the bottom.

"I did better. Now, don't all scream at once over these beauties;" and Frank shook out some evergreen sprigs, half a dozen saxifrages, and two or three forlorn violets with hardly any stems.

"I don't brag, but here's the best of all the three," chuckled Jack, producing a bunch of feathery carrot-tops, with a few half-shut dandelions trying to look brave and gay.

"Oh, boys, is that all?"

"What *shall* we do?"

"We've only a few house-flowers, and all those baskets to fill," cried the girls, in despair; for Merry's contribution had been small, and Molly had only a handful of artificial flowers "to fill up," she said.

"It isn't our fault: it is the late spring. We can't make flowers, can we?" asked Frank, in a tone of calm resignation.

"Couldn't you buy some, then?" said Molly, smoothing her crumpled morning-glories, with a sigh.

"Who ever heard of a fellow having any money left the last day of the month?" demanded Gus, severely.

"Or girls either. I spent all mine in ribbon and paper for my baskets, and now they are of no use. It's a shame!"

lamented Jill, while Merry began to thin out her full baskets to fill the empty ones.

"Hold on!" cried Frank, relenting. "Now, Jack, make their minds easy before they begin to weep and wail."

"Left the box outside. You tell while I go for it;" and Jack bolted, as if afraid the young ladies might be too demonstrative when the tale was told.

"Tell away," said Frank, modestly passing the story along to Gus, who made short work of it.

"We rampaged all over the country, and got only that small mess of greens. Knew you'd be disgusted, and sat down to see what we could do. Then Jack piped up, and said he'd show us a place where we could get a plenty. 'Come on,' said we, and after leading us a nice tramp, he brought us out at Morse's greenhouse. So we got a few on tick, as we had but four cents among us, and there you are. Pretty clever of the little chap, wasn't it?"

A chorus of delight greeted Jack as he popped his head in, was promptly seized by his elders and walked up to the table, where the box was opened, displaying gay posies enough to fill most of the baskets if distributed with great economy and much green.

"You are the dearest boy that ever was!" began Jill, with her nose luxuriously buried in the box, though the flowers were more remarkable for color than perfume.

"No, I'm not; there's a much dearer one coming upstairs now, and he's got something that will make you howl for joy," said Jack, ignoring his own prowess as Ed came in with a bigger box, looking as if he had done nothing but go a Maying all his days.

"Don't believe it!" cried Jill, hugging her own treasure jealously.

"It's only another joke. I won't look," said Molly, still struggling to make her cambric roses bloom again.

"I know what it is! Oh, how sweet!" added Merry, sniffing, as Ed set the box before her, saying pleasantly,—

"You shall see first, because you had faith."

Up went the cover, and a whiff of the freshest fragrance regaled the seven eager noses bent to inhale it, as a general murmur of pleasure greeted the nest of great, rosy mayflowers that lay before them.

"The dear things, how lovely they are!" and Merry looked as if greeting her cousins, so blooming and sweet was her own face.

Molly pushed her dingy garlands away, ashamed of such poor attempts beside these perfect works of nature, and Jill stretched out her hand involuntarily, as she said, forgetting her exotics, "Give me just one to smell of, it is so woodsy and delicious."

"Here you are, plenty for all. Real Pilgrim Fathers, right from Plymouth. One of our fellows lives there, and I told him to bring me a good lot; so he did, and you can do what you like with them," explained Ed, passing round bunches and shaking the rest in a mossy pile upon the table.

"Ed always gets ahead of us in doing the right thing at the right time. Hope you've got some first-class baskets ready for him," said Gus, refreshing the Washingtonian nose with a pink blossom or two.

"Not much danger of *his* being forgotten," answered Molly; and every one laughed, for Ed was much beloved by all the girls, and his door-steps always bloomed like a flower-bed on May eve.

"Now we must fly round and fill up. Come, boys, sort out the green and hand us the flowers as we want them.

Then we must direct them, and, by the time that is done, you can go and leave them," said Jill, setting all to work.

"Ed must choose his baskets first. These are ours; but any of those you can have;" and Molly pointed to a detachment of gay baskets, set apart from those already partly filled.

Ed chose a blue one, and Merry filled it with the rosiest mayflowers, knowing that it was to hang on Mabel's door-handle.

The others did the same, and the pretty work went on, with much fun, till all were filled, and ready for the names or notes.

"Let us have poetry, as we can't get wild flowers. That will be rather fine," proposed Jill, who liked jingles.

All had had some practice at the game parties, and pencils went briskly for a few minutes, while silence reigned, as the poets racked their brains for rhymes, and stared at the blooming array before them for inspiration.

"Oh, dear! I can't find a word to rhyme to 'geranium,' " sighed Molly, pulling her braid, as if to pump the well of her fancy dry.

"Cranium," said Frank, who was getting on bravely with "Annette" and "violet."

"That is elegant!" and Molly scribbled away in great glee, for her poems were always funny ones.

"How do you spell *anemoly*, — the wild flower, I mean?" asked Jill, who was trying to compose a very appropriate piece for her best basket, and found it easier to feel love and gratitude than to put them into verse.

"Anemone; do spell it properly, or you'll get laughed at," answered Gus, wildly struggling to make his lines express great ardor, without being "too spoony," as he expressed it.

"No, I shouldn't. This person never laughs at other persons' mistakes, as some persons do," replied Jill, with dignity.

Jack was desperately chewing his pencil, for he could not get on at all; but Ed had evidently prepared his poem, for his paper was half full already, and Merry was smiling as she wrote a friendly line or two for Ralph's basket, as she feared he would be forgotten, and knew he loved kindness even more than he did beauty.

"Now let's read them," proposed Molly, who loved to laugh even at herself.

The boys politely declined, and scrambled their notes into the chosen baskets in great haste; but the girls were less bashful. Jill was invited to begin, and gave her little piece, with the pink hyacinth basket before her, to illustrate her poem.

"TO MY LADY.

"There are no flowers in the fields,
No green leaves on the tree,
No columbines, no violets,
No sweet anemone.
So I have gathered from my pots
All that I have to fill
The basket that I hang to-night,
With heaps of love from Jill."

"That's perfectly sweet! Mine isn't; but I meant it to be funny," said Molly, as if there could be any doubt about the following ditty: —

"Dear Grif,
Here is a whiff
Of beautiful spring flowers;
The big red rose

Is for your nose,
As toward the sky it towers.

"Oh, do not frown
Upon this crown
Of green pinks and blue geranium;
But think of me
When this you see,
And put it on your cranium."

"O Molly, you will never hear the last of that if Grif gets it," said Jill, as the applause subsided, for the boys pronounced it "tip-top."

"Don't care, he gets the worst of it any way, for there is a pin in that rose, and if he goes to smell the mayflowers underneath he will find a thorn to pay for the tack he put in my rubber-boot. I know he will play me some joke tonight, and I mean to be first if I can," answered Molly, settling the artificial wreath round the orange-colored canoe which held her effusion.

"Now, Merry, read yours: you always have sweet poems;" and Jill folded her hands to listen with pleasure to something sentimental.

"I can't read the poems in some of mine, because they are for you; but this little verse you can hear, if you like: I'm going to give that basket to Ralph. He said he should hang one for his grandmother, and I thought that was so nice of him, I'd love to surprise him with one all to himself. He's always so good to us;" and Merry looked so innocently earnest that no one smiled at her kind thought or the unconscious paraphrase she had made of a famous stanza in her own "little verse."

"To one who teaches me
The sweetness and the beauty

> Of doing faithfully
> And cheerfully my duty."

"He will like that, and know who sent it, for none of us have pretty pink paper but you, or write such an elegant hand," said Molly, admiring the delicate white basket shaped like a lily, with the flowers inside and the note hidden among them, all daintily tied up with the palest blush-colored ribbon.

"Well, that's no harm. He likes pretty things as much as I do, and I made my basket like a flower because I gave him one of my callas, he admired the shape so much;" and Merry smiled as she remembered how pleased Ralph looked as he went away carrying the lovely thing.

"I think it would be a good plan to hang some baskets on the doors of other people who don't expect or often have any. I'll do it if you can spare some of these, we have so many. Give me only one, and let the others go to old Mrs. Tucker, and the little Irish girl who has been sick so long, and lame Neddy, and Daddy Munson. It would please and surprise them so. Will we?" asked Ed, in that persuasive voice of his.

All agreed at once, and several people were made very happy by a bit of spring left at their doors by the May elves who haunted the town that night playing all sorts of pranks. Such a twanging of bells and rapping of knockers; such a scampering of feet in the dark; such droll collisions as boys came racing round corners, or girls ran into one another's arms as they crept up and down steps on the sly; such laughing, whistling, flying about of flowers and friendly feeling, — it was almost a pity that May-day did not come oftener.

Molly got home late, and found that Grif had been be-

fore her, after all; for she stumbled over a market-basket at
her door, and on taking it in found a mammoth nosegay of
purple and white cabbages, her favorite vegetable. Even
Miss Bat laughed at the funny sight, and Molly resolved to
get Ralph to carve her a bouquet out of carrots, beets, and
turnips for next time, as Grif would never think of that.

Merry ran up the garden-walk alone, for Frank left her
at the gate, and was fumbling for the latch when she felt
something hanging there. Opening the door carefully, she
found it gay with offerings from her mates; and among them
was one long quiver-shaped basket of birch bark, with
something heavy under the green leaves that lay at the top.
Lifting these, a slender bas-relief of a calla lily in plaster appeared, with this couplet slipped into the blue cord by
which it was to hang:—

> "That mercy you to others show
> That Mercy Grant to me."

"How lovely! and this one will never fade, but always
be a pleasure hanging there. Now, I really have something
beautiful all my own," said Merry to herself as she ran up to
hang the pretty thing on the dark wainscot of her room,
where the graceful curve of its pointed leaves and the depth
of its white cup would be a joy to her eyes as long as they
lasted.

"I wonder what that means," and Merry read over the
lines again, while a soft color came into her cheeks and
a little smile of girlish pleasure began to dimple round
her lips; for she was so romantic, this touch of sentiment
showed her that her friendship was more valued than she
dreamed. But she only said, "How glad I am I remembered
him, and how surprised he will be to see mayflowers in return for the lily."

He was, and worked away more happily and bravely for the thought of the little friend whose eyes would daily fall on the white flower which always reminded him of her.

Good Templars
CHAPTER 19 ☞

"*H*i there! bell's rung! get up, lazy-bones!" called Frank from his room as the clock struck six one bright morning, and a great creaking and stamping proclaimed that he was astir.

"All right, I'm coming," responded a drowsy voice, and Jack turned over as if to obey; but there the effort ended, and he was off again, for growing lads are hard to rouse, as many a mother knows to her sorrow.

Frank made a beginning on his own toilet, and then took a look at his brother, for the stillness was suspicious.

"I thought so! he told me to wake him, and I guess this will do it;" and, filling his great sponge with water, Frank stalked into the next room and stood over the unconscious victim like a stern executioner, glad to unite business with pleasure in this agreeable manner.

A woman would have relented and tried some milder means, for when his broad shoulders and stout limbs were hidden, Jack looked very young and innocent in his sleep. Even Frank paused a moment to look at the round, rosy face, the curly eyelashes, half-open mouth, and the peaceful expression of a dreaming baby. "I *must* do it, or he won't be ready for breakfast," said the Spartan brother, and down came the sponge, cold, wet, and choky, as it was briskly rubbed to and fro regardless of every obstacle.

"Come, I say! that's not fair! Leave me alone!" sputtered Jack, hitting out so vigorously that the sponge flew across the room, and Frank fell back to laugh at the indignant sufferer.

"I promised to wake you, and you believe in keeping promises, so I'm doing my best to get you up."

"Well, you needn't pour a quart of water down a fellow's neck, and rub his nose off, need you? I'm awake, so take your old sponge and go along," growled Jack, with one eye open and a mighty gape.

"See that you keep so, then, or I'll come and give you another sort of a rouser," said Frank, retiring well pleased with his success.

"I shall have one good stretch, if I like. It is strengthening to the muscles, and I'm as stiff as a board with all that foot-ball yesterday," murmured Jack, lying down for one delicious moment. He shut the open eye to enjoy it thoroughly, and forgot the stretch altogether, for the bed was warm, the pillow soft, and a half-finished dream still hung about his drowsy brain. Who does not know the fatal charm of that stolen moment,—for once yield to it, and one is lost.

Jack was miles away "in the twinkling of a bedpost," and the pleasing dream seemed about to return, when a ruthless hand tore off the clothes, swept him out of bed, and he really did awake to find himself standing in the middle of his bath-pan with both windows open, and Frank about to pour a pail of water over him.

"Hold on! Yah, how cold the water is! Why, I thought I *was* up;" and, hopping out, Jack rubbed his eyes and looked about with such a genuine surprise that Frank put down the pail, feeling that the deluge would not be needed this time.

"You are now, and I'll see that you keep so," he said, as he stripped the bed and carried off the pillows.

"I don't care. What a jolly day!" and Jack took a little promenade to finish the rousing process.

"You'd better hurry up, or you won't get your chores done before breakfast. No time for a 'go as you please' now," said Frank; and both boys laughed, for it was an old joke of theirs, and rather funny.

Going up to bed one night expecting to find Jack asleep, Frank discovered him tramping round and round the room airily attired in a towel, and so dizzy with his brisk revolutions that as his brother looked he tumbled over and lay panting like a fallen gladiator.

"What on earth are you about?"

"Playing Rowell. Walking for the belt, and I've got it too," laughed Jack, pointing to an old gilt chandelier chain hanging on the bedpost.

"You little noodle, you'd better revolve into bed before you lose your head entirely. I never saw such a fellow for taking himself off his legs."

"Well, if I didn't exercise, do you suppose I should be able to do that—or that?" cried Jack, turning a somersault and striking a fine attitude as he came up, flattering himself that he was the model of a youthful athlete.

"You look more like a clothes-pin than a Hercules," was the crushing reply of this unsympathetic brother, and Jack meekly retired with a bad headache.

"I don't do such silly things now: I'm as broad across the shoulders as you are, and twice as strong on my pins, thanks to my gymnastics. Bet you a cent I'll be dressed first, though you have got the start," said Jack, knowing that Frank always had a protracted wrestle with his collar-buttons, which gave his adversary a great advantage over him.

"Done!" answered Frank, and at it they went. A wild scramble was heard in Jack's room, and a steady tramp in the other as Frank worked away at the stiff collar and the unaccommodating button till every finger ached. A clashing of boots followed, while Jack whistled "Polly Hopkins," and Frank declaimed in his deepest voice,—

"Arma virumque cano, Trojae qui primus ab oris Italiam, fato profugus, Laviniaque venit litora."

Hair-brushes came next, and here Frank got ahead, for Jack's thick crop would stand straight up on the crown, and only a good wetting and a steady brush would make it lie down.

"Play away, No. 2," called out Frank as he put on his vest, while Jack was still at it with a pair of the stiffest brushes procurable for money.

"Hold hard, No. 11, and don't forget your teeth," answered Jack, who had done his.

Frank took a hasty rub and whisked on his coat, while Jack was picking up the various treasures which had flown out of his pockets as he caught up his round-about.

"Ready! I'll trouble you for a cent, sonny;" and Frank held out his hand as he appeared equipped for the day.

"You haven't hung up your night-gown, nor aired the bed, nor opened the windows. That's part of the dressing; mother said so. I've got you there, for you did all that for me, except this," and Jack threw his gown over a chair with a triumphant flourish as Frank turned back to leave his room in the order which they had been taught was one of the signs of a good bringing-up in boys as well as girls.

"Ready! I'll trouble *you* for a cent, old man;" and Jack held out his hand, with a chuckle.

He got the money and a good clap beside; then they retired to the shed to black their boots, after which Frank filled the wood-boxes and Jack split kindlings, till the daily allowance was ready. Both went at their lessons for half an hour, Jack scowling over his algebra in the sofa corner, while Frank, with his elbows on and his legs round the little stand which held his books, seemed to be having a wrestling-match with Herodotus.

When the bell rang they were glad to drop the lessons and fall upon their breakfast with the appetite of wolves, especially Jack, who sequestered oatmeal and milk with such rapidity that one would have thought he had a leathern bag hidden somewhere to slip it into, like his famous namesake when he breakfasted with the giant.

"I declare I don't see what he does with it! He really ought not to 'gobble' so, mother," said Frank, who was eating with great deliberation and propriety.

"Never you mind, old quiddle. I'm so hungry I could tuck away a bushel," answered Jack, emptying a glass of milk and holding out his plate for more mush, regardless of his white moustache.

"Temperance in all things is wise, in speech as well as eating and drinking,—remember that, boys," said Mamma from behind the urn.

"That reminds me! We promised to do the 'Observer' this week, and here it is Tuesday and I haven't done a thing: have you?" asked Frank.

"Never thought of it. We must look up some bits at noon instead of playing. Dare say Jill has got some: she always saves all she finds for me."

"I have one or two good items, and can do any copying there may be. But I think if you undertake the paper you should give some time and labor to make it good," said Mamma, who was used to this state of affairs, and often edited the little sheet read every week at the Lodge. The boys seldom missed going, but the busy lady was often unable to be there, so helped with the paper as her share of the labor.

"Yes, we ought, but somehow we don't seem to get up much steam about it lately. If more people belonged, and we could have a grand time now and then, it would be jolly;" and Jack sighed at the lack of interest felt by outsiders in the loyal little Lodge which went on year after year kept up by the faithful few.

"I remember when in this very town we used to have a Cold Water Army, and in the summer turn out with processions, banners, and bands of music to march about, and end with a picnic, songs, and speeches in some grove or hall. Nearly all the children belonged to it, and the parents also, and we had fine times here twenty-five or thirty years ago."

"It didn't do much good, seems to me, for people still drink, and we haven't a decent hotel in the place," said Frank, as his mother sat looking out of the window as if she saw again the pleasant sight of old and young working together against the great enemy of home peace and safety.

"Oh yes, it did, my dear; for to this day many of those children are true to their pledge. One little girl was, I am sure, and now has two big boys to fight for the reform she has upheld all her life. The town is better than it was in those days, and if we each do our part faithfully, it will improve yet more. Every boy and girl who joins is one gained, perhaps, and your example is the best temperance lecture you can give. Hold fast, and don't mind if it isn't 'jolly:' it is *right,* and that should be enough for us."

Mamma spoke warmly, for she heartily believed in young people's guarding against this dangerous vice before it became a temptation, and hoped her boys would never break the pledge they had taken; for, young as they were, they were old enough to see its worth, feel its wisdom, and pride themselves on the promise which was fast growing into a principle. Jack's face brightened as he listened, and Frank said, with the steady look which made his face manly,—

"It shall be. Now I'll tell you what I was going to keep as a surprise till to-night, for I wanted to have my secret as well as other folks. Ed and I went up to see Bob Sunday, and he said he'd join the Lodge, if they'd have him. I'm going to propose him to-night."

"Good! good!" cried Jack, joyfully, and Mrs. Minot clapped her hands, for every new member was rejoiced over by the good people, who were not discouraged by ridicule, indifference, or opposition.

"We've got him now, for no one will object, and it is just the thing for him. He wants to belong somewhere, he says, and he'll enjoy the fun, and the good things will help him, and we will look after him. The Captain was so pleased, and you ought to have seen Ed's face when Bob said, 'I'm ready, if you'll have me.' "

Frank's own face was beaming, and Jack forgot to "gobble," he was so interested in the new convert, while Mamma said, as she threw down her napkin and took up the newspaper,—

"We must not forget our 'Observer,' but have a good one to-night in honor of the occasion. There may be something here. Come home early at noon, and I'll help you get your paper ready."

"I'll be here, but if you want Frank, you'd better tell him not to dawdle over Annette's gate half an hour," began Jack, who could not resist teasing his dignified brother about one of the few foolish things he was fond of doing.

"Do you want your nose pulled?" demanded Frank,

who never would stand joking on that tender point from his brother.

"No, I don't; and if I did, you couldn't do it;" with which taunt he was off and Frank after him, having made a futile dive at the impertinent little nose which was turned up at him and his sweetheart.

"Boys, boys, not through the parlor!" implored Mamma, resigned to skirmishes, but trembling for her piano legs as the four stout boots pranced about the table and then went thundering down the hall, through the kitchen where the fat cook cheered them on, and Mary, the maid, tried to head off Frank as Jack rushed out into the garden. But the pursuer ducked under her arm and gave chase with all speed. Then there was a glorious race all over the place; for both were good runners, and, being as full of spring vigor as frisky calves, they did astonishing things in the way of leaping fences, dodging round corners, and making good time down the wide walks.

But Jack's leg was not quite strong yet, and he felt that his round nose was in danger of a vengeful tweak as his breath began to give out and Frank's long arms drew nearer and nearer to the threatened feature. Just when he was about to give up and meet his fate like a man, old Bunny, who had been much excited by the race, came scampering across the path with such a droll skip into the air and shake of the hind legs that Frank had to dodge to avoid stepping on him, and to laugh in spite of himself. This momentary check gave Jack a chance to bolt up the back stairs and take refuge in the Bird Room, from the window of which Jill had been watching the race with great interest.

No romping was allowed there, so a truce was made by locking little fingers, and both sat down to get their breath.

"I am to go on the piazza, for an hour, by and by, Doctor said. Would you mind carrying me down before you go
to school, you do it so nicely, I'm not a bit afraid," said Jill,
as eager for the little change as if it had been a long and
varied journey.

"Yes, indeed! Come on, Princess," answered Jack,
glad to see her so well and happy.

The boys made an arm-chair, and away she went, for a
pleasant day downstairs. She thanked Frank with a posy for
his button-hole, well knowing that it would soon pass into
other hands, and he departed to join Annette. Having told
Jill about Bob, and set her to work on the "Observer," Jack
kissed his mother, and went whistling down the street, a
gay little bachelor, with a nod and smile for all he met, and
no turned-up hat or jaunty turban bobbing along beside him
to delay his steps or trouble his peace of mind.

At noon they worked on their paper, which was a
collection of items, cut from other papers, concerning temperance, a few anecdotes, a bit of poetry, a story, and, if
possible, an original article by the editor. Many hands make
light work, and nothing remained but a little copying,
which Jill promised to do before night. So the boys had time
for a game of foot-ball after school in the afternoon, which
they much enjoyed. As they sat resting on the posts, Gus
said, —

"Uncle Fred says he will give us a hay-cart ride to-
night, as it is moony, and after it you are all to come to our
house and have games."

"Can't do it," answered Frank, sadly.

"Lodge," groaned Jack, for both considered a drive in
the cart, where they all sat in a merry bunch among the hay,
one of the joys of life, and much regretted that a prior en-
gagement would prevent their sharing in it.

"That's a pity! I forgot it was Tuesday, and can't put it off, as I've asked all the rest. Give up your old Lodge and come along," said Gus, who had not joined yet.

"We might for once, perhaps, but I don't like to"— began Jack, hesitating.

"*I* won't. Who's to propose Bob if we don't? I want to go awfully; but I wouldn't disappoint Bob for a good deal, now he is willing to come." And Frank sprang off his post as if anxious to flee temptation, for it *was* very pleasant to go singing, up hill and down dale, in the spring moonlight, with—well, the fellows of his set.

"Nor Ed, I forgot that. No, we can't go. We want to be Good Templars, and we mustn't shirk," added Jack, following his brother.

"Better come. Can't put it off. Lots of fun," called Gus, disappointed at losing two of his favorite mates.

But the boys did not turn back, and as they went steadily away they felt that they *were* doing their little part in the good work, and making their small sacrifices, like faithful members.

They got their reward, however, for at home they found Mr. Chauncey, a good and great man, from England, who had known their grandfather, and was an honored friend of the family. The boys loved to hear him talk, and all tea-time listened with interest to the conversation, for Mr. Chauncey was a reformer as well as a famous clergyman, and it was like inspiring music to hear him tell about the world's work, and the brave men and women who were carrying it on. Eager to show that they had, at least, begun, the boys told him about their Lodge, and were immensely pleased when their guest took from his pocket-book a worn paper, proving that he too was a Good Templar, and belonged to the same army as they did. Nor was that all, for when they reluctantly excused themselves, Mr. Chauncey gave each a hearty "grip," and said, holding their hands in his, as he smiled at the young faces looking up at him with so much love and honor in them, —

"Tell the brothers and sisters that if I can serve them in any way while here, to command me. I will give them a lecture at their Lodge or in public, whichever they like; and I wish you God-speed, dear boys."

Two prouder lads never walked the streets than Frank and Jack as they hurried away, nearly forgetting the poor little paper in their haste to tell the good news; for it was seldom that such an offer was made the Lodge, and they felt the honor done them as bearers of it.

As the secrets of the association cannot be divulged to the uninitiated, we can only say that there was great rejoicing over the new member, for Bob was unanimously welcomed, and much gratitude both felt and expressed for Mr. Chauncey's interest in this small division of the grand army; for these good folk met with little sympathy from the great people of the town, and it was very cheering to have a well-known and much-beloved man say a word for them. All agreed that the lecture should be public, that others might share the pleasure with them, and perhaps be converted by a higher eloquence than any they possessed.

So the services that night were unusually full of spirit and good cheer; for all felt the influence of a friendly word, the beauty of a fine example. The paper was much applauded, the songs were very hearty, and when Frank, whose turn it was to be chaplain, read the closing prayer, every one felt that they had much to give thanks for, since one more had joined them, and the work was slowly getting on with unexpected helpers sent to lend a hand. The lights shone out from the little hall across the street, the music

reached the ears of passers-by, and the busy hum of voices
up there told how faithfully some, at least, of the villagers
tried to make the town a safer place for their boys to grow
up in, though the tavern still had its private bar and the
saloon-door stood open to invite them in.

There are many such quiet lodges, and in them many
young people learning as these lads were learning something of the duty they owed their neighbors as well as themselves, and being fitted to become good men and sober
citizens by practising and preaching the law and gospel of
temperance.

The next night Mr. Chauncey lectured, and the town
turned out to hear the distinguished man, who not only told
them of the crime and misery produced by this terrible vice
which afflicted both England and America, but of the great
crusade against it going on everywhere, and the need of
courage, patience, hard work, and much faith, that in time
it might be overcome. Strong and cheerful words that all
liked to hear and many heartily believed, especially the
young Templars, whose boyish fancies were won by the
idea of fighting as knights of old did in the famous crusades
they read about in their splendid, new young folks' edition
of Froissart.

"We can't pitch into people as the Red Cross fellows
did, but we can smash rum-jugs when we get the chance,
and stand by our flag as our men did in the war," said Frank,
with sparkling eyes, as they went home in the moonlight
arm in arm, keeping step behind Mr. Chauncey, who led
the way with their mother on his arm, a martial figure
though a minister, and a good captain to follow, as the boys
felt after hearing his stirring words.

"Let's try and get up a company of boys like those
mother told us about, and show people that we mean what

we say. I'll be color-bearer, and you may drill us as much as you like. A real Cold Water Army, with flags flying, and drums, and all sorts of larks," said Jack, much excited, and taking a dramatic view of the matter.

"We'll see about it. Something ought to be done, and perhaps we shall be the men to do it when the time comes," answered Frank, feeling ready to shoulder a musket or be a minute-man in good earnest.

Boyish talk and enthusiasm, but it was of the right sort; and when time and training had fitted them to bear arms, these young knights would be worthy to put on the red cross and ride away to help right the wrongs and slay the dragons that afflict the world.

A Sweet Memory
CHAPTER 20

*N*ow the lovely June days had come, everything began to look really summer-like; school would soon be over, and the young people were joyfully preparing for the long vacation.

"We are all going up to Bethlehem. We take the seashore one year and the mountains the next. Better come along," said Gus, as the boys lay on the grass after beating the Lincolns at one of the first matches of the season.

"Can't; we are off to Pebbly Beach the second week in July. Our invalids need sea air. That one looks delicate, doesn't he?" asked Frank, giving Jack a slight rap with his bat as that young gentleman lay in his usual attitude admiring the blue hose and russet shoes which adorned his sturdy limbs.

"Stop that, Captain! you needn't talk about invalids,

when you know mother says you are not to look at a book for a month because you have studied yourself thin and headachy. I'm all right;" and Jack gave himself a sounding slap on the chest, where shone the white star of the H. B. B. C.

"Hear the little cockerel crow! you just wait till you get into the college class, and see if you don't have to study like fun," said Gus, with unruffled composure, for he was going to Harvard next year, and felt himself already a Senior.

"Never shall; I don't want any of your old colleges. I'm going into business as soon as I can. Ed says I may be his book-keeper, if I am ready when he starts for himself. That is much jollier than grinding away for four years, and then having to grind ever so many more at a profession," said Jack, examining with interest the various knocks and bruises with which much ball-playing had adorned his hands.

"Much you know about it. Just as well you don't mean to try, for it would take a mighty long pull and strong pull to get you in. Business would suit you better, and you and Ed would make a capital partnership. Devlin, Minot, & Co. sounds well, hey, Gus?"

"Very, but they are such good-natured chaps, they'd never get rich. By the way, Ed came home at noon to-day sick. I met him, and he looked regularly knocked up," answered Gus, in a sober tone.

"I told him he'd better not go down Monday, for he wasn't well Saturday, and couldn't come to sing Sunday evening, you remember. I must go right round and see what the matter is;" and Jack jumped up, with an anxious face.

"Let him alone till to-morrow. He won't want any one fussing over him now. We are going for a pull; come along and steer," said Frank, for the sunset promised to be fine, and the boys liked a brisk row in their newly painted boat, the "Rhodora."

"Go ahead and get ready, I'll just cut round and ask at the door. It will seem kind, and I must know how Ed is. Won't be long;" and Jack was off at his best pace.

The others were waiting impatiently when he came back with slower steps and a more anxious face.

"How is the old fellow?" called Frank from the boat, while Gus stood leaning on an oar in a nautical attitude.

"Pretty sick. Had the doctor. May have a fever. I didn't go in, but Ed sent his love, and wanted to know who beat," answered Jack, stepping to his place, glad to rest and cool himself.

"Guess he'll be all right in a day or two;" and Gus pushed off, leaving all care behind.

"Hope he won't have typhoid,—that's no joke, I tell you," said Frank, who knew all about it, and did not care to repeat the experience.

"He's worked too hard. He's so faithful he does more than his share, and gets tired out. Mother asked him to come down and see us when he has his vacation; we are going to have high old times fishing and boating. Up or down?" asked Jack, as they glided out into the river.

Gus looked both ways, and seeing another boat with a glimpse of red in it just going round the bend, answered, with decision, "Up, of course. Don't we always pull to the bridge?"

"Not when the girls are going down," laughed Jack, who had recognized Juliet's scarlet boating-suit as he glanced over his shoulder.

"Mind what you are about, and don't gabble," commanded Captain Frank, as the crew bent to their oars and the slender boat cut through the water leaving a long furrow trembling behind.

"Oh, ah! I see! there is a blue jacket as well as a red one, so it's all right.

> " 'Lady Queen Anne, she sits in the sun,
>   As white as a lily, as brown as a bun,' "

sung Jack, recovering his spirits, and wishing Jill was there too.

"Do you want a ducking?" sternly demanded Gus, anxious to preserve discipline.

"Shouldn't mind, it's so warm."

But Jack said no more, and soon the "Rhodora" was alongside the "Water Witch," exchanging greetings in the most amiable manner.

"Pity this boat won't hold four. We'd put Jack in yours, and take you girls a nice spin up to the Hemlocks," said Frank, whose idea of bliss was floating down the river with Annette as coxswain.

"You'd better come in here, this will hold four, and we are tired of rowing," returned the "Water Witch," so invitingly that Gus could not resist.

"I don't think it is safe to put four in there. You'd better change places with Annette, Gus, and then we shall be ship-shape," said Frank, answering a telegram from the eyes that matched the blue jacket.

"Wouldn't it be *more* ship-shape still if you put me ashore at Grif's landing? I can take his boat, or wait till you come back. Don't care what I do," said Jack, feeling himself sadly in the way.

The good-natured offer being accepted with thanks, the changes were made, and, leaving him behind, the two

boats went gayly up the river. He really did not care what
he did, so sat in Grif's boat awhile watching the red sky, the
shining stream, and the low green meadows, where the
blackbirds were singing as if they too had met their little
sweethearts and were happy.

Jack remembered that quiet half-hour long afterward,
because what followed seemed to impress it on his memory. As he sat enjoying the scene, he very naturally thought
about Ed; for the face of the sister whom he saw was very
anxious, and the word "fever" recalled the hard times when
Frank was ill, particularly the night it was thought the boy
would not live till dawn, and Jack cried himself to sleep,
wondering how he ever could get on without his brother.
Ed was almost as dear to him, and the thought that he was
suffering destroyed Jack's pleasure for a little while. But,
fortunately, young people do not know how to be anxious
very long, so our boy soon cheered up, thinking about the
late match between the Stars and the Lincolns, and after a
good rest went whistling home, with a handful of mint for
Mrs. Pecq, and played games with Jill as merrily as if there
was no such thing as care in the world.

Next day Ed was worse, and for a week the answer
was the same, when Jack crept to the back door with his
eager question. Others came also, for the dear boy lying upstairs had friends everywhere, and older neighbors thought
of him even more anxiously and tenderly than his mates. It
was not fever, but some swifter trouble, for when Saturday
night came, Ed had gone home to a longer and more peaceful Sabbath than any he had ever known in this world.

Jack had been there in the afternoon, and a kind message had come down to him that his friend was not suffering
so much, and he had gone away, hoping, in his boyish igno-
rance, that all danger was over. An hour later he was read-

ing in the parlor, having no heart for play, when Frank came
in with a look upon his face which would have prepared Jack
for the news if he had seen it. But he did not look up, and
Frank found it so hard to speak, that he lingered a moment
at the piano, as he often did when he came home. It stood
open, and on the rack was the "Jolly Brothers' Galop," which
he had been learning to play with Ed. Big boy as he was, the
sudden thought that never again would they sit shoulder to
shoulder, thundering the marches or singing the songs both
liked so well, made his eyes fill as he laid away the music,
and shut the instrument, feeling as if he never wanted to
touch it again. Then he went and sat down beside Jack with
an arm round his neck, trying to steady his voice by a natural question before he told the heavy news.

"What are you reading, Jackey?"

The unusual caress, the very gentle tone, made Jack
look up, and the minute he saw Frank's face he knew
the truth.

"Is Ed——?" he could not say the hard word, and Frank
could only answer by a nod as he winked fast, for the tears
would come. Jack said no more, but as the book dropped
from his knee he hid his face in the sofa-pillow and lay quite
still, not crying, but trying to make it seem true that his dear
Ed had gone away for ever. He could not do it, and presently
turned his head a little to say, in a despairing tone,—

"I don't see what I *shall* do without him!"

"I know it's hard for you. It is for all of us."

"You've got Gus, but now I haven't anybody. Ed was
always *so* good to me!" and with the name so many tender
recollections came, that poor Jack broke down in spite of
his manful attempts to smother the sobs in the red pillow.

There was an unconscious reproach in the words,
Frank thought; for he was not as gentle as Ed, and he did not

wonder that Jack loved and mourned for the lost friend like a brother.

"You've got me. I'll be good to you; cry if you want to, I don't mind."

There was such a sympathetic choke in Frank's voice that Jack felt comforted at once, and when he had had his cry out, which was very soon, he let Frank pull him up with a bear-like but affectionate hug, and sat leaning on him as they talked about their loss, both feeling that there might have been a greater one, and resolving to love one another very much hereafter.

Mrs. Minot often called Frank the "father-boy," because he was now the head of the house, and a sober, reliable fellow for his years. Usually he did not show much affection except to her, for, as he once said, "I shall never be too old to kiss my mother," and she often wished that he had a little sister, to bring out the softer side of his character. He domineered over Jack and laughed at his affectionate little ways, but now when trouble came, he was as kind and patient as a girl; and when Mamma came in, having heard the news, she found her "father-boy" comforting his brother so well that she slipped away without a word, leaving them to learn one of the sweet lessons sorrow teaches, — to lean on one another, and let each trial bring them closer together.

It is often said that there should be no death or grief in children's stories. It is not wise to dwell on the dark and sad side of these things; but they have also a bright and lovely side, and since even the youngest, dearest, and most guarded child cannot escape some knowledge of the great mystery, is it not well to teach them in simple, cheerful ways that affection sweetens sorrow, and a lovely life can make death beautiful? I think so, therefore try to tell the last scene in the history of a boy who really lived and really left behind him a memory so precious that it will not be soon forgotten by those who knew and loved him. For the influence of this short life was felt by many, and even this brief record of it may do for other children what the reality did for those who still lay flowers on his grave, and try to be "as good as Elly."

Few would have thought that the death of a quiet lad of seventeen would have been so widely felt, so sincerely mourned; but virtue, like sunshine, works its own sweet miracles, and when it was known that never again would the bright face be seen in the village streets, the cheery voice heard, the loving heart felt in any of the little acts which so endeared Ed Devlin to those about him, it seemed as if young and old grieved alike for so much promise cut off in its spring-time. This was proved at the funeral, for, though it took place at the busy hour of a busy day, men left their affairs, women their households, young people their studies and their play, and gave an hour to show their affection, respect, and sympathy for those who had lost so much.

The girls had trimmed the church with all the sweetest flowers they could find, and garlands of lilies of the valley robbed the casket of its mournful look. The boys had brought fresh boughs to make the grave a green bed for their comrade's last sleep. Now they were all gathered together, and it was a touching sight to see the rows of young faces sobered and saddened by their first look at sorrow. The girls sobbed, and the boys set their lips tightly as their glances fell upon the lilies under which the familiar face lay full of solemn peace. Tears dimmed older eyes when the hymn the dead boy loved was sung, and the pastor told with how much pride and pleasure he had watched the gracious growth of this young parishioner since he first met the lad of twelve and was attracted by the shining face, the pleasant manners. Dutiful and loving; ready to help; patient to bear and forbear; eager to excel; faithful to the smallest task, yet full of high ambitions; and, better still, possessing the child-like piety that can trust and believe, wait and hope. Good and happy,—the two things we all long for and so few of us truly are. This he was, and this single fact was the best eulogy his pastor could pronounce over the beloved youth gone to a nobler manhood whose promise left so sweet a memory behind.

As the young people looked, listened, and took in the scene, they felt as if some mysterious power had changed their playmate from a creature like themselves into a sort of saint or hero for them to look up to, and imitate if they could. "What has he done, to be so loved, praised, and mourned?" they thought, with a tender sort of wonder; and the answer seemed to come to them as never before, for never had they been brought so near the solemn truth of life and death." It was not what he did but what he was that made him so beloved. All that was sweet and noble in him still lives; for goodness is the only thing we can take with us when we die, the only thing that can comfort those we leave behind, and help us to meet again hereafter."

This feeling was in many hearts when they went away to lay him, with prayer and music, under the budding oak that leaned over his grave, a fit emblem of the young life just beginning its new spring. As the children did their part, the beauty of the summer day soothed their sorrow, and something of the soft brightness of the June sunshine seemed to gild their thoughts, as it gilded the flower-strewn mound they left behind. The true and touching words spoken cheered as well as impressed them, and made them feel that their friend was not lost but gone on into a higher class of the great school whose Master is eternal love and wisdom. So the tears soon dried, and the young faces looked up like flowers after rain. But the heaven-sent shower sank into the earth, and they were the stronger, sweeter for it, more eager to make life brave and beautiful, because death had gently shown them what it should be.

When the boys came home they found their mother already returned, and Jill upon the parlor sofa listening to her account of the funeral with the same quiet, hopeful look which their own faces wore; for somehow the sadness seemed to have gone, and a sort of Sunday peace remained.

"I'm glad it was all so sweet and pleasant. Come and rest, you look so tired;" and Jill held out her hands to greet them,—a crumpled handkerchief in one and a little bunch of fading lilies in the other.

Jack sat down in the low chair beside her and leaned his head against the arm of the sofa, for he was tired. But Frank walked slowly up and down the long rooms with a serious yet serene look on his face, for he felt as if he had learned something that day, and would always be the better for it. Presently he said, stopping before his mother, who leaned in the easy-chair looking up at the picture of her boys' father,—

"I should like to have just such things said about me when I die."

"So should I, if I deserved them as Ed did!" cried Jack, earnestly.

"You may if you try. I should be proud to hear them, and if they were true, they would comfort me more than anything else. I am glad you see the lovely side of sorrow, and are learning the lesson such losses teach us," answered their mother, who believed in teaching young people to face trouble bravely, and find the silver lining in the clouds that come to all of us.

"I never thought much about it before, but now dying doesn't seem dreadful at all,—only solemn and beautiful. Somehow everybody seems to love everybody else more for it, and try to be kind and good and pious. I can't say what I mean, but you know, mother;" and Frank went pacing on again with the bright look his eyes always wore when he listened to music or read of some noble action.

"That's what Merry said when she and Molly came in on their way home. But Molly felt dreadfully, and so did Mabel. She brought me these flowers to press, for we are all going to keep some to remember dear Ed by," said Jill, carefully smoothing out the little bells as she laid the lilies in her hymn-book, for she too had had a thoughtful hour while she lay alone, imagining all that went on in the church, and shedding a few tender tears over the friend who was always so kind to her.

"I don't want anything to remember him by. I was so fond of him, I couldn't forget if I tried. I know I ought not to say it, but I *don't* see why God let him die," said Jack, with a quiver in his voice, for his loving heart could not help aching still.

"No, dear, we cannot see or know many things that grieve us very much, but we *can* trust that it is right, and try to believe that all is meant for our good. That is what faith means, and without it we are miserable. When you were little, you were afraid of the dark, but if I spoke or touched you, then you were sure all was well, and fell asleep holding my hand. God is wiser and stronger than any father or mother, so hold fast to Him, and you will have no doubt or fear, however dark it seems."

"As you do," said Jack, going to sit on the arm of

Mamma's chair, with his cheek to hers, willing to trust as she bade him, but glad to hold fast the living hand that had led and comforted him all his life.

"Ed used to say to me when I fretted about getting well, and thought nobody cared for me, which was very naughty, 'Don't be troubled, God won't forget you; and if you must be lame, He will make you able to bear it,'" said Jill, softly, her quick little mind all alive with new thoughts and feelings.

"He believed it, and that's why he liked that hymn so much. I'm glad they sung it to-day," said Frank, bringing his heavy dictionary to lay on the book where the flowers were pressing.

"Oh, thank you! Could you play that tune for me? I didn't hear it, and I'd love to, if you are willing," asked Jill.

"I didn't think I ever should want to play again, but I do. Will you sing it for her, mother? I'm afraid I shall break down if I try alone."

"We will all sing, music is good for us now," said Mamma; and in rather broken voices they did sing Ed's favorite words:—

> "Not a sparrow falleth but its God doth know,
> Just as when his mandate lays a monarch low;
> Not a leaflet moveth, but its God doth see,—
> Think not, then, O mortal, God forgetteth thee.
> Far more precious surely than the birds that fly
> Is a Father's image to a Father's eye.
> E'en thy hairs are numbered; trust Him full and free.
> Cast thy cares before Him, He will comfort thee;
> For the God that planted in thy breast a soul,
> On his sacred tables doth thy name enroll.
> Cheer thine heart, then, mortal, never faithless be,
> He that marks the sparrows will remember thee."

Pebbly Beach

CHAPTER 21

"Now, Mr. Jack, it is a moral impossibility to get all those things into one trunk, and you mustn't ask it of me," said Mrs. Pecq, in a tone of despair, as she surveyed the heap of treasures she was expected to pack for the boys.

"Never mind the clothes, we only want a boating-suit apiece. Mamma can put a few collars in her trunk for us; but these necessary things *must* go," answered Jack, adding his target and air-pistol to the pile of bats, fishing-tackle, games, and a choice collection of shabby balls.

"Those are the necessaries and clothes the luxuries, are they? Why don't you add a velocipede, wheel-barrow, and printing-press, my dear?" asked Mrs. Pecq, while Jill turned up her nose at "boys' rubbish."

"Wish I could. Dare say we shall want them. Women don't know what fellows need, and always must put in a lot of stiff shirts and clean handkerchiefs and clothes-brushes and pots of cold cream. We are going to rough it, and don't want any fuss and feathers," said Jack, beginning to pack the precious balls in his rubber-boots, and strap them up with the umbrellas, rods, and bats, seeing that there was no hope of a place in the trunk.

Here Frank came in with two big books, saying calmly, "Just slip these in somewhere, we shall need them."

"But you are not to study at all, so you won't want those great dictionaries," cried Jill, busily packing her new travelling-basket with all sorts of little rolls, bags, and boxes.

"They are not dics, but my Encyclopedia. We shall want to know heaps of things, and this tells about everything. With those books, and a microscope and a telescope, you could travel round the world, and learn all you wanted to. Can't possibly get on without them," said Frank, fondly patting his favorite work.

"My patience! what queer cattle boys are!" exclaimed Mrs. Pecq, while they all laughed. "It can't be done, Mr. Frank; all the boxes are brim full, and you'll have to leave those fat books behind, for there's no place anywhere."

"Then I'll carry them myself;" and Frank tucked one under each arm, with a determined air, which settled the matter.

"I suppose you'll study cockleology instead of boating, and read up on polywogs while we play tennis, or go poking round with your old spy-glass instead of having a jolly good time," said Jack, hauling away on the strap till all was taut and ship-shape with the bundle.

"Tadpoles don't live in salt water, my son, and if you mean conchology, you'd better say so. I shall play as much as I wish, and when I want to know about any new or curious thing, I shall consult my Cyclo, instead of bothering other people with questions, or giving it up like a dunce;" with which crushing reply Frank departed, leaving Jill to pack and unpack her treasures a dozen times, and Jack to dance jigs on the lids of the trunks till they would shut.

A very happy party set off the next day, leaving Mrs. Pecq waving her apron on the steps. Mrs. Minot carried the lunch, Jack his precious bundle with trifles dropping out by the way, and Jill felt very elegant bearing her new basket with red worsted cherries bobbing on the outside. Frank actually did take the Encyclopedia, done up in the roll of shawls, and whenever the others wondered about anything, — tides, light-houses, towns, or natural productions, — he brought forth one of the books and triumphantly read therefrom, to the great merriment, if not edification, of his party.

A very short trip by rail and the rest of the journey by boat, to Jill's great contentment, for she hated to be shut up; and while the lads roved here and there she sat under the awning, too happy to talk. But Mrs. Minot watched with real satisfaction how the fresh wind blew the color back into the pale cheeks, how the eyes shone and the heart filled with delight at seeing the lovely world again, and being able to take a share in its active pleasures.

The Willows was a long, low house close to the beach, and as full as a beehive of pleasant people, all intent on having a good time. A great many children were swarming about, and Jill found it impossible to sleep after her journey, there was such a lively clatter of tongues on the piazzas, and so many feet going to and fro in the halls. She lay down obediently while Mrs. Minot settled matters in the two airy rooms and gave her some dinner, but she kept popping up her head to look out of the window to see what she could see. Just opposite stood an artist's cottage and studio, with all manner of charming galleries, towers, steps, and even a sort of drawbridge to pull up when the painter wished to be left in peace. He was absent now, and the visitors took possession of this fine play-place. Children were racing up and down the galleries, ladies sitting in the tower, boys disporting themselves on the roof, and young gentlemen preparing for theatricals in the large studio.

"What fun I'll have over there," thought Jill, watching the merry scene with intense interest, and wondering if the little girls she saw were as nice as Molly and Merry.

Then there were glimpses of the sea beyond the green bank where a path wound along to the beach, whence came the cool dash of waves, and now and then the glimmer of a passing sail.

"Oh, when can I go out? It looks *so* lovely, I can't wait long," she said, looking as eager as a little gull shut up in a cage and pining for its home on the wide ocean.

"As soon as it is a little cooler, dear. I'm getting ready for our trip, but we must be careful and not do too much at once. 'Slow and sure' is our motto," answered Mrs. Minot, busily collecting the camp-stools, the shawls, the air-cushions, and the big parasols.

"I'll be good, only do let me have my sailor-hat to wear, and my new suit. I'm not a bit tired, and I do want to be like other folks right off," said Jill, who had been improving rapidly of late, and felt much elated at being able to drive out nearly every day, to walk a little, and sit up some hours without any pain or fatigue.

To gratify her, the blue flannel suit with its white trimming was put on, and Mamma was just buttoning the stout boots when Jack thundered at the door, and burst in with all sorts of glorious news.

"Do come out, mother, it's perfectly splendid on the beach! I've found a nice place for Jill to sit, and it's only a step. Lots of capital fellows here; one has a bicycle, and is going to teach us to ride. No end of fun up at the hotel, and every one seems glad to see us. Two ladies asked about Jill, and one of the girls has got some shells all ready for her, Gerty Somebody, and her mother is so pretty and jolly, I like her ever so much. They sit at our table, and Wally is the boy, younger than I am, but very pleasant. Bacon is the fellow in knickerbockers; just wish you could see what stout legs he's got! Cox is the chap for me, though; we are going fishing to-morrow. He's got a sweet-looking mother, and a sister for you, Jill. Now, then, *do* come on, I'll take the traps."

Off they went, and Jill thought that very short walk to the shore the most delightful she ever took; for people smiled at the little invalid as she went slowly by leaning on Mrs. Minot's arm, while Jack pranced in front, doing the honors, as if he owned the whole Atlantic. A new world opened to her eyes as they came out upon the pebbly beach full of people enjoying their afternoon promenade. Jill gave one rapturous "Oh!" and then sat on her stool, forgetting everything but the beautiful blue ocean rolling away to meet the sky, with nothing to break the wide expanse but a sail here and there, a point of rocks on one hand, the little pier on the other, and white gulls skimming by on their wide wings.

While she sat enjoying herself, Jack showed his mother the place he had found, and a very nice one it was. Just under the green bank lay an old boat propped up with some big stones. A willow drooped over it, the tide rippled up within a few yards of it, and a fine view of the waves could be seen as they dashed over the rocks at the point.

"Isn't it a good cubby-house? Ben Cox and I fixed it for Jill, and she can have it for hers. Put her cushions and things there on the sand the children have thrown in, — that will make it soft; then these seats will do for tables; and up in the bow I'm going to have that old rusty tin boiler full of salt water, so she can put sea-weed and crabs and all sorts of chaps in it for an aquarium, you know," explained Jack, greatly interested in establishing his family comfortably before he left them.

"There couldn't be a nicer place, and it is very kind of you to get it ready. Spread the shawls and settle Jill, then you needn't think of us any more, but go and scramble with

Frank. I see him over there with his spy-glass and some pleasant-looking boys," said Mamma, bustling about in great spirits.

So the red cushions were placed, the plaids laid, and the little work-basket set upon the seat, all ready for Jill, who was charmed with her nest, and cuddled down under the big parasol, declaring she would keep house there every day.

Even the old boiler pleased her, and Jack raced over the beach to begin his search for inhabitants for the new aquarium, leaving Jill to make friends with some pretty babies digging in the sand, while Mamma sat on the camp-stool and talked with a friend from Harmony Village.

It seemed as if there could not be anything more delightful than to lie there lulled by the sound of the sea, watching the sunset and listening to the pleasant babble of little voices close by. But when they went to tea in the great hall, with six tables full of merry people, and half a dozen maids flying about, Jill thought that was even better, because it was so new to her. Gerty and Wally nodded to her, and their pretty mamma was so kind and so gay, that Jill could not feel bashful after the first few minutes, and soon looked about her, sure of seeing friendly faces everywhere. Frank and Jack ate as if the salt air had already improved their appetites, and talked about Bacon and Cox as if they had been bosom friends for years. Mamma was as happy as they, for her friend, Mrs. Hammond, sat close by; and this rosy lady, who had been a physician, cheered her up by predicting that Jill would soon be running about as well as ever.

But the best of all was in the evening, when the elder people gathered in the parlors and played Twenty Questions, while the children looked on for an hour before going to bed, much amused at the sight of grown people laughing, squabbling, dodging, and joking as if they had all become young again; for, as every one knows, it is impossible to help lively skirmishes when that game is played. Jill lay in the sofa corner enjoying it all immensely; for she never saw anything so droll, and found it capital fun to help guess the thing, or try to puzzle the opposite side. Her quick wits and bright face attracted people, and in the pauses of the sport she held quite a levee, for everybody was interested in the little invalid. The girls shyly made friends in their own way, the mammas told thrilling tales of the accidents their darlings had survived, several gentlemen kindly offered their boats, and the boys, with the best intentions in life, suggested strolls of two or three miles to Rafe's Chasm and Norman's Woe, or invited her to tennis and archery, as if violent exercise was the cure for all human ills. She was very grateful, and reluctantly went away to bed, declaring, when she got upstairs, that these new friends were the dearest people she ever met, and the Willows the most delightful place in the whole world.

Next day a new life began for the young folks,—a very healthy, happy life; and all threw themselves into it so heartily, that it was impossible to help getting great good from it, for these summer weeks, if well spent, work miracles in tired bodies and souls. Frank took a fancy to the bicycle boy, and, being able to hire one of the breakneck articles, soon learned to ride it; and the two might be seen wildly working their long legs on certain smooth stretches of road, or getting up their muscle rowing about the bay till they were almost as brown and nautical in appearance and language as the fishermen who lived in nooks and corners along the shore.

Jack struck up a great friendship with the sturdy Bacon and the agreeable Cox: the latter, being about his own age, was his especial favorite; and they soon were called Box and Cox by the other fellows, which did not annoy them a bit, as both had played parts in that immortal farce. They had capital times fishing, scrambling over the rocks, playing ball and tennis, and rainy days they took possession of the studio opposite, drew up the portcullis, and gallantly defended the castle, which some of the others besieged with old umbrellas for shields, bats for battering-rams, and bunches of burrs for cannon-balls. Great larks went on over there, while the girls applauded from the piazza or chamber windows, and made a gay flag for the victors to display from the tower when the fight was over.

But Jill had the best time of all, for each day brought increasing strength and spirits, and she improved so fast it was hard to believe that she was the same girl who lay so long almost helpless in the Bird Room at home. Such lively letters as she sent her mother, all about her new friends, her fine sails, drives, and little walks; the good times she had in the evening, the lovely things people gave her, and she was learning to make with shells and sea-weed, and what splendid fun it was to keep house in a boat.

This last amusement soon grew quite absorbing, and her "cubby," as she called it, rapidly became a pretty grotto, where she lived like a little mermaid, daily loving more and more the beauty of the wonderful sea. Finding the boat too sunny at times, the boys cut long willow boughs and arched them over the seats, laying hemlock branches across till a green roof made it cool and shady inside. There Jill sat or lay among her cushions reading, trying to sketch, sorting shells, drying gay sea-weeds, or watching her crabs, jelly-fish, and anemones in the old boiler, now buried in sand and edged about with moss from the woods.

Nobody disturbed her treasures, but kindly added to

them, and often when she went to her nest she found fruit
or flowers, books or bon-bons, laid ready for her. Every
one pitied and liked the bright little girl who could not run
and frisk with the rest, who was so patient and cheerful
after her long confinement, ready to help others, and so
grateful for any small favor. She found now that the weary
months had not been wasted, and was very happy to discover in herself a new sort of strength and sweetness that
was not only a comfort to her, but made those about her
love and trust her. The songs she had learned attracted the
babies, who would leave their play to peep at her and listen
when she sung over her work. Passers-by paused to hear the
blithe voice of the bird in the green cage, and other invalids,
strolling on the beach, would take heart when they saw the
child so happy in spite of her great trial.

The boys kept all their marine curiosities for her, and
were always ready to take her a row or a sail, as the bay was
safe and that sort of travelling suited her better than driving.
But the girls had capital times together, and it did Jill good
to see another sort from those she knew at home. She had
been so much petted of late, that she was getting rather vain
of her small accomplishments, and being with strangers
richer, better bred and educated than herself, made her
more humble in some things, while it showed her the worth
of such virtues as she could honestly claim. Mamie Cox
took her to drive in the fine carriage of her mamma, and Jill
was much impressed by the fact that Mamie was not a bit
proud about it, and did not put on any airs, though she had
a maid to take care of her. Gerty wore pretty costumes, and
came down with pink and blue ribbons in her hair that Jill
envied very much; yet Gerty liked her curls, and longed to
have some, while her mother, "the lady from Philadelphia,"
as they called her, was so kind and gay that Jill quite adored

her, and always felt as if sunshine had come into the room
when she entered. Two little sisters were very interesting
to her, and made her long for one of her own when she saw
them going about together and heard them talk of their
pleasant home, where the great silk factories were. But they
invited her to come and see the wonderful cocoons, and
taught her to knot pretty gray fringe on a cushion, which
delighted her, being so new and easy. There were several
other nice little lasses, and they all gathered about Jill with
the sweet sympathy children are so quick to show toward
those in pain or misfortune. She thought they would not
care for a poor little girl like herself, yet here she was the
queen of the troupe, and this discovery touched and pleased
her very much.

In the morning they camped round the boat on the
stones with books, gay work, and merry chatter, till
bathing-time. Then the beach was full of life and fun, for
every one looked so droll in the flannel suits, it was hard to
believe that the neat ladies and respectable gentlemen who
went into the little houses could be the same persons as the
queer, short-skirted women with old hats tied down, and
bareheaded, barefooted men in old suits, who came skipping over the sand to disport themselves in the sea in the
most undignified ways. The boys raced about, looking like
circus-tumblers, and the babies were regular little cupids,
running away from the waves that tried to kiss their flying feet.

Some of the young ladies and girls were famous swim-
mers, and looked very pretty in their bright red and blue
costumes, with loose hair and gay stockings, as they danced
into the water and floated away as fearlessly as real mer-
maidens. Jill had her quiet dip and good rubbing each fine
day, and then lay upon the warm sand watching the pranks

of the others, and longing to run and dive and shout and tumble with the rest. Now that she was among the well and active, it seemed harder to be patient than when shut up and unable to stir. She felt so much better, and had so little pain to remind her of past troubles, it was almost impossible to help forgetting the poor back and letting her recovered spirits run away with her. If Mrs. Minot had not kept good watch, she would have been off more than once, so eager was she to be "like other girls" again, so difficult was it to keep the restless feet quietly folded among the red cushions.

One day she did yield to temptation, and took a little voyage which might have been her last, owing to the carelessness of those whom she trusted. It was a good lesson, and made her as meek as a lamb during the rest of her stay. Mrs. Minot drove to Gloucester one afternoon, leaving Jill safely established after her nap in the boat, with Gerty and Mamie making lace beside her.

"Don't try to walk or run about, my dear. Sit on the piazza if you get tired of this, and amuse yourself quietly till I come back. I'll not forget the worsted and the canvas," said Mamma, peeping over the bank for a last word as she waited for the omnibus to come along.

"Oh, *don't* forget the Gibraltars!" cried Jill, popping her head out of the green roof.

"Nor the bananas, please!" added Gerty, looking round one end.

"Nor the pink and blue ribbon to tie our shell-baskets," called Mamie, nearly tumbling into the aquarium at the other end.

Mrs. Minot laughed, and promised, and rumbled away, leaving Jill to an experience which she never forgot.

For half an hour the little girls worked busily, then the

boys came for Gerty and Mamie to go to the Chasm with a party of friends who were to leave next day. Off they went, and Jill felt very lonely as the gay voices died away. Every one had gone somewhere, and only little Harry Hammond and his maid were on the beach. Two or three sand-pipers ran about among the pebbles, and Jill envied them their nimble legs so much, that she could not resist getting up to take a few steps. She longed to run straight away over the firm, smooth sand, and feel again the delight of swift motion; but she dared not try it, and stood leaning on her tall parasol with her book in her hand, when Frank, Jack, and the bicycle boy came rowing lazily along and hailed her.

"Come for a sail, Jill? Take you anywhere you like," called Jack, touched by the lonely figure on the beach.

"I'd love to go, if you will row. Mamma made me promise not to go sailing without a man to take care of me. Would it spoil your fun to have me?" answered Jill, eagerly.

"Not a bit; come out on the big stones and we'll take you aboard," said Frank, as they steered to the place where she could embark the easiest.

"All the rest are gone to the Chasm. I wanted to go, because I've never seen it; but, of course, I had to give it up, as I do most of the fun;" and Jill sat down with an impatient sigh.

"We'll row you round there. Can't land, but you can see the place and shout to the others, if that will be any comfort to you," proposed Frank, as they pulled away round the pier.

"Oh, yes, that would be lovely!" and Jill smiled at Jack, who was steering, for she found it impossible to be dismal now with the fresh wind blowing in her face, the blue waves slapping against the boat, and three good-natured lads ready to gratify her wishes.

Away they went, laughing and talking gayly till they came to Goodwin's Rocks, where an unusual number of people were to be seen though the tide was going out, and no white spray was dashing high into the air to make a sight worth seeing.

"What do you suppose they are about? Never saw such a lot of folks at this time. Shouldn't wonder if something had happened. I say, put me ashore, and I'll cut up and see," said the bicycle boy, who was of an inquiring turn.

"I'll go with you," said Frank; "it won't take but a minute, and I'd like to discover what it is. May be something we ought to know about."

So the boys pulled round into a quiet nook, and the two elder ones scrambled up the rocks, to disappear in the crowd. Five, ten, fifteen minutes passed, and they did not return. Jack grew impatient, so did Jill, and bade him run up and bring them back. Glad to know what kept them, Jack departed, to be swallowed up in his turn, for not a sign of a boy did she see after that; and, having vainly strained her eyes to discover the attraction which held them, she gave it up, lay down on their jackets, and began to read.

Then the treacherous tide, as it ebbed lower and lower down the beach, began to lure the boat away; for it was not fastened, and when lightened of its load was an easy prize to the hungry sea, always ready to steal all it can. Jill knew nothing of this, for her story was dull, the gentle motion proved soothing, and before she knew it she was asleep. Little by little the runaway boat slid farther from the shore, and presently was floating out to sea with its drowsy freight, while the careless boys, unconscious of the time they were wasting, lingered to see group after group photographed by the enterprising man who had trundled his camera to the rocks.

In the midst of a dream about home, Jill was roused by a loud shout, and, starting up so suddenly that the sun-umbrella went overboard, she found herself sailing off alone, while the distracted lads roared and beckoned vainly from the cove. The oars lay at their feet, where they left them; and the poor child was quite helpless, for she could not manage the sail, and even the parasol, with which she might have paddled a little, had gone down with all sail set. For a minute, Jill was so frightened that she could only look about her with a scared face, and wonder if drowning was a very disagreeable thing. Then the sight of the bicycle boy struggling with Jack, who seemed inclined to swim after her, and Frank shouting wildly, "Hold on! Come back!" made her laugh in spite of her fear, it was so comical, and their distress so much greater than hers, since it was their own carelessness which caused the trouble.

"I can't come back! There's nothing to hold on to! You didn't fasten me, and now I don't know where I'm going!" cried Jill, looking from the shore to the treacherous sea that was gently carrying her away.

"Keep cool! We'll get a boat and come after you," roared Frank, before he followed Jack, who had collected his wits and was tearing up the rocks like a chamois hunter.

The bicycle boy calmly sat down to keep his eye on the runaway, calling out from time to time such cheering remarks as "All aboard for Liverpool! Give my love to Victoria! Luff and bear away when you come to Halifax! If you are hard up for provisions, you'll find an apple and some bait in my coat-pocket," and other directions for a comfortable voyage, till his voice was lost in the distance as a stronger current bore her swiftly away and the big waves began to tumble and splash.

At first Jill had laughed at his efforts to keep up her

spirits, but when the boat floated round a point of rock that shut in the cove, she felt all alone, and sat quite still, wondering what would become of her. She turned her back to the sea and looked at the dear, safe land, which never had seemed so green and beautiful before. Up on the hill rustled the wood through which the happy party were wandering to the Chasm. On the rocks she still saw the crowd all busy with their own affairs, unconscious of her danger. Here and there artists were sketching in picturesque spots, and in one place an old gentleman sat fishing peacefully. Jill called and waved her handkerchief, but he never looked up, and an ugly little dog barked at her in what seemed to her a most cruel way.

"Nobody sees or hears or cares, and those horrid boys will never catch up!" she cried in despair, as the boat began to rock more and more, and the loud swash of water dashing in and out of the chasm drew nearer and nearer. Holding on now with both hands she turned and looked straight before her, pale and shivering, while her eyes tried to see some sign of hope among the steep cliffs that rose up on the left. No one was there, though usually at this hour they were full of visitors, and it was time for the walkers to have arrived.

"I wonder if Gerty and Mamie will be sorry if I'm drowned," thought Jill, remembering the poor girl who had been lost in the Chasm not long ago. Her lively fancy pictured the grief of her friends at her loss; but that did not help or comfort her now, and as her anxious gaze wandered along the shore, she said aloud, in a pensive tone, —

"Perhaps I shall be wrecked on Norman's Woe, and somebody will make poetry about me. It would be pretty to read, but I don't want to die that way. Oh, why did I come! Why didn't I stay safe and comfortable in my own boat?"

At the thought a sob rose, and poor Jill laid her head down on her lap to cry with all her heart, feeling very helpless, small, and forsaken alone there on the great sea. In the midst of her tears came the thought, "When people are in danger, they ask God to save them;" and, slipping down upon her knees, she said her prayer as she had never said it before, for when human help seems gone we turn to Him as naturally as lost children cry to their father, and feel sure that He will hear and answer them.

After that she felt better, and wiped away the drops that blinded her, to look out again like a shipwrecked mariner watching for a sail. And there it was! close by, coming swiftly on with a man behind it, a sturdy brown fisher, busy with his lobster-pots, and quite unconscious how like an angel he looked to the helpless little girl in the rudderless boat.

"Hi! hi! oh, please do stop and get me! I'm lost, no oars, nobody to fix the sail! Oh, oh! please come!" screamed Jill, waving her hat frantically as the other boat skimmed by and the man stared at her as if she really was a mermaid with a fishy tail.

"Keep still! I'll come about and fetch you!" he called out; and Jill obeyed, sitting like a little image of faith, till with a good deal of shifting and flapping of the sail the other boat came alongside and took her in tow.

A few words told the story, and in five minutes she was sitting snugly tucked up watching an unpleasant mass of lobsters flap about dangerously near her toes, while the boat bounded over the waves with a delightful motion, and every instant brought her nearer home. She did not say much, but felt a good deal; and when they met two boats coming to meet her, manned by very anxious crews of men and boys, she was so pale and quiet that Jack was quite bowed down with remorse, and Frank nearly pitched the bicycle boy overboard because he gayly asked Jill how she left her friends in England. There was great rejoicing over her, for the people on the rocks had heard of her loss, and ran about like ants when their hill is disturbed. Of course half a dozen amiable souls posted off to the Willows to tell the family that the little girl was drowned, so that when the rescuers appeared quite a crowd was assembled on the beach to welcome her. But Jill felt so used up with her own share of the excitement that she was glad to be carried to the house by Frank and Jack, and laid upon her bed, where Mrs. Hammond soon restored her with sugar-coated pills, and words even sweeter and more soothing.

Other people, busied with their own pleasures, forgot all about it by the next day; but Jill remembered that hour long afterward, both awake and asleep, for her dreams were troubled, and she often started up imploring some one to save her. Then she would recall the moment when, feeling most helpless, she had asked for help, and it had come as quickly as if that tearful little cry had been heard and answered, though her voice had been drowned by the dash of the waves that seemed ready to devour her. This made a deep impression on her, and a sense of childlike faith in the Father of all began to grow up within her; for in that lonely voyage, short as it was, she had found a very precious treasure to keep for ever, to lean on, and to love during the longer voyage which all must take before we reach our home.

A Happy Day

CHAPTER 22

"Oh dear! only a week more, and then we must go back. Don't you hate the thoughts of it?" said Jack, as he was giving Jill her early walk on the beach one August morning.

"Yes, it will be dreadful to leave Gerty and Mamie and all the nice people. But I'm so much better I won't have to be shut up again, even if I don't go to school. How I long to see Merry and Molly. Dear things, if it wasn't for them I should hate going home more than you do," answered Jill, stepping along quite briskly, and finding it very hard to resist breaking into a skip or a run, she felt so well and gay.

"Wish they could be here to-day to see the fun," said Jack, for it was the anniversary of the founding of the place, and the people celebrated it by all sorts of festivity.

"I did want to ask Molly, but your mother is so good to me I couldn't find courage to do it. Mammy told me not to ask for a thing, and I'm sure I don't get a chance. I feel just as if I was your truly born sister, Jack."

"That's all right, I'm glad you do," answered Jack, comfortably, though his mind seemed a little absent and his eyes twinkled when she spoke of Molly. "Now, you sit in the cubby-house, and keep quiet till the boat comes in. Then the fun will begin, and you must be fresh and ready to enjoy it. Don't run off, now, I shall want to know where to find you by and by."

"No more running off, thank you. I'll stay here till you come, and finish this box for Molly; she has a birthday this week, and I've written to ask what day, so I can send it right up and surprise her."

Jack's eyes twinkled more than ever as he helped Jill settle herself in the boat, and then with a whoop he tore over the beach, as if practising for the race which was to come off in the afternoon.

Jill was so busy with her work that time went quickly, and the early boat came in just as the last pink shell was stuck in its place. Putting the box in the sun to dry, she leaned out of her nook to watch the gay parties land, and go streaming up the pier along the road that went behind the bank that sheltered her. Flocks of children were running about on the sand, and presently strangers appeared, eager to see and enjoy all the delights of this gala-day.

"There's a fat little boy who looks ever so much like Boo," said Jill to herself, watching the people and hoping they would not come and find her, since she had promised to stay till Jack returned.

The fat little boy was staring about him in a blissful sort of maze, holding a wooden shovel in one hand and the skirts of a young girl with the other. Her back was turned to Jill, but something in the long brown braid with a fly-away blue bow hanging down her back looked very familiar to Jill. So did the gray suit and the Japanese umbrella; but the hat was strange, and while she was thinking how natural the boots looked the girl turned round.

"Why, how much she looks like Molly! It can't be— yes, it might, I do believe it *is!*" cried Jill, starting up and hardly daring to trust her own eyes.

As she came out of her nest and showed herself, there could be no doubt about the other girl, for she gave one shout and came racing over the beach with both arms out, while her hat blew off unheeded, and the gay umbrella flew away, to the great delight of all the little people except Boo, who was upset by his sister's impetuous rush, and lay upon his back howling. Molly did not do all the running, though, and Jill got her wish, for, never stopping to think of herself, she was off at once, and met her friend half-way with an answering cry. It was a pretty sight to see them run into one another's arms and hug and kiss and talk and skip in such a state of girlish joy they never cared who saw or laughed at their innocent raptures.

"You darling dear! where did you come from?" cried Jill, holding Molly by both shoulders, and shaking her a little to be sure she was real.

"Mrs. Minot sent for us to spend a week. You look so well, I can't believe my eyes!" answered Molly, patting Jill's cheeks and kissing them over and over, as if to make sure the bright color would not come off.

"A week? How splendid! Oh, I've such heaps to tell and show you; come right over to my cubby and see how lovely it is," said Jill, forgetting everybody else in her delight at getting Molly.

"I must get poor Boo, and my hat and umbrella. I left them all behind me when I saw you," laughed Molly, looking back.

But Mrs. Minot and Jack had consoled Boo and collected the scattered property, so the girls went on arm in arm, and had a fine time before any one had the heart to disturb them. Molly was charmed with the boat, and Jill very glad the box was done in season. Both had so much to tell and hear and plan, that they would have sat there for ever if bathing-time had not come, and the beach suddenly looked like a bed of red and yellow tulips, for every one took a dip, and the strangers added much to the fun.

Molly could swim like a duck, and quite covered herself with glory by diving off the pier. Jack undertook to teach Boo, who was a promising pupil, being so plump that he could not sink if he tried. Jill was soon through, and lay on the sand enjoying the antics of the bathers till she was so faint with laughter she was glad to hear the dinner-horn and do the honors of the Willows to Molly, whose room was next hers.

Boat-races came first in the afternoon, and the girls watched them, sitting luxuriously in the nest, with the ladies and children close by. The sailing-matches were very pretty to see; but Molly and Jill were more interested in the rowing, for Frank and the bicycle boy pulled one boat, and the friends felt that this one must win. It did, though the race was not very exciting nor the prize of great worth; but the boys and girls were satisfied, and Jack was much exalted, for he always told Frank he could do great things if he would only drop books and "go in on his muscle."

Foot-races followed, and, burning to distinguish himself also, Jack insisted on trying, though his mother warned him that the weak leg might be harmed, and he had his own doubts about it, as he was all out of practice. However, he took his place with a handkerchief tied round his head, red shirt and stockings, and his sleeves rolled up as if he meant business. Jill and Molly could not sit still during this race, and stood on the bank quite trembling with excitement as the half-dozen runners stood in a line at the starting-post waiting for the word "Go!"

Off they went at last over the smooth beach to the pole with the flag at the further end, and every one watched them with mingled interest and merriment, for they were a droll set, and the running not at all scientific with most of them. One young fisherman with big boots over his trousers started off at a great pace, pounding along in the most dogged way, while a little chap in a tight bathing-suit with very thin legs skimmed by him, looking so like a sand-piper

it was impossible to help laughing at both. Jack's former
training stood him in good stead now; for he went to work
in professional style, and kept a steady trot till the flag-pole
had been passed, then he put on his speed and shot ahead
of all the rest, several of whom broke down and gave up.
But Cox and Bacon held on gallantly; and soon it was evident that the sturdy legs in the knickerbockers were gain-
ing fast, for Jack gave his ankle an ugly wrench on a round
pebble, and the weak knee began to fail. He did his best,
however, and quite a breeze of enthusiasm stirred the spec-
tators as the three boys came down the course like mettle-
some horses, panting, pale, or purple, but each bound to
win at any cost.

"Now, Bacon!" "Go it, Minot!" "Hit him up, Cox!"
"Jack's ahead!" "No, he isn't!" "Here they come!" "Bacon's
done it!" shouted the other boys, and they were right; Bacon
had won, for the gray legs came in just half a yard ahead
of the red ones, and Minot tumbled into his brother's
arms with hardly breath enough left to gasp out, good-
humoredly, "All right, I'm glad he beat!"

Then the victor was congratulated and borne off by his
friends to refresh himself, while the lookers-on scattered to
see a game of tennis and the shooting of the Archery Club
up at the hotel. Jack was soon rested, and, making light of
his defeat, insisted on taking the girls to see the fun. So they
drove up in the old omnibus, and enjoyed the pretty sight
very much; for the young ladies were in uniform, and the
broad green ribbons over the white dresses, the gay quivers,
long bows, and big targets, made a lively scene. The shooting was good; a handsome damsel got the prize of a dozen
arrows, and every one clapped in the most enthusiastic
manner.

Molly and Jill did not care about tennis, so they went

home to rest and dress for the evening, because to their minds the dancing, the illumination, and the fireworks were the best fun of all. Jill's white bunting with cherry ribbons was very becoming, and the lively feet in the new slippers patted the floor impatiently as the sound of dance music came down to the Willows after tea, and the other girls waltzed on the wide piazza because they could not keep still.

"No dancing for me, but Molly must have a good time. You'll see that she does, won't you, boys?" said Jill, who knew that her share of the fun would be lying on a settee and watching the rest enjoy her favorite pastime.

Frank and Jack promised, and kept their word handsomely; for there was plenty of room in the great dancing-hall at the hotel, and the band in the pavilion played such inspiring music that, as the bicycle boy said, "Every one who had a leg couldn't help shaking it." Molly was twirled about to her heart's content, and flew hither and thither like a blue butterfly; for all the lads liked her, and she kept running up to tell Jill the funny things they said and did.

As night darkened from all the houses in the valley, on the cliffs and along the shore lights shone and sparkled; for every one decorated with gay lanterns, and several yachts in the bay strung colored lamps about the little vessels, making a pretty picture on the quiet sea. Jill thought she had never seen anything so like fairy-land, and felt very like one in a dream as she drove slowly up and down with Mamie, Gerty, Molly, and Mrs. Cox in the carriage, so that she might see it all without too much fatigue. It was very lovely; and when rockets began to whizz, filling the air with golden rain, a shower of colored stars, fiery dragons, or glittering wheels, the girls could only shriek with delight, and beg to stay a little longer each time the prudent lady proposed going home.

It had to be at last; but Molly and Jill comforted themselves by a long talk in bed, for it was impossible to sleep with glares of light coming every few minutes, flocks of people talking and tramping by in the road, and bursts of music floating down to them as the older but not wiser revellers kept up the merriment till a late hour. They dropped off at last; but Jill had the nightmare, and Molly was waked up by a violent jerking of her braid as Jill tried to tow her along, dreaming she was a boat.

They were too sleepy to laugh much then, but next morning they made merry over it, and went to breakfast with such happy faces that all the young folks pronounced Jill's friend a most delightful girl. What a good time Molly did have that week! Other people were going to leave also, and therefore much picnicking, boating, and driving was crowded into the last days. Clambakes on the shore, charades in the studio, sewing-parties at the boat, evening frolics in the big dining-room, farewell calls, gifts, and invitations, all sorts of plans for next summer, and vows of eternal friendship exchanged between people who would soon forget each other. It was very pleasant, till poor Boo innocently added to the excitement by poisoning a few of his neighbors with a bad lobster.

The ambitious little soul pined to catch one of these mysterious but lovely red creatures, and spent days fishing on the beach, investigating holes and corners, and tagging after the old man who supplied the house. One day after a high wind he found several "lobs" washed up on the beach, and, though disappointed at their color, he picked out a big one, and set off to show his prize to Molly. Half-way home he met the old man on his way with a basket of fish, and being tired of lugging his contribution laid it with the others, meaning to explain later. No one saw him do it, as the old man was busy with his pipe; and Boo ran back to get more dear lobs, leaving his treasure to go into the kettle and appear at supper, by which time he had forgotten all about it.

Fortunately none of the children ate any, but several older people were made ill, and quite a panic prevailed that night as one after the other called up the doctor, who was boarding close by; and good Mrs. Grey, the hostess, ran about with hot flannels, bottles of medicine, and distracted messages from room to room. All were comfortable by morning, but the friends of the sufferers lay in wait for the old fisherman, and gave him a good scolding for his carelessness. The poor man was protesting his innocence when Boo, who was passing by, looked into the basket, and asked what had become of *his* lob. A few questions brought the truth to light, and a general laugh put every one in good humor, when poor Boo mildly said, by way of explanation, —

"I fought I was helpin' Mrs. Dray, and I did want to see the dreen lob come out all red when she boiled him. But I fordot, and I don't fink I'll ever find such a nice big one any more."

"For our sakes, I hope you won't, my dear," said Mrs. Hammond, who had been nursing one of the sufferers.

"It's lucky we are going home to-morrow, or that child would be the death of himself and everybody else. He is perfectly crazy about fish, and I've pulled him out of that old lobster-pot on the beach a dozen times," groaned Molly, much afflicted by the mishaps of her young charge.

There was a great breaking up next day, and the old

omnibus went off to the station with Bacon hanging on behind, the bicycle boy and his iron whirligig atop, and heads
popping out of all the windows for last good-byes. Our
party and the Hammonds were going by boat, and were all
ready to start for the pier when Boo and little Harry were
missing. Molly, the maid, and both boys ran different ways
to find them; and all sorts of dreadful suggestions were
being made when shouts of laughter were heard from the
beach, and the truants appeared, proudly dragging in Harry's
little wagon a dead devil-fish, as the natives call that ugly
thing which looks like a magnified tadpole,—all head and
no body.

"We've dot him!" called the innocents, tugging up
their prize with such solemn satisfaction it was impossible to
help laughing.

"I always wanted to tatch a whale, and this is a baby
one, I fink. A boy said, when they wanted to die they comed
on the sand and did it, and we saw this one go dead just
now. Ain't he pretty?" asked Boo, displaying the immense
mouth with fond pride, while his friend flapped the tail.

"What are you going to do with him?" said Mrs. Hammond, regarding her infant as if she often asked herself the
same question about her boy.

"Wap him up in a paper and tate him home to pay
wid," answered Harry, with such confidence in his big blue
eyes that it was very hard to disappoint his hopes and tell
him the treasure must be left behind.

Wails of despair burst from both children as the hard-
hearted boys tipped out the little whale, and hustled the indignant fishermen on board the boat, which had been
whistling for them impatiently. Boo recovered his spirits
first, and gulping down a sob that nearly shook his hat off,

consoled his companion in affliction and convulsed his friends by taking from his pocket several little crabs, the remains of a jelly-fish, and such a collection of pebbles that Frank understood why he found the fat boy such a burden when he shouldered him, kicking and howling, in the late run to the boat. These delicate toys healed the wounds of Boo and Harry, and they were soon happily walking the little "trabs" about inside a stone wall of their own building, while the others rested after their exertions, and laid plans for coming to the Willows another year, as people usually did who had once tasted the wholesome delights and cordial hospitality of this charming place.

Cattle Show

CHAPTER 23

*T*he children were not the only ones who had learned something at Pebbly Beach. Mrs. Minot had talked a good deal with some very superior persons, and received light upon various subjects which had much interested or perplexed her. While the ladies worked or walked together, they naturally spoke oftenest and most earnestly about their children, and each contributed her experience. Mrs. Hammond, who had been a physician for many years, was wise in the care of healthy little bodies, and the cure of sick ones. Mrs. Channing, who had read, travelled, and observed much in the cause of education, had many useful hints about the training of young minds and hearts. Several teachers reported their trials, and all the mothers were eager to know how to bring up their boys and girls to be healthy, happy, useful men and women.

As young people do not care for such discussions, we

will not describe them, but as the impression they made upon one of the mammas affected our hero and heroine, we must mention the changes which took place in their life when they all got home again.

"School begins to-morrow. Oh, dear!" sighed Jack, as he looked up his books in the Bird Room, a day or two after their return.

"Don't you want to go? I long to, but don't believe I shall. I saw our mothers talking to the doctor last night, but I haven't dared to ask what they decided," said Jill, affectionately eying the long-unused books in her little library.

"I've had such a jolly good time, that I hate to be shut up all day worse than ever. Don't you, Frank?" asked Jack, with a vengeful slap at the arithmetic which was the torment of his life.

"Well, I confess I don't hanker for school as much as I expected. I'd rather take a spin on the old bicycle. Our roads are so good, it is a great temptation to hire a machine, and astonish the natives. That's what comes of idleness. So brace up, my boy, and go to work, for vacation is over," answered Frank, gravely regarding the tall pile of books before him, as if trying to welcome his old friends, or tyrants, rather, for they ruled him with a rod of iron when he once gave himself up to them.

"Ah, but vacation is not over, my dears," said Mrs. Minot, hearing the last words as she came in prepared to surprise her family.

"Glad of it. How much longer is it to be?" asked Jack, hoping for a week at least.

"Two or three years for some of you."

"What?" cried all three, in utter astonishment, as they stared at Mamma, who could not help smiling, though she was very much in earnest.

"For the next two or three years I intend to cultivate my boys' bodies, and let their minds rest a good deal, from books at least. There is plenty to learn outside of school-houses, and I don't mean to shut you up just when you most need all the air and exercise you can get. Good health, good principles, and a good education are the three blessings I ask for you, and I am going to make sure of the first, as a firm foundation for the other two."

"But, mother, what becomes of college?" asked Frank, rather disturbed at this change of base.

"Put it off for a year, and see if you are not better fitted for it then than now."

"But I am already fitted: I've worked like a tiger all this year, and I'm sure I shall pass."

"Ready in one way, but not in another. That hard work is no preparation for four years of still harder study. It has cost you these round shoulders, many a headache, and consumed hours when you had far better have been on the river or in the fields. I cannot have you break down, as so many boys do, or pull through at the cost of ill-health after-ward. Eighteen is young enough to begin the steady grind, if you have a strong constitution to keep pace with the eager mind. Sixteen is too young to send even my good boy out into the world, just when he most needs his mother's care to help him be the man she hopes to see him."

Mrs. Minot laid her hand on his shoulder as she spoke, looking so fond and proud that it was impossible to rebel, though some of his most cherished plans were spoilt.

"Other fellows go at my age, and I was rather pleased to be ready at sixteen," he began. But she added, quickly,—

"They go, but how do they come out? Many lose health of body, and many what is more precious still, moral strength, because too young and ignorant to withstand temptations of all sorts. The best part of education does not come from books, and the good principles I value more than either of the other things are to be carefully watched over till firmly fixed; then you may face the world, and come to no real harm. Trust me, dear, I do it for your sake; so bear the disappointment bravely, and in the end I think you will say I'm right."

"I'll do my best; but I don't see what is to become of us if we don't go to school. You will get tired of it first," said Frank, trying to set a good example to the others, who were looking much impressed and interested.

"No danger of that, for I never sent my children to school to get rid of them, and now that they are old enough to be companions, I want them at home more than ever. There are to be some lessons, however, for busy minds must be fed, but not crammed; so you boys will go and recite at certain hours such things as seem most important. But there is to be no studying at night, no shutting up all the best hours of the day, no hurry and fret of getting on fast, or skimming over the surface of many studies without learning any thoroughly."

"So I say!" cried Jack, pleased with the new idea, for he never did love books. "I do hate to be driven so I don't half understand, because there is no time to have things explained. School is good fun as far as play goes; but I don't see the sense of making a fellow learn eighty questions in geography one day, and forget them the next."

"What is to become of me, please?" asked Jill, meekly.

"You and Molly are to have lessons here. I was a teacher when I was young, you know, and liked it, so I shall be school-ma'am, and leave my house-keeping in better hands than mine. I always thought that mothers should teach their girls during these years, and vary their studies to suit the growing creatures as only mothers can."

"That will be splendid! Will Molly's father let her come?" cried Jill, feeling quite reconciled to staying at home, if her friend was to be with her.

"He likes the plan very much, for Molly is growing fast, and needs a sort of care that Miss Dawes cannot give her. I am not a hard mistress, and I hope you will find my school a pleasant one."

"I know I shall; and I'm not disappointed, because I was pretty sure I couldn't go to the old school again, when I heard the doctor say I must be very careful for a long time. I thought he meant months; but if it must be years, I can bear it, for I've been happy this last one though I was sick," said Jill, glad to show that it had not been wasted time by being cheerful and patient now.

"That's my good girl!" and Mrs. Minot stroked the curly black head as if it was her own little daughter's. "You have done so well, I want you to go on improving, for care now will save you pain and disappointment by-and-by. You all have got a capital start during these six weeks, so it is a good time to begin my experiment. If it does not work well, we will go back to school and college next spring."

"Hurrah for Mamma and the long vacation!" cried Jack, catching up two big books and whirling them round like clubs, as if to get his muscles in order at once.

"Now I shall have time to go to the Gymnasium and straighten out my back," said Frank, who was growing so tall he needed more breadth to make his height symmetrical.

"And to ride horseback. I am going to hire old Jane and get out the little phaeton, so we can all enjoy the fine weather while it lasts. Molly and I can drive Jill, and you can take turns in the saddle when you are tired of ball and boating. Exercise of all sorts is one of the lessons we are to learn," said Mrs. Minot, suggesting all the pleasant things she could to sweeten the pill for her pupils, two of whom did love their books, not being old enough to know that even an excellent thing may be overdone.

"Won't that be gay? I'll get down the saddle to-day, so we can begin right off. Lem rides, and we can go together. Hope old Jane will like it as well as I shall," said Jack, who had found a new friend in a pleasant lad lately come to town.

"You must see that she does, for you boys are to take care of her. We will put the barn in order, and you can decide which shall be hostler and which gardener, for I don't intend to hire labor on the place any more. Our estate is not a large one, and it will be excellent work for you, my men."

"All right! I'll see to Jane. I love horses," said Jack, well pleased with the prospect.

"My horse won't need much care. I prefer a bicycle to a beast, so I'll get in the squashes, pick the apples, and cover the strawberry bed when it is time," added Frank, who had enjoyed the free life at Pebbly Beach so much that he was willing to prolong it.

"You may put me in a hen-coop, and keep me there a year, if you like. I won't fret, for I'm sure you know what is best for me," said Jill, gayly, as she looked up at the good friend who had done so much for her.

"I'm not sure that I won't put you in a pretty cage and send you to Cattle Show, as a sample of what we can do in the way of taming a wild bird till it is nearly as meek as a dove," answered Mrs. Minot, much gratified at the amiability of her flock.

"I don't see why there should not be an exhibition of
children, and prizes for the good and pretty ones, as well as
for fat pigs, fine horses, or handsome fruit and flowers,—I
don't mean a baby show, but boys and girls, so people can
see what the prospect is of a good crop for the next genera-
tion," said Frank, glancing toward the tower of the building
where the yearly Agricultural Fair was soon to be held.

"Years ago, there was a pretty custom here of collecting all the schools together in the spring, and having a festi-
val at the Town Hall. Each school showed its best pupils,
and the parents looked on at the blooming flower show. It
was a pity it was ever given up, for the schools have never
been so good as then, nor the interest in them so great;" and
Mrs. Minot wondered, as many people do, why farmers
seem to care more for their cattle and crops than for their
children, willingly spending large sums on big barns and
costly experiments, while the school-houses are shabby and
inconvenient, and the cheapest teachers preferred.

"Ralph is going to send my bust. He asked if he might,
and mother said Yes. Mr. German thinks it very good, and I
hope other people will," said Jill, nodding toward the little
plaster head that smiled down from its bracket with her
own merry look.

"I could send my model; it is nearly done. Ralph told
me it was a clever piece of work, and he knows," added
Frank, quite taken with the idea of exhibiting his skill in
mechanics.

"And I could send my star bedquilt! They always have
things of that kind at Cattle Show;" and Jill began to rum-
mage in the closet for the pride of her heart, burning to display it to an admiring world.

"I haven't got anything. Can't sew rags together; or
make baby engines, and I have no live-stock—yes, I have

too! There's old Bun. I'll send him, for the fun of it; he really is a curiosity, for he is the biggest one I ever saw, and hopping into the lime has made his fur such a queer color, he looks like a new sort of rabbit. I'll catch and shut him up before he gets wild again;" and off rushed Jack to lure unsuspecting old Bun, who had grown tame during their absence, into the cage which he detested.

They all laughed at his ardor, but the fancy pleased them; and as Mamma saw no reason why their little works of art should not be sent, Frank fell to work on his model, and Jill resolved to finish her quilt at once, while Mrs. Minot went off to see Mr. Acton about the hours and studies for the boys.

In a week or two, the young people were almost resigned to the loss of school, for they found themselves delightfully fresh for the few lessons they did have, and not weary of play, since it took many useful forms. Old Jane not only carried them all to ride, but gave Jack plenty of work keeping her premises in nice order. Frank mourned privately over the delay of college, but found a solace in his whirligig and the Gymnasium, where he set himself to developing a chest to match the big head above, which head no longer ached with eight or ten hours of study. Harvesting beans and raking up leaves seemed to have a soothing effect upon his nerves, for now he fell asleep at once instead of thumping his pillow with vexation because his brain would go on working at difficult problems and passages when he wanted it to stop.

Jill and Molly drove away in the little phaeton every fair morning over the sunny hills and through the changing woods, filling their hands with asters and golden-rod, their lungs with the pure, invigorating air, and their heads with all manner of sweet and happy fancies and feelings born of

the wholesome influences about them. People shook their
heads, and said it was wasting time; but the rosy-faced girls
were content to trust those wiser than themselves, and
found their new school very pleasant. They read aloud a
good deal, rapidly acquiring one of the rarest and most
beautiful accomplishments; for they could stop and ask
questions as they went along, so that they understood what
they read, which is half the secret. A thousand things came
up as they sewed together in the afternoon, and the eager
minds received much general information in an easy and
well-ordered way. Physiology was one of the favorite studies, and Mrs. Hammond often came in to give them a little
lecture, teaching them to understand the wonders of their
own systems, and how to keep them in order, — a lesson of
far more importance just then than Greek or Latin, for girls
are the future mothers, nurses, teachers, of the race, and
should feel how much depends on them. Merry could not
resist the attractions of the friendly circle, and soon per-
suaded her mother to let her do as they did; so she got more
exercise and less study, which was just what the delicate girl
needed.

The first of the new ideas seemed to prosper, and the
second, though suggested in joke, was carried out in
earnest, for the other young people were seized with a
strong desire to send something to the Fair. In fact, all sorts
of queer articles were proposed, and much fun prevailed,
especially among the boys, who ransacked their gardens for
mammoth vegetables, sighed for five-legged calves, blue
roses, or any other natural curiosity by means of which they
might distinguish themselves. Ralph was the only one who
had anything really worth sending; for though Frank's
model seemed quite perfect, it obstinately refused to go,

and at the last moment blew up with a report like a pop-gun. So it was laid away for repairs, and its disappointed maker devoted his energies to helping Jack keep Bun in order; for that indomitable animal got out of every prison they put him in, and led Jack a dreadful life during that last week. At all hours of the day and night that distracted boy would start up, crying, "There he is again!" and dart out to give chase and capture the villain now grown too fat to run as he once did.

The very night before the Fair, Frank was awakened by a chilly draught, and, getting up to see where it came from, found Jack's door open and bed empty, while the vision of a white ghost flitting about the garden suggested a midnight rush after old Bun. Frank watched laughingly, till poor Jack came toward the house with the gentleman in gray kicking lustily in his arms, and then whispered in a sepulchral tone,—

"Put him in the old refrigerator, he can't get out of that."

Blessing him for the suggestion, the exhausted hunter shut up his victim in the new cell, and found it a safe one, for Bun could not burrow through a sheet of zinc, or climb up the smooth walls.

Jill's quilt was a very elaborate piece of work, being bright blue with little white stars all over it; this she finished nicely, and felt sure no patient old lady could outdo it. Merry decided to send butter, for she had been helping her mother in the dairy that summer, and rather liked the light part of the labor. She knew it would please her very much if she chose that instead of wild flowers, so she practised moulding the yellow pats into pretty shapes, that it might please both eye and taste.

Molly declared she would have a little pen, and put Boo in it, as the prize fat boy,—a threat which so alarmed the innocent that he ran away, and was found two or three miles from home, asleep under the wall, with two seedcakes and a pair of socks done up in a bundle. Being with difficulty convinced that it was a joke, he consented to return to his family, but was evidently suspicious, till Molly decided to send her cats, and set about preparing them for exhibition. The Minots' deserted Bunny-house was rather large; but as cats cannot be packed as closely as much-enduring sheep, Molly borrowed this desirable family mansion, and put her darlings into it, where they soon settled down, and appeared to enjoy their new residence. It had been scrubbed up and painted red, cushions and plates put in, and two American flags adorned the roof. Being barred all round, a fine view of the Happy Family could be had, now twelve in number, as Molasses had lately added three white kits to the varied collection.

The girls thought this would be the most interesting spectacle of all, and Grif proposed to give some of the cats extra tails, to increase their charms, especially poor Mortification, who would appreciate the honor of two, after having none for so long. But Molly declined, and Grif looked about him for some attractive animal to exhibit, so that he too might go in free and come to honor, perhaps.

A young lady in the town owned a donkey, a small, gray beast, who insisted on tripping along the sidewalks and bumping her rider against the walls as she paused to browse at her own sweet will, regardless of blows or cries, till ready to move on. Expressing great admiration for this rare animal, Grif obtained leave to display the charms of Graciosa at the Fair. Little did she guess the dark designs entertained against her dignity, and happily she was not as sensitive to

ridicule as a less humble-minded animal, so she went willingly with her new friend, and enjoyed the combing and
trimming up which she received at his hands, while he prepared for the great occasion.

When the morning of September 28th arrived, the
town was all astir, and the Fair ground a lively scene. The
air was full of the lowing of cattle, the tramp of horses,
squealing of indignant pigs, and clatter of tongues, as people
and animals streamed in at the great gate and found their
proper places. Our young folks were in a high state of excitement, as they rumbled away with their treasures in a
hay-cart. The Bunny-house might have been a cage of tigers,
so rampant were the cats at this new move. Old Bun, in a
small box, brooded over the insult of the refrigerator, and
looked as fierce as a rabbit could. Gus had a coop of rare
fowls, who clucked wildly all the way, while Ralph, with
the bust in his arms, stood up in front, and Jill and Molly
bore the precious bedquilt, as they sat behind.

These objects of interest were soon arranged, and the
girls went to admire Merry's golden butter cups among the
green leaves, under which lay the ice that kept the pretty
flowers fresh. The boys were down below, where the cack-
ling was very loud, but not loud enough to drown the
sonorous bray which suddenly startled them as much as it
did the horses outside. A shout of laughter followed, and
away went the lads, to see what the fun was, while the girls
ran out on the balcony, as some one said, "It's that rogue of
a Grif with some new joke."

It certainly was, and, to judge from the peals of merriment, the joke was a good one. In at the gate came a two-
headed donkey, ridden by Grif, in great spirits at his
success, for the gate-keeper laughed so he never thought to
ask for toll. A train of boys followed him across the ground,

lost in admiration of the animal and the cleverness of her rider. Among the stage properties of the Dramatic Club was the old ass's head once used in some tableaux from "Midsummer Night's Dream." This Grif had mended up, and fastened by means of straps and a collar to poor Graciosa's neck hiding his work with a red cloth over her back. One eye was gone, but the other still opened and shut, and the long ears wagged by means of strings, which he slyly managed with the bridle, so the artificial head looked almost as natural as the real one. The funniest thing of all was the innocent air of Graciosa, and the mildly inquiring expression with which she now and then turned to look at or to smell of the new ornament as if she recognized a friend's face, yet was perplexed by its want of animation. She vented her feelings in a bray, which Grif imitated, convulsing all hearers by the sound as well as by the wink the one eye gave, and the droll waggle of one erect ear, while the other pointed straight forward.

The girls laughed so at the ridiculous sight that they nearly fell over the railing, and the boys were in ecstasies, especially when Grif, emboldened by his success, trotted briskly round the race-course, followed by the cheers of the crowd. Excited by the noise, Graciosa did her best, till the false head, loosened by the rapid motion, slipped round under her nose, causing her to stop so suddenly that Grif flew off, alighting on his own head with a violence which would have killed any other boy. Sobered by his downfall, he declined to mount again, but led his steed to repose in a shed, while he rejoined his friends, who were waiting impatiently to congratulate him on his latest and best prank.

The Committee went their rounds soon after, and, when the doors were again opened, every one hurried to see if their articles had received a premium. A card lay on the butter cups, and Mrs. Grant was full of pride because *her* butter always took a prize, and this proved that Merry was walking in her mother's steps, in this direction at least. Another card swung from the blue quilt, for the kindly judges knew who made it, and were glad to please the little girl, though several others as curious but not so pretty hung near by. The cats were admired, but, as they were not among the animals usually exhibited, there was no prize awarded. Gus hoped his hens would get one; but somebody else outdid him, to the great indignation of Laura and Lotty, who had fed the white biddies faithfully for months. Jack was sure his rabbit was the biggest there, and went eagerly to look for his premium. But neither card nor Bun were to be seen, for the old rascal had escaped for the last time, and was never seen again; which was a great comfort to Jack, who was heartily tired of him.

Ralph's bust was the best of all, for not only did it get a prize, and was much admired, but a lady, who found Jill and Merry rejoicing over it, was so pleased with the truth and grace of the little head, that she asked about the artist, and whether he would do one of her own child, who was so delicate she feared he might not live long.

Merry gladly told the story of her ambitious friend, and went to find him, that he might secure the order. While she was gone, Jill took up the tale, gratefully telling how kind he had been to her, how patiently he worked and waited, and how much he longed to go abroad. Fortunately the lady was rich and generous, as well as fond of art, and being pleased with the bust, and interested in the young sculptor, gave him the order when he came, and filled his soul with joy by adding, that, if it suited her when done, it should be put into marble. She lived in the city, and Ralph soon arranged his work so that he could give up his noon hour, and go to model the child; for every penny he could earn or save now was very precious, as he still hoped to go abroad.

The girls were so delighted with this good fortune, that they did not stay for the races, but went home to tell the happy news, leaving the boys to care for the cats, and enjoy the various matches to come off that day.

"I'm so glad I tried to look pleasant when I was lying on the board while Ralph did my head, for the pleasantness got into the clay face, and that made the lady like it," said Jill, as she lay resting on the sofa.

"I always thought it was a dear, bright little face, but now I love and admire it more than ever," cried Merry, kissing it gratefully, as she remembered the help and pleasure it had given Ralph.

Down the River
CHAPTER 24 ⏃

A fortnight later, the boys were picking apples one golden October afternoon, and the girls were hurrying to finish their work, that they might go and help the harvesters. It was six weeks now since the new school began, and they had learned to like it very much, though they found that it was not all play, by any means. But lessons, exercise, and various sorts of housework made an agreeable change, and they felt that they were learning things which would be useful to them all their lives. They had been making underclothes for themselves, and each had several neatly finished garments cut, fitted, and sewed by herself, and trimmed with the pretty tatting Jill made in such quantities while she lay on her sofa.

Now they were completing new dressing sacks, and had enjoyed this job very much, as each chose her own material, and suited her own taste in the making. Jill's was white, with tiny scarlet leaves all over it, trimmed with red braid and buttons so like checkerberries she was tempted to eat them. Molly's was gay, with bouquets of every sort of flower, scalloped all round, and adorned with six buttons, each of a different color, which she thought the last touch of elegance. Merry's, though the simplest, was the daintiest of the three, being pale blue, trimmed with delicate edging, and beautifully made.

Mrs. Minot had been reading from Miss Strickland's "Queens of England" while the girls worked, and an illustrated Shakspeare lay open on the table, as well as several fine photographs of historical places for them to look at as they went along. The hour was over now, the teacher gone, and the pupils setting the last stitches as they talked over the lesson, which had interested them exceedingly.

"I really believe I have got Henry's six wives into my head right at last. Two Annes, three Katherines, and one Jane. Now I've seen where they lived and heard their stories, I quite feel as if I knew them," said Merry, shaking the threads off her work before she folded it up to carry home.

" 'King Henry the Eighth to six spouses was wedded,—
One died, one survived, two divorced, two beheaded,'

was all I knew about them before. Poor things, what a bad time they did have," added Jill, patting down the red braid, which would pucker a bit at the corners.

"Katherine Parr had the best of it, because she outlived the old tyrant and so kept her head on," said Molly, winding the thread round her last button, as if bound to fasten it on so firmly that nothing should decapitate that.

"I used to think I'd like to be a queen or a great lady,
and wear velvet and jewels, and live in a palace, but now I
don't care much for that sort of splendor. I like to make
things pretty at home, and know that they all depend on
me, and love me very much. Queens are not happy, and I
am," said Merry, pausing to look at Anne Hathaway's cottage as she put up the pictures, and to wonder if it was very
pleasant to have a famous man for one's husband.

"I guess your missionarying has done you good; mine
has, and I'm getting to have things my own way more and
more every day. Miss Bat is so amiable, I hardly know her,
and father tells her to ask Miss Molly when she goes to him
for orders. Isn't that fun?" laughed Molly, in high glee, at
the agreeable change. "I like it ever so much, but I don't
want to stay so all my days. I mean to travel, and just as
soon as I can I shall take Boo and go all round the world, and
see everything," she added, waving her gay sack, as if
it were the flag she was about to nail to the masthead of
her ship.

"Well, I should like to be famous in some way, and
have people admire me very much. I'd like to act, or dance,
or sing, or be what I heard the ladies at Pebbly Beach call a
'queen of society.' But I don't expect to be anything, and
I'm not going to worry, for I shall *not* be a Lucinda, so I
ought to be contented and happy all my life," said Jill, who
was very ambitious in spite of the newly acquired meekness,
which was all the more becoming because her natural liveli-
ness often broke out like sunshine through a veil of light
clouds.

If the three girls could have looked forward ten years
they would have been surprised to see how different a fate
was theirs from the one each had chosen, and how happy

each was in the place she was called to fill. Merry was not making the old farmhouse pretty, but living in Italy, with a young sculptor for her husband, and beauty such as she never dreamed of all about her. Molly was not travelling round the world, but contentedly keeping house for her father and still watching over Boo, who was becoming her pride and joy as well as care. Neither was Jill a famous woman, but a very happy and useful one, with the two mothers leaning on her as they grew old, the young men better for her influence over them, many friends to love and honor her, and a charming home, where she was queen by right of her cheery spirit, grateful heart, and unfailing devotion to those who had made her what she was.

If any curious reader, not content with this peep into futurity, asks, "Did Molly and Jill ever marry?" we must reply, for the sake of peace, — Molly remained a merry spinster all her days, one of the independent, brave, and busy creatures of whom there is such need in the world to help take care of other peoples' wives and children, and do the many useful jobs that the married folk have no time for. Jill certainly did wear a white veil on the day she was twenty-five and called her husband Jack. Further than that we cannot go, except to say that this leap did not end in a catastrophe, like the first one they took together.

That day, however, they never dreamed of what was in store for them, but chattered away as they cleared up the room, and then ran off ready for play, feeling that they had earned it by work well done. They found the lads just finishing, with Boo to help by picking up the windfalls for the cider-heap, after he had amused himself by putting about a bushel down the various holes old Bun had left behind him.

Jack was risking his neck climbing in the most dangerous places, while Frank, with a long-handled apple-picker, nipped off the finest fruit with care, both enjoying the pleasant task and feeling proud of the handsome red and yellow piles all about the little orchard. Merry and Molly caught up baskets and fell to work with all their might, leaving Jill to sit upon a stool and sort the early apples ready to use at once, looking up now and then to nod and smile at her mother who watched her from the window, rejoicing to see her lass so well and happy.

It was such a lovely day, they all felt its cheerful influence; for the sun shone bright and warm, the air was full of an invigorating freshness which soon made the girls' faces look like rosy apples, and their spirits as gay as if they had been stealing sips of new cider through a straw. Jack whistled like a blackbird as he swung and bumped about, Frank orated and joked, Merry and Molly ran races to see who would fill and empty fastest, and Jill sung to Boo, who reposed in a barrel, exhausted with his labors.

"These are the last of the pleasant days, and we ought to make the most of them. Let's have one more picnic before the frost spoils the leaves," said Merry, resting a minute at the gate to look down the street, which was a glorified sort of avenue, with brilliant maples lining the way and carpeting the ground with crimson and gold.

"Oh, yes! go down the river once more and have supper on the Island. I couldn't go to some of your picnics, and I do long for a last good time before winter shuts me up again," cried Jill, eager to harvest all the sunshine she could, for she was not yet quite her old self again.

"I'm your man, if the other fellows agree. We can't barrel these up for a while, so to-morrow will be a holiday for us. Better make sure of the day while you can, this weather can't last long;" and Frank shook his head like one on intimate terms with Old Prob.

"Don't worry about those high ones, Jack. Give a shake and come down and plan about the party," called Molly, throwing up a big Baldwin with what seemed a remarkably good aim, for a shower of apples followed, and a boy came tumbling earthward to catch on the lowest bough and swing down like a caterpillar, exclaiming, as he landed, —

"I'm glad that job is done! I've rasped every knuckle I've got and worn out the knees of my pants. Nice little crop though, isn't it?"

"It will be nicer if this young man does not bite every apple he touches. Hi there! stop it, Boo," commanded Frank, as he caught his young assistant putting his small teeth into the best ones, to see if they were sweet or sour.

Molly set the barrel up on end, and that took the boy out of the reach of mischief, so he retired from view and peeped through a crack as he ate his fifth pearmain, regardless of consequences.

"Gus will be at home to-morrow. He always comes up early on Saturday, you know. We can't get on without him," said Frank, who missed his mate very much, for Gus had entered college, and so far did not like it as much as he had expected.

"Or Ralph; he is very busy every spare minute on the little boy's bust, which is getting on nicely, he says; but he will be able to come home in time for supper, I think," added Merry, remembering the absent, as usual.

"I'll ask the girls on my way home, and all meet at two o'clock for a good row while it's warm. What shall I bring?" asked Molly, wondering if Miss Bat's amiability would

extend to making goodies in the midst of her usual Saturday's baking.

"You bring coffee and the big pot and some buttered
crackers. I'll see to the pie and cake, and the other girls can
have anything else they like," answered Merry, glad and
proud that she could provide the party with her own inviting handiwork.

"I'll take my zither, so we can have music as we sail,
and Grif will bring his violin, and Ralph can imitate a banjo
so that you'd be sure he had one. I do hope it will be fine, it
is so splendid to go round like other folks and enjoy myself,"
cried Jill, with a little bounce of satisfaction at the prospect
of a row and ramble.

"Come along, then, and make sure of the girls," said
Merry, catching up her roll of work, for the harvesting
was done.

Molly put her sack on as the easiest way of carrying it,
and, extricating Boo, they went off, accompanied by the
boys, "to make sure of the fellows" also, leaving Jill to sit
among the apples, singing and sorting like a thrifty little
housewife.

Next day eleven young people met at the appointed
place, basket in hand. Ralph could not come till later, for he
was working now as he never worked before. They were a
merry flock, for the mellow autumn day was even brighter
and clearer than yesterday, and the river looked its loveliest, winding away under the sombre hemlocks, or through
the fairyland the gay woods made on either side. Two large
boats and two small ones held them all, and away they
went, first up through the three bridges and round the
bend, then, turning, they floated down to the green island,
where a grove of oaks rustled their sere leaves and the squirrels were still gathering acorns. Here they often met to

keep their summer revels, and here they now spread their feast on the flat rock which needed no cloth beside its own gray lichens. The girls trimmed each dish with bright leaves, and made the supper look like a banquet for the elves, while the boys built a fire in the nook where ashes and blackened stones told of many a rustic meal. The big tin coffee-pot was not so romantic, but more successful than a kettle slung on three sticks, gypsy fashion; so they did not risk a downfall, but set the water boiling, and soon filled the air with the agreeable perfume associated in their minds with picnics, as most of them never tasted the fascinating stuff at any other time, being the worst children can drink.

Frank was cook, Gus helped cut bread and cake, Jack and Grif brought wood, while Bob Walker took Joe's place and made himself generally useful, as the other gentleman never did, and so was quite out of favor lately.

All was ready at last, and they were just deciding to sit down without Ralph, when a shout told them he was coming, and down the river skimmed a wherry at such a rate the boys wondered whom he had been racing with.

"Something has happened, and he is coming to tell us," said Jill, who sat where she could see his eager face.

"Nothing bad, or he wouldn't smile so. He is glad of a good row and a little fun after working so hard all the week;" and Merry shook a red napkin as a welcoming signal.

Something certainly had happened, and a very happy something it must be, they all thought, as Ralph came on with flashing oars, and leaping out as the boat touched the shore, ran up the slope, waving his hat, and calling in a glad voice, sure of sympathy in his delight,—

"Good news! good news! Hurrah for Rome, next month!"

The young folks forgot their supper for a moment, to

congratulate him on his happy prospect, and hear all about it, while the leaves rustled as if echoing the kind words, and the squirrels sat up aloft, wondering what all the pleasant clamor was about.

"Yes, I'm really going in November. German asked me to go with him to-day, and if there is any little hitch in my getting off, he'll lend a hand, and I—I'll black his boots, wet his clay, and run his errands the rest of my life to pay for this!" cried Ralph, in a burst of gratitude; for, independent as he was, the kindness of this successful friend to a deserving comrade touched and won his heart.

"I call that a handsome thing to do!" said Frank, warmly, for noble actions always pleased him. "I heard my mother say that making good or useful men was the best sort of sculpture, so I think David German may be proud of this piece of work, whether the big statue succeeds or not."

"I'm very glad, old fellow. When I run over for my trip four years from now, I'll look you up, and see how you are getting on," said Gus, with a hearty shake of the hand; and the younger lads grinned cheerfully, even while they wondered where the fun was in shaping clay and chipping marble.

"Shall you stay four years?" asked Merry's soft voice, while a wistful look came into her happy eyes.

"Ten, if I can," answered Ralph, decidedly, feeling as if a long lifetime would be all too short for the immortal work he meant to do. "I've got so much to learn, that I shall do whatever David thinks best for me at first, and when I *can* go alone, I shall just shut myself up and forget that there is any world outside my den."

"Do write and tell us how you get on now and then; I like to hear about other people's good times while I'm waiting for my own," said Molly, too much interested to observe that Grif was sticking burrs up and down her braids.

"Of course I shall write to some of you, but you mustn't expect any great things for years yet. People don't grow famous in a hurry, and it takes a deal of hard work even to earn your bread and butter, as you'll find if you ever try it," answered Ralph, sobering down a little as he remembered the long and steady effort it had taken to get even so far.

"Speaking of bread and butter reminds me that we'd better eat ours before the coffee gets quite cold," said Annette, for Merry seemed to have forgotten that she had been chosen to play matron, as she was the oldest.

The boys seconded the motion, and for a few minutes supper was the all-absorbing topic, as the cups went round and the goodies vanished rapidly, accompanied by the usual mishaps which make picnic meals such fun. Ralph's health was drunk with all sorts of good wishes; and such splendid prophecies were made, that he would have far surpassed Michael Angelo, if they could have come true. Grif gave him an order on the spot for a full-length statue of himself, and stood up to show the imposing attitude in which he wished to be taken, but unfortunately slipped and fell forward with one hand in the custard pie, the other clutching wildly at the coffee-pot, which inhospitably burnt his fingers.

"I think I grasp the idea, and will be sure to remember not to make your hair blow one way and the tails of your coat another, as a certain sculptor made those of a famous man," laughed Ralph, as the fallen hero scrambled up, amidst general merriment.

"Will the little bust be done before you go?" asked Jill,

anxiously, feeling a personal interest in the success of that order.

"Yes: I've been hard at it every spare minute I could get, and have a fortnight more. It suits Mrs. Lennox, and she will pay well for it, so I shall have something to start with, though I haven't been able to save much. I'm to thank you for that, and I shall send you the first pretty thing I get hold of," answered Ralph, looking gratefully at the bright face, which grew still brighter as Jill exclaimed,—

"I do feel *so* proud to know a real artist, and have my bust done by him. I only wish *I* could pay for it as Mrs. Lennox does; but I haven't any money, and you don't need the sort of things I can make," she added, shaking her head, as she thought over knit slippers, wall-pockets, and crochet in all its forms, as offerings to her departing friend.

"You can write often, and tell me all about everybody, for I shall want to know, and people will soon forget me when I'm gone," said Ralph, looking at Merry, who was making a garland of yellow leaves for Jill's black hair.

Jill promised, and kept her word; but the longest letters went from the farmhouse on the hill, though no one knew the fact till long afterward. Merry said nothing now, but she smiled, with a pretty color in her cheeks, and was very much absorbed in her work, while the talk went on.

"I wish I was twenty, and going to seek my fortune, as you are," said Jack; and the other boys agreed with him, for something in Ralph's new plans and purposes roused the manly spirit in all of them, reminding them that playtime would soon be over, and the great world before them, where to choose.

"It is easy enough to say what you'd like; but the trouble is, you have to take what you can get, and make the best of it," said Gus, whose own views were rather vague as yet.

"No you don't, always; you can *make* things go as you want them, if you only try hard enough, and walk right over whatever stands in the way. I don't mean to give up my plans for any man; but, if I live, I'll carry them out,—you see if I don't;" and Frank gave the rock where he lay a blow with his fist, that sent the acorns flying all about.

One of them hit Jack, and he said, sorrowfully, as he held it in his hand so carefully it was evident he had some association with it,—

"Ed used to say that, and he had some splendid plans, but they didn't come to anything."

"Perhaps they did; who can tell? Do your best while you live, and I don't believe anything good is lost, whether we have it a long or a short time," said Ralph, who knew what a help and comfort high hopes were, and how they led to better things, if worthily cherished.

"A great many acorns are wasted, I suppose; but some of them sprout and grow, and make splendid trees," added Merry, feeling more than she knew how to express, as she looked up at the oaks overhead.

Only seven of the party were sitting on the knoll now, for the rest had gone to wash the dishes and pack the baskets down by the boats. Jack and Jill, with the three elder boys, were in a little group, and as Merry spoke, Gus said to Frank,—

"Did you plant yours?"

"Yes, on the lawn, and I mean it shall come up if I can make it," answered Frank, gravely.

"I put mine where I can see it from the window, and

not forget to water and take care of it," added Jack, still turning the pretty brown acorn to and fro as if he loved it.

"What do they mean?" whispered Merry to Jill, who was leaning against her knee to rest.

"The boys were walking in the Cemetery last Sunday, as they often do, and when they came to Ed's grave, the place was all covered with little acorns from the tree that grows on the bank. They each took up some as they stood talking, and Jack said he should plant his, for he loved Ed very much, you know. The others said they would, too; and I hope the trees will grow, though we don't need anything to remember him by," answered Jill, in a low tone, thinking of the pressed flowers the girls kept for his sake.

The boys heard her, but no one spoke for a moment as they sat looking across the river toward the hill where the pines whispered their lullabies and pointed heavenward, steadfast and green, all the year round. None of them could express the thought that was in their minds as Jill told the little story; but the act and the feeling that prompted it were perhaps as beautiful an assurance as could have been given that the dear dead boy's example had not been wasted, for the planting of the acorns was a symbol of the desire budding in those young hearts to be what he might have been, and to make their lives nobler for the knowledge and the love of him.

"It seems as if a great deal had happened this year," said Merry, in a pensive tone, for this quiet talk just suited her mood.

"So I say, for there's been a Declaration of Independence and a Revolution in our house, and I'm commander-in-chief now; and don't I like it!" cried Molly, complacently surveying the neat new uniform she wore of her own choosing.

"I feel as if I never learned so much in my life as I have since last December, and yet I never did so little," added Jill, wondering why the months of weariness and pain did not seem more dreadful to her.

"Well, pitching on my head seems to have given me a good shaking up, somehow, and I mean to do great things next year in better ways than breaking my bones coasting," said Jack, with a manly air.

"I feel like a Siamese twin without his mate now you are gone, but I'm under orders for a while, and mean to do my best. Guess it won't be lost time;" and Frank nodded at Gus, who nodded back with the slightly superior expression all Freshmen wear.

"Hope you won't find it so. My work is all cut out for me, and I intend to go in and win, though it is more of a grind than you fellows know."

"I'm sure I have everything to be grateful for. It won't be plain sailing,—I don't expect it; but, if I live, I'll do something to be proud of," said Ralph, squaring his shoulders as if to meet and conquer all obstacles as he looked into the glowing west, which was not fairer than his ambitious dreams.

Here we will say good-by to these girls and boys of ours as they sit together in the sunshine talking over a year that was to be forever memorable to them, not because of any very remarkable events, but because they were just beginning to look about them as they stepped out of childhood into youth, and some of the experiences of the past months had set them to thinking, taught them to see the use and beauty of the small duties, joys, and sorrows which make up our lives, and inspired them to resolve that the coming year should be braver and brighter than the last.

There are many such boys and girls, full of high hopes,

lovely possibilities, and earnest plans, pausing a moment before they push their little boats from the safe shore. Let
those who launch them see to it that they have good health
to man the oars, good education for ballast, and good principles as pilots to guide them as they voyage down an ever-
widening river to the sea.